THE SUMMER ESCAPE

THE ISLES OF SCILLY SERIES: BOOK THREE

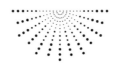

HANNAH ELLIS

Published by Hannah Ellis
www.authorhannahellis.com
Postfach 900309, 81503 München
Germany

Cover design by Mario Ellis

THE SUMMER ESCAPE

CHAPTER ONE

B each holidays were supposed to be sunny. An entire week of rain hadn't even occurred to Beth as a possibility. Apparently it was something of a rarity for the Isles of Scilly in July, but that fact was of little comfort. Her first solo trip with her five-year-old daughter had been a washout. She'd need another holiday to recover from the two of them being cooped up inside all week.

Wandering through to the living room with a steaming mug of coffee in her hand, Beth smiled at Ellie, who was in her usual spot by the window. Out of boredom, her little girl had taken to gazing out of the window, looking out for people to wave at.

Their holiday home – quaintly named Peswera Cottage – was the last in a row of four cottages on a narrow lane, Peswera being the Cornish word for fourth. The lane ended shortly after the cottage, and a larger house stood up on the headland where the owner of the cottages lived.

Beth perched beside Ellie on the deep windowsill. Finally, the fog had lifted so they at least had a view over the bay, even if the rain and wind had remained.

"Do you think Noah will come to see us today?" Ellie asked, looking up at Beth.

"I'm not sure."

"He said he'd come another day," Ellie remarked, her eyes flicking back outside as though she expected the owner's son to appear at any moment. He lived in the cottage next door, and Ellie had invited him in for a tea party the previous day. Not so much invited as dragged him inside by the hand.

"He said he *might,*" Beth said. "And I think he was just being polite." The poor guy had spent twenty minutes sitting around the coffee table with Ellie and her dolls and teddies. Once she'd got over her embarrassment, Beth had been grateful of the adult company.

"I think he had a nice time," Ellie said confidently. "Can we go on Kit's train today?"

Kit was another of the owner's sons, who'd been over to fix a leaky tap earlier in the week. He'd told Ellie she could go for a ride on his tourist train once the rain stopped, but at this rate it didn't seem as though that was going to happen.

"I'd like to." Beth licked her thumb and rubbed at the dirty mark on her daughter's chin. "Kit said the train doesn't run when it's raining though."

"I don't like this holiday." Ellie looked accusingly at Beth. "It's boring."

"It was just bad luck that it rained all week."

"When are we going home?"

"Tomorrow." Beth gazed longingly out to the long strip of pale sand. If the weather had been decent for their stay, it would have been the perfect holiday spot. "We need to go up to Mirren's house to check that she can drive us to the airport tomorrow."

"Let's go now," Ellie said, hopping down from the windowsill.

"Can I finish my coffee first?"

"I want to go now, Mummy. I'm bored."

"Okay." She took another sip of her drink before taking the mug to the kitchen. By the time she came back, Ellie had her shoes on and was stepping out of the door. "You'll need your raincoat," Beth called after her.

Ellie turned on the doorstep and grinned. "It's stopped raining."

"Oh my goodness. Finally!" Following Ellie outside, Beth craned her neck to look overhead. "There's blue sky over there."

"Does that mean we can go on Kit's train?"

"Maybe. Let's go and talk to Mirren, then we can walk into town and see if there's a train trip."

The wind had dropped to a gentle breeze as they wandered up to Mirren's house, dodging puddles as they went. Dark clouds were dispersing fast and a shaft of sunlight emerged like a spotlight on the sea, causing the tips of gentle waves to sparkle.

Beth had just knocked on the back door when Ellie spotted a butterfly and chased after it.

"I thought it was never going to stop," Mirren remarked, glancing skywards as she opened the door. "I can't believe it's rained for the entire week." She beckoned Beth inside. "I'm so sorry for you."

From the kitchen window, Beth kept an eye on Ellie, who was happily exploring the garden. "It hasn't felt like a holiday at all. More like the opposite." Her eyes widened as she looked at Mirren. "Sorry. That sounded terrible. The cottage is fantastic, and you and your family have been lovely." Kit had even dropped a box of toys off for Ellie, so she definitely couldn't complain about her hosts. "It's only the weather I have a problem with."

"I understand." Mirren smiled warmly. "I feel for you."

"It definitely wasn't the week I was expecting." If Beth was honest, she'd known the week would be difficult, but she'd ended up feeling sorry for herself for different reasons than she'd anticipated.

"I'm sorry," Mirren said. "I hope you'll come back another time. I'll give you a discount if you do."

"I can't believe we're leaving tomorrow. The weather forecast for the next week is glorious."

Mirren winced. "It's such a shame. Little Ellie would have loved playing on the beach."

"I don't suppose the cottage happens to be available next week so we can extend our stay?" When Mirren wrinkled her brow, Beth felt her cheeks heat up. Apparently a week stuck inside with Ellie had impeded her social skills. "I was joking. Sorry. Of course you're booked up … and we can't really extend our stay anyway."

"Can't you?" Mirren asked, her features serious.

"Well … we're booked on a flight tomorrow."

Mirren moved to the window, her eyes following Ellie. "It probably wouldn't be easy to rebook the flight in peak season. You might be able to get on the ferry though."

Beth stared at her in confusion. "*Do* you have availability?"

"I might be able to organise something." Mirren looked thoughtful. "Peswera Cottage is owned by my son, Trystan. He lives in London, so I rent it out for him. He's arriving home this afternoon and he was going to be staying in the cottage after you leave. He's here for the summer. I don't see why he can't stay with me for a few nights … that way you could stay on in the cottage and have a few days of sunshine."

"Oh … I'm not sure …" Outside, more clouds parted and bright sunshine made the pale sand glow while illuminating the water to a tantalising shade of turquoise. "Wouldn't your son mind?"

"Trystan will be fine with it." There was a twinkle in Mirren's eyes which made Beth wonder whether he really would be fine with it. "I'll make us a cuppa and you can have a look at changing your travel plans."

They moved out to the patio and Mirren dried a couple of chairs for them to sit down. While they sipped cups of coffee, Beth tapped away on her phone, checking their travel options.

Mirren was right that the flights were full, but there was plenty of availability on the ferry. It would mean getting a train from the ferry port in Penzance, but the slightly longer journey would be worth it for a few days of actual holiday. Besides, there had been a purpose to her trip that she hadn't yet fulfilled.

"Are you going to drive us to the plane tomorrow?" Ellie asked Mirren when she gave up exploring the garden and joined them on the patio.

"I think we might stay for a few more days," Beth told her, then looked to Mirren. "Are you sure it's okay? I'm concerned your son isn't going to be happy. Do you need to call and check with him?"

"No." She chuckled. "I'll surprise him with the news when he arrives."

"Why do I get the feeling he's going to be annoyed and you're going to take pleasure in his irritation?"

"I promise he won't be annoyed. Not with you, anyway. There might be some eye-rolling and muttering in my direction. Cancel your flight and enjoy a few more days. Shall we say until Wednesday? That gives you a full four days to see the islands."

"Thank you." Beth felt instantly lighter at not having to leave so soon. "Isn't that great?" she asked Ellie, pulling her onto her lap. "We get to stay for longer."

"It's good if it doesn't rain." Ellie pushed her hair off her face with the palm of her hand. "Can we go on the train now?"

"Do you think it will be going?" Beth asked Mirren.

"I'd imagine so." She checked her watch. "I'm not convinced you'll make it in time though."

"How about we go tomorrow?" Beth asked Ellie. "We've got lots of time now that we're staying for longer."

"I want to go now." She pouted. "You said we can go as soon as it stops raining."

Mirren chuckled lightly. "Let me give Kit a call. See what we can do." She reached for her phone, and after a brief exchange, she ended the call and smiled at Ellie. "You're in luck. He says he'll wait for you. I'll drive you down there."

"We could have gone tomorrow," Beth said apologetically.

"The poor little mite's been stuck inside all week. No wonder she's desperate to get out and do something fun."

While Mirren fetched her car keys, Beth nipped back to the cottage for her bag. She was completely embarrassed when they arrived at the promenade in Hugh Town to find the train full of waiting passengers. Kit opened the front door and beckoned them onto the seat beside him.

"We get to sit right at the front!" Ellie said excitedly.

"Thank you for waiting," Beth said to Kit. "It's really kind of you."

"No problem." He tickled Ellie's tummy. "I have to tell the passengers about the island, but I'll talk to you in a little while, okay?"

Ellie nodded solemnly and stared at Kit in wonder as he put a microphone headset on and announced to the entire train that they were ready to go now that the VIP guests had arrived. Beth felt her cheeks flush and was glad when they set off and Kit switched to talking about the scenery.

Initially, she was concerned that Ellie might get restless, but they were both enthralled by Kit's commentary. When Ellie inched closer to him, Beth pulled her back along the bench seat, quietly telling her not to distract him.

"I hope she isn't bothering you too much," Beth said, when Kit stopped the train on the northern tip of the island, giving the passengers five minutes to enjoy the view and take photographs.

Kit looked confused as he slipped his headset off. "I forgot she was there, she's so quiet." He stepped out of the train and stretched his neck. "Do you want to take some photos?"

"I wish I'd thought to bring my camera," Beth said, getting out to stretch her legs.

"You forgot your phone?" Kit asked, smiling down at Ellie as she leaned against his leg.

Distracted by her flirt of a daughter, it took Beth a moment to register his words. "Oh, yes, I could use my phone." She pulled it from her pocket and opened the camera. "I'm a photographer for my job, so I usually have a better camera than my phone."

"I'd say you can come with me again tomorrow and bring it then, but it's your last day today, isn't it?"

"We're actually staying a few more days." Beth raised her phone to take a few photos of the crystal-clear water and the smaller islands in the distance. "Your mum took pity on us because it rained all week. She said we can stay on until Wednesday."

"At Mum's house?"

"No, in Peswera Cottage."

He smiled widely. "Trystan's going to love that."

"Oh god. Is he going to be annoyed? Mirren said it was fine, but I get the feeling I might not be very popular with your brother."

"He won't mind," Kit said. "I'd like to be there when he finds out though."

"That definitely sounds as though he *will* mind."

"Don't worry about it." Kit looked down at Ellie, who'd curled herself around his leg. "Why don't you hop into my seat for a minute and your mum can get a photo of you driving the train?"

"Can I really drive it?" Ellie asked.

"No!" Beth laughed. "Just pretend for the photo."

Once Ellie had posed for a photo, Kit pointed beside the steering wheel. "Press the button for the horn," he instructed Ellie. "That will make everyone get back on the train." He slipped in beside her and lifted her onto his lap. "How about helping me drive the train?"

The look of glee on Ellie's face filled Beth with joy. She took a few photos with her phone while Ellie proudly clutched the steering wheel as they drove the rest of the route.

When the train came to a stop back at Porthcressa Beach, Kit hopped out to chat to the passengers while deftly creating balloon animals for a bunch of eager children.

"Please can I have one?" Ellie asked once the crowd had dispersed.

He smiled down at her and began to pump air into the long thin balloon. "How about a giraffe?"

"Yes. Can I have a dog as well so the giraffe doesn't get lonely?"

"That's a good idea," Kit said, before Beth could jump in and tell Ellie it wasn't polite to ask for two.

"How much do I owe you?" Beth asked Kit, pulling out her purse as he handed over a yellow giraffe to Ellie.

"Nothing," he said. "VIPs get to ride for free."

"What's a VIP?" Ellie asked, gazing up at him.

"Very important person."

"Are you sure?" Beth said.

"Yep." He focused on twisting the next balloon, then handed it over to Ellie. "Thank you for helping me drive. You can come and work for me when you're older."

"I'd like to be a train driver," she said.

"I think you'd be very good at it." He took his phone from his pocket and tapped away. "Sorry. I'm being summoned. Trystan's just arrived back and the whole family is meeting in the pub for a drink. Do you fancy joining us?"

Beth stared at him, surprised and touched by the offer. "Thank you, but I think we're going to find a cafe for dinner."

"The food in the pub is good."

"I don't want to intrude on your family reunion. Especially since I probably won't be your brother's favourite person when he finds out that Mirren's letting us stay longer in his house."

Kit chuckled. "I promise you he'll be fine with it."

"The amusement on your face makes me think he's actually going to hate me."

"No chance!" Kit backed away from them. "Are you sure I can't tempt you?"

She shook her head. "Thanks for the offer. And for the train trip. We had a great time."

The Trenearys had all been so kind, but there was no way she could impose on their family time.

CHAPTER TWO

I t took Trystan a minute to spot his mum through the crowd at the Mermaid Inn. The start of the school holidays always meant an influx of holidaymakers, and the bustle in the nautical-themed pub reflected it. Mirren was sitting at a long table at the back of the room with his youngest brother, Kit.

"What happened to my welcome committee at the airport?" Trystan asked as he embraced his mum.

"Keira was supposed to pick you up," she told him. "But she got held up on a work call. Kit was working, as are Noah and Seren." She glanced behind the bar at them. "I had a dentist appointment."

"I felt very unloved," he said jokily, giving Kit a hug before they all took a seat.

"How was the flight?" his mum asked.

"Fine. It's nice to be back." Usually, he'd just fly in for short visits. This time he was staying for a whole month, and the extended stay was welcome.

"I have something to tell you …" His mum took a sip of her wine and looked slightly sheepish.

He rolled his eyes. "Why do I get the feeling I'm not going to like it?"

"Because you're not," Kit said, amused.

"Not going to like what?" Seren asked, appearing behind Trystan. She gave him a playful kiss on the side of his head in greeting, then moved around the table and slipped onto the bench beside Kit, discreetly entwining her fingers with his. It was the first time Trystan had seen them as a couple, and it took him off guard for a moment before his lips twitched to a discreet smile.

Kit gave Seren a sidelong glance that was full of mirth. "Mum was just about to tell him about … *you know?*"

"Oh, *that!*"

Trystan sighed. "Someone better just tell me."

"There's a small problem with the cottage," his mum began, shrinking back into her seat.

"*My* cottage?" he asked.

Kit chuckled. "Mum told the guests they could stay longer … so you're stuck at Mum's place."

"*Stuck* there?" Mirren said, clicking her tongue. "No need to make it sound quite so terrible."

"Are you serious?" Trystan asked. "You've promised my cottage to someone without checking with me first?"

"I'm in charge of bookings," Mirren said.

"Yes. But it's still my house, and you knew I was coming back. It's supposed to be empty from tomorrow for the rest of the summer."

"Don't get your knickers in a twist!"

Trystan let out an exasperated sigh. "I'll just go over there and explain your mistake and kick them out." There was no way he'd do it, but he wanted to make a point to his mum.

"You'd never be able to kick them out," Kit said with a smirk.

"Is he massive?" Trystan asked, his lips pulling to a smile.

"No. A tiny little girl."

"I could kick a kid out," Trystan said, full of bravado.

"You couldn't," Kit replied confidently. "She's got gorgeous big blue eyes and she's as cute as anything. You'd melt as soon as she looked at you."

Mirren wrinkled her brow. "It rained all week for them, the poor things. Not much of a holiday. That's why I said they could stay longer. It's just the mum and her little girl. They're ever so sweet."

"How long are they staying?" Trystan asked. Staying with his mum was fine for a while, but he'd been looking forward to spending the summer in the cottage.

"Just until Wednesday," Mirren said. "Although I was half thinking of offering for them to stay in the house with me after that."

"You should," Seren said. "It'd be nice for you to have the company."

Trystan shook his head. "Don't do it. Having a kid around the house will drive you mad after a couple of days. And it's always weird when you have strangers staying in the house."

"I say go for it," Kit said. "It's a bit of extra money. And the kid's super cute. Her mum's nice too."

"I'll think about it," Mirren said.

They all looked up as Keira arrived.

"I'm really sorry I didn't pick you up from the airport," she said, dropping onto the stool beside Trystan. "My boss forgot to let me know about a conference call until the last minute. I couldn't get out of it."

He gave her a steely look. "It was pretty annoying to walk from the airport with my luggage."

"Was it really?" Seren said, her tone making it clear she knew he hadn't walked from the airport at all. "So my dad didn't drive past and give you a lift?"

"There are no secrets around here, are there? Did he call you just to tell you that?"

"Yep."

"Were you just trying to make me feel bad?" Keira said, giving him a playful shove.

HANNAH ELLIS

"I might not have had to walk home with my luggage," he said with a smile. "But I did have the embarrassment of explaining to Ben how my family don't care enough to pick me up from the airport."

"I had a work thing," Keira said, shaking her head. "I'd have come otherwise."

"I'll forgive you. But you owe me a dance …"

She glanced around the busy pub. "I'm not dancing with you now. There's no room."

"No, but the next time I ask you to dance, you have to do it. Without rolling your eyes. Deal?"

"Fine. You're weird about dancing, you know."

"I'm not," he insisted, shaking her hand to seal the deal. "It's the rest of you who are weirdly unenthusiastic about dancing with me." He pulled her into a side hug. "It's nice to see you, by the way."

"You too," Keira said, chuckling. She hadn't been together with Noah for very long, but she fit right in with their family. It felt as though she'd been around for years, not just a matter of months.

Craning his neck, he caught Noah's eye and beckoned for him to bring him a drink. "How's it going working on the train?" he asked Keira.

"I love it," she replied. "I'm very excited for next week. I'll be taking the train tours every morning in August."

Trystan looked at Kit. "You're helping with the kids' club?"

"Yeah. And teaching some swimming lessons too."

"That'll be good," Trystan said, just as Noah reached over and put a drink in front of him. He stood to hug him.

"I heard Keira failed at picking you up?" Noah said.

"You need to choose your girlfriends better in future."

"Tell me about it," he joked, then dodged out of the way as Keira swiped at his leg.

"Have you finished your shift?" Keira asked him.

"Yeah, finally. It seemed to go on forever today."

18

Seren groaned as she stood up. "If you're finished, I should probably get back to work." She gave Kit a quick kiss before leaving them.

"You two are so cute," Keira said to Kit. "I'm really happy you finally got together."

"You and me both," Kit said. "Though it still feels a bit surreal."

Their mum squeezed his shoulder. "I think you make a lovely couple."

"Are you ready to go?" Noah asked Keira.

"Aren't we eating here?"

"I'd rather not. We've got leftovers at home."

"Trystan's just arrived," she pointed out.

"You don't mind if we catch up another time, do you?" Noah looked down at Trystan and put a hand over his mouth to cover a yawn.

"No. We've got all summer."

Noah tipped his chin at Keira. "Let's go home."

"You're very lucky," Trystan said, raising his eyebrows at his mum. "I'd really like to go home too."

Noah slapped a hand on his shoulder. "I heard Mum told Beth and Ellie they can stay longer."

"It seems as though they've made friends with everyone," Trystan remarked.

"The little girl's very sweet," Noah said. "She spent most of the week sitting in the window, getting excited when she saw any of us pass by. Yesterday she invited me in for a tea party with her teddies. Practically dragged me inside. Her mum was mortified."

"So long as they know it's just a couple of extra days," Trystan said, shooting his mum a quizzical look.

"I told you it's only until Wednesday."

"Good." He could cope with that.

After dinner in the pub, he left his mum chatting with a couple of her friends and set off for home alone. He'd pretty much forgotten about the guests in his cottage as he ambled through Hugh Town and out towards Old Town. Staying with his mum for a few days wasn't such a bad thing anyway. A smile pulled at his lips as he walked the familiar lanes. The salty air in his lungs seemed to take all his stress with it.

Over the last few months, his breakup with Jenny had taken up most of his mental energy. After ten years together it was hard to process being without her, but once he'd finally got it in his head that it really was over, there was a part of him that felt relieved. He missed her, but the fact that he wasn't compelled to do whatever it took to fix things between them seemed like a sign that it wasn't meant to be.

Rounding the corner, the sea came into view, along with screeching gulls gliding on the wind. Being back on St Mary's always felt refreshing, but this time it felt more uplifting than usual. Maybe it was because he was staying for longer than he normally would, or maybe because it signalled the start of a new chapter in his life. Whatever it was, there was a definite spring in his step as he approached his childhood home.

As he neared Peswera Cottage, he glanced at the living room window, where a couple of balloon animals stood on the sill looking out. Kit's handiwork, no doubt.

A faint knocking drew his attention to the upstairs window, where a little girl in pink pyjamas waved eagerly. He raised a hand in reply. When he continued on his way, the knocking came again, louder. Pushing her teddy against the glass, the girl flapped its arm to make it wave too. Trystan chuckled as he waved back. She looked over her shoulder, then gave another frantic wave before running away from the window.

Kit had been right; there was no way he'd have been able to demand she leave.

CHAPTER THREE

A few days of sunshine was just the pick-me-up Beth needed. She and Ellie both had some colour in their cheeks after their days exploring the beautiful beaches that St Mary's had to offer. The whole island was like a child's paradise, and the time in nature was refreshing for them both.

"Can you come and eat your breakfast?" Beth called to Ellie, who was in her usual spot in the living room window on Tuesday morning.

"I haven't seen the running man yet," she replied.

"Who?"

"The man who runs past in the mornings. Yesterday he pulled a funny face at me, but I haven't seen him today."

Beth suspected she was referring to the guy who owned the cottage and wondered if his funny face had been him scowling at the people who'd taken over his house.

"Just come and eat," Beth called, setting a plate of toast on the kitchen counter.

Ellie appeared and clambered up onto the stool. "What are we going to do today?"

"It's our last day here. What do you want to do?"

"I thought we were staying longer." She took a bite of toast and left a stripe of strawberry jam across her top lip.

"We did stay longer, but we have to leave tomorrow."

"I don't want to go home yet," Ellie mumbled while crunching on her toast.

"I'm afraid we have to." Beth hoped Ellie didn't start asking questions about *why* they had to get home. There wasn't a particularly good answer to that. With four-and-a-half more weeks of school holidays, they had very little on their schedule.

"I'd like to stay longer," Ellie said, looking her right in the eyes.

"We were lucky that we got to stay for a few extra days, but the cottage isn't available for us to stay in for any longer. Maybe we can come again next year."

"Okay. But let's not come on rainy days."

Beth smiled gently. "Finish your breakfast. Then I'll have a shower and we can go and talk to Mirren about coming again next year."

"Can we go on the train again after that?"

"We've already been on it twice. I think Kit will be sick of the sight of us."

Ellie shook her head. "He says I'm very important *and* I help him drive the train."

"I'm not sure he should really let you do that. It's a bit naughty. Anyway, we're not going on the train again. I'd like a lazy beach day." On autopilot, Beth opened the cupboard above the microwave and gazed up at the top shelf. A jolt hit her stomach at the thought of the task she still had to tackle before they left. If she was going to do what she'd come to do, she couldn't put it off any longer.

"Are you sad, Mummy?"

Closing the cupboard, she pasted on a smile and swallowed the lump in her throat. "Of course not," she said as she turned to her daughter. "How could I be sad when we're going to spend the day at the beach?"

"I don't want to do lots of walking," Ellie said, in a tone that was more suited to a teenager than a five-year old.

Beth grinned. "It's a good job we have a beach right on the doorstep then, isn't it?"

"It's not right on the doorstep, Mummy."

"I realise that, clever clogs. It's just a saying." Beth headed for the stairs. "I'm going to shower and get dressed. Why don't you draw a picture for me? There's paper and crayons in the living room."

"Okay, Mummy," Ellie replied sweetly.

Trystan hopped out of bed on Tuesday and straight into his running gear. Jogging along the coastal path with a cool breeze in his hair beat sweating it out on the treadmill any day.

"Isn't running every day a bit much?" his mum asked when he walked into the kitchen.

"I don't run every day. I run five days a week."

"It seems excessive. Especially when you're on holiday." She had her hands wrapped around a mug of coffee as she stared out of the window.

"I'm not really on holiday. I have to work, remember?" He'd been with the relocation firm for six years and had good relationships with his colleagues. It hadn't been a problem to organise for them to take over any face-to-face work for him while he concentrated on the behind-the-scenes stuff and liaising with clients over phone and video calls.

"I hope you'll have a break too. You work too hard."

"I have a perfectly balanced work and social life," he told her with a smile. "And things will feel even more balanced when I'm back in my own house tomorrow."

"I've been thinking about that …"

"Don't even think about renting the place out for longer."

"I'm not." She turned to look at him. "I just wondered

whether to offer Beth and Ellie one of the spare bedrooms here if they'd like to extend their stay."

"Did she say she wanted to?"

"No. I just got the feeling she'd like to avoid going home for a while. She seemed a bit sad somehow. But maybe I was imagining it." Mirren shook her head. "I don't know, I just like her. She has a nice vibe."

"You already let them stay longer than they planned. I'd say you've done enough. And I really think you'd be annoyed with having people around the house after a couple of days. Especially a noisy kid."

"She's sweet."

"She certainly looks like butter wouldn't melt," Trystan conceded. He'd waved to her every morning as he set off for a jog. "It's different having people stay in the house though – sharing the kitchen and the living room. It's awkward."

"You might be right. I thought the company might be nice, but it probably would be annoying."

Trystan took a couple of steps to his mum and wrapped her in a hug. "I'll be here all summer. We'll get Noah and Keira and Kit and Seren over for dinners and barbecues. It'll be fun."

"I know." Her eyes brightened as she pulled away from him. "I'm glad you're back."

"Me too."

"Off you go and run around the island then." She dismissed him with a flick of her hand. As he set off out the door he had a pang of guilt at talking his mum out of inviting guests to stay in her house. Selfishly, he just didn't like the thought of there being random people around whenever he called up to see her.

Outside the door, he paused to feel the tingle of sunshine on his face and listen to the shrieks from gulls gliding high on the wind. The gusty sea air smelled of seaweed and blew any lingering guilt away as he stretched on the lawn before setting off through the gate and onto the lane.

Turning to greet the little girl in the window of Peswera Cottage was automatic, but this time she wasn't grinning out at him. Today, her face was contorted with sadness. Her tear-filled eyes made him stop in his tracks.

As she slipped off the windowsill, he contemplated continuing on his way. Kids cried all the time, and her mum was there to take care of her, so there was really no need for him to waylay himself. At least until the front door opened and the sound of her gentle crying hit his ears.

"Are you okay?" he asked.

She shook her head in short jerky movements.

Gravel crunched underfoot as he stepped onto the short path to the door. "Where's your mum?"

"In the shower." Her chest hitched as she sniffed.

He stopped before he got too close and crouched to her level. "You're Ellie, right?"

"Yes. Do you know Mirren?"

"She's my mum," he said with a smile.

She wiped her nose with the back of her hand. "She's Kit's mummy too, and Noah's."

"They're my brothers," he told her. "Why are you crying? Did you hurt yourself?"

"No." More tears flooded her eyes and her chin twitched wildly. "Granny fell down and I don't know what to do."

"Granny?" he said, confused. "I thought it was just you and your mum on holiday?"

She shook her head, causing her blond locks to swing around her shoulders. "Granny came too. She fell over in the kitchen."

"Show me," he said, trying not to convey his panic.

She reached for his hand, wrapping her delicate fingers around his to lead him into the cottage.

"See," she said, pointing to the floor at the other side of the kitchen island.

One of the tall stools had been moved against the counter

and was covered in … what was it? Sand? Or dust maybe? It was all over the counter, and a pile of it was on the floor.

Picking up a handful to inspect it was automatic. "What is this?"

"That's Granny."

A shudder ran through Trystan when he spotted the urn upended on the floor. He let the ashes slip through his fingers, then brushed his palms against each other. "This is your grandma?"

"Yes." Ellie gazed up at him. "She's dead."

He chewed his lip. "I see."

"She was up on the high shelf. But she fell."

"Just fell? All on her own?"

"I wanted to have a look while Mummy was in the shower, but it's very heavy."

"Yeah."

"I'm going to be in trouble," she said solemnly.

"It was an accident."

"Mummy's already sad that Granny died. She'll be even more sad that she's all over the kitchen."

Trystan registered the sound of water running through the pipes. "How about we clean this up before Mummy gets out of the shower?"

The suggestion brought a smile to Ellie's blotchy little face and she nodded eagerly. Quickly, Trystan surveyed the scene again, then knelt to pick up the urn and carefully pushed the ashes from the counter back inside the container. He did the same for the layer covering the chair, then got the dustpan and brush from under the sink and knelt to the mound on the floor.

"You're very good at cleaning." Ellie crouched beside him as he swept ashes onto the dustpan.

"Thank you."

"It tickles."

"What does?" He was funnelling the ashes from the dustpan

into the urn but stopped when he saw Ellie's nose twitching violently.

Her sneeze sent a cloud of ash rising up around Trystan. He closed his eyes and froze for a moment. Eventually, he blinked a few times, then locked eyes with Ellie. Neither of them moved, and the only sound was the rush of water in the pipes, until that came to an abrupt stop.

"I'll be down in two minutes!" a voice called from upstairs.

Ellie's eyes filled with big fat tears.

"Don't cry," Trystan said in a rush. Gently, he brushed a sheen of dust from the front of her T-shirt. "We've almost cleaned it all up. I don't think your mummy would be cross with you anyway."

Turning back to the urn, he poured the remaining ashes in and replaced the lid.

"It goes up on the high shelf," Ellie said, pointing.

He frowned as he returned it to the cereal shelf. Maybe it wouldn't be the cereal shelf any more. In fact, he probably wouldn't put any food on that shelf from now on.

After wiping down the surfaces, he returned his attention to Ellie. "It's all clean." Hesitantly, he followed when she pulled him back through the living room. "I should stay and explain to your mum," he protested at the door.

She shook her head. "Let's not tell her."

"You shouldn't keep secrets," he said, not comfortable with the thought of leaving without making her mum aware of his presence. "I can explain if you want."

"I don't want to make Mummy more sad."

"But—"

She cut him off, shoving at his leg. For a tiny thing, she was forceful in pushing him outside.

"Bye," she said as she closed the door on him.

He stood still on the path, wondering whether he ought to be more adamant about staying to explain the situation. But maybe it was fine not to; the ashes were all cleaned up as though nothing had happened. Did he want to get more involved? Not really. What he wanted to do was get back to his jog.

As the sun broke through a gap in fluffy cumulus clouds, he glanced down at his navy-blue T-shirt, which was covered in grey ash. He brushed it off as best he could, then set off along the lane at a steady pace.

CHAPTER FOUR

"Who were you talking to?" Beth asked, towelling her shoulder-length hair dry as she came down the stairs.

Ellie didn't look up from the picture she was drawing while kneeling at the coffee table. "My new friend."

"Who's your new friend?" Beth assumed they were a figment of her daughter's imagination. Although after the way she'd invited Noah in for a tea party last week, it was hard to know.

"I don't know his name, but he's very kind."

"Okay." Beth smiled dismissively and continued rubbing her hair as she perched on the edge of the couch. "We need to go and talk to Mirren to settle the bill this morning. We have to pack all our things today too. I might start on that now while you're busy. Then we'll be able to enjoy the beach without worrying about having to come back and pack later."

Ellie remained engrossed in her picture, and Beth realised she may as well be talking to herself. Slinging the towel across the end of the couch, she crossed the room and once again opened the cupboard where she'd stashed her mum's ashes. If she was going to scatter them on the island it had to be today, but her stomach clenched at the thought of parting with them.

"Are you okay, Mummy?"

She smiled down at Ellie. "Yes. I'm okay."

"Do you miss Granny?"

"Yes," she whispered, her bottom lip quivering. Her throat felt like sandpaper, and she had to swallow hard before she could speak. "I think it's a very good idea to come back here again next year."

"Will we bring Granny with us again?"

"Yes." She couldn't face scattering the ashes yet. "We'll come back with Granny next year." The decision filled her with a sense of relief. All she wanted to do was spend their final day on the beach without thinking about her mum's ashes.

After some hasty packing, they set off to Mirren's house. Beth would enquire about booking for next year while she settled the bill. As they approached the back door, laughter from the kitchen stopped Beth in her tracks. She was about to suggest they come back later, but Ellie boldly opened the door and marched inside.

"Sorry," Beth said as she followed. "I need to teach her about knocking."

"Don't worry about it." Mirren's smile stretched wide. "Come in and meet Trystan. Another of my sons."

"Hi," Beth said to the guy in shorts and T-shirt sitting up on the kitchen counter. His blonde hair highlighted his tanned skin and a sheen of sweat glistened at his hairline. "It's your cottage we've taken over, isn't it?"

"Yes." The skin around his eyes crinkled as he smiled.

"I hope you didn't mind too much that we stayed longer."

"It's fine. I had a few days of being pampered by my mum." He beamed down at Ellie, who was standing by his legs. "Hello again."

"You look hot," Ellie told him.

Doesn't he just? Beth thought, hoping her cheeks hadn't betrayed her by flushing bright red.

"I've been for a run."

"Have you two already met?" Beth asked, registering the fact that he'd greeted Ellie as though they'd seen each other before.

"Kind of. Briefly. We've waved at each other through the window a few times and then ..." He glanced down at Ellie, who stared up at him. Whipping his head up again, he extended his hand. "Beth, was it?"

"Yes." She felt slightly flustered as she shook his hand. The weather had definitely made a turnaround from the previous week. The room felt stuffy even so early in the day.

"Why are you sitting up there?" Ellie asked.

"That's a very good question." Mirren rolled her eyes. "I've been asking the same since he was about nine years old."

Ignoring his mum, Trystan kept his eyes on Ellie. "It's a better height up here."

Out of nowhere, Beth had an image of standing between his legs and kissing his beautiful lips. That probably wasn't what he meant about the height. Taking a step backwards, she wiped her hands on her shorts and cleared her throat. The heat was getting to her.

"Come here," Trystan said, reaching down and lifting Ellie to sit beside him. He tilted his head as though telling her a secret. "I have four brothers, and when I was growing up, the kitchen was always full of people. We liked to annoy each other, so it was always better to sit up here so no one could sneak up behind you and thwack you on the back of the head or flick your ears."

"Did your brothers hit you?" Ellie asked with wide eyes.

"Yeah." He put his hand in front of his mouth as he mock-whispered, "But most of the time it was my mum giving me a clip."

"That's true," Mirren said with a smile. "But you should have heard how cheeky he was."

Trystan flashed Beth a smile that made butterflies dance in her stomach. "I heard it rained a lot for your holiday," he said, changing the subject.

"We were very unlucky with the weather." Beth's voice

sounded slightly unnatural, and she had the feeling her sweat glands were in overdrive. "The last few days have been gorgeous though."

"I don't want to go home," Ellie said grumpily. "But Mummy says we can't stay in the cottage any more so we have to."

"Well now I feel bad." Trystan looked at Beth with a pained expression. "Sorry."

She gave a quick shake of the head. "Don't apologise. I'm grateful we got to stay a few extra days."

"Yesterday we went on a boat trip and saw seals," Ellie announced happily.

"That sounds like fun," Trystan replied. "Did you swim with them?"

"I can't swim," she said, gazing up at him. "I liked seeing them from the boat though. Some of them were sunbathing on a beach. I don't like sunbathing, but I like making sandcastles. That's why I don't want to go home."

"We have beautiful beaches at home too," Beth said.

"Whereabouts do you live?" Trystan asked.

"Plymouth."

He nodded.

"I like it more here." Ellie leaned close to Trystan, then pulled back, nostrils flaring. "You smell funny."

"Ellie!" Beth hissed, while Mirren chuckled.

"I'm a bit sweaty," Trystan said.

Beth cast Ellie an impatient look. "It's not very nice to tell someone they smell."

"To be fair, she's not the first person to tell me that today." Trystan cast a glance in his mum's direction.

Mirren pulled a face. "I was trying to convince him to go and shower right before you arrived."

"I'm going for a swim in a minute," Trystan said.

"We're going to the beach today," Ellie said, grinning up at him.

"To build sandcastles?" he asked.

She nodded. "And have a picnic."

"That's right." Beth took a step forwards. "We should go now and leave Mirren in peace."

Ellie rested her head against Trystan's bicep, the casual gesture making Beth's heart swell. "But you haven't asked Mirren if we can come again next year."

"Right. Yes." Beth swung around. "I wanted to ask if we could book in for next year. I think Ellie might refuse to leave the island unless she knows we'll definitely be coming back. I also need to pay for our extra time in the cottage."

"I'd love to have you back." Mirren went to the table and opened her laptop. "Let's see what's available."

"Where do *you* live?" Ellie asked Trystan.

"Most of the time I live in London," he told her. "And sometimes I come back here. The cottage you've been staying in belongs to me."

Her nose crinkled. "Why did we stay in your house?"

"Because when I'm not staying here, I rent it out to people who want a holiday."

"You have two houses?" she asked.

"Kind of."

"We only have one," she told him.

"One is usually enough," he said, amused.

"Why do you have two then?"

"Sorry," Beth said, shooting Trystan an apologetic look before switching her attention to Ellie. "I think that's enough questions. And I think we also need to have a conversation about personal space." Her fingers grazed Trystan's arm as she lifted Ellie from the counter.

Mirren looked up from the laptop. "Did you have a particular time in mind?"

"The beginning of the school holidays would be perfect if you have something available then. I think we'll come for two weeks next time. A week wasn't long enough."

Beth pulled up the calendar on her phone as she took a seat at the kitchen table with Mirren.

"Will I still be five the next time we come?" Ellie asked.

"No," Beth replied. "You'll be a big six-year-old."

Ellie screwed up her face in displeasure. "That's a very long time."

"You really don't want to go home tomorrow, do you?" Trystan muttered.

"No. I want to stay here."

Beth ran a hand over Ellie's hair. "I'm afraid that's the problem with holidays. They always have to come to an end. But we'll be back next year. That's something to look forward to."

Mirren shifted her gaze from the laptop screen to Trystan, giving him a look Beth couldn't decipher.

Trystan let out a breath that was part chuckle. "Isn't there a guest room in the house they could stay in?"

Smiling widely, Mirren looked at Beth. "There's a double room upstairs. It's basic but there's an en suite. You'd be welcome to use the kitchen and living room. You could make yourselves at home. It's not as nice as the cottage, and you obviously don't have the same privacy, but if you really do want to stay for longer it's an option."

"Oh, wow." Beth blinked rapidly as she tried to digest the offer. "Do you usually rent out rooms in your house?"

"I haven't for a while. And it's not something I advertise. Like I say, it's basic, but it's also cheap."

"You should take her up on it," Trystan said. "That way I won't have to feel bad for being the reason you can't stay longer."

"I'm not sure," Beth said, feeling flustered.

"Have you got work to get back to?" Mirren asked.

"No. I took the school holidays off."

Ellie moved to stand beside Mirren. "Granny was going to look after me in the summer holidays, but she died so she can't now."

"I'm sorry to hear that," Mirren said gently. "That's really sad."

"Yes, it is," Ellie said, matter-of-factly. "It made Mummy *very* sad. I miss Granny too. She was very kind and she played with me a lot."

Given the lump in her throat, Beth didn't trust herself to speak. When Mirren gave her hand a squeeze, she was sure she was going to burst into tears.

"Are we going to stay at Mirren's house?" Ellie asked, tilting her head.

"I'm not sure." Beth's voice was weak.

"Why don't you think about it today," Mirren suggested. "Let me know what you decide."

"Yes." Beth's thoughts were all over the place, and she needed time to mull it over. "I'll have a think about it while we're at the beach." Standing, she took Ellie's hand, then snapped her gaze back to Mirren. "I need to sort out the bill, too."

"We can do that later. You get out and enjoy the sunshine."

"Thank you," Beth said, needing to get away for fear she was about to start crying.

"Have fun at the beach," Trystan called as Beth encouraged Ellie out of the door.

Mirren waited until the door had closed behind the two of them before turning and giving Trystan a knowing look.

"What?" he asked, a grin creeping over his face as he tried to look innocent.

"I thought having guests staying in the house would be annoying. Especially noisy kids!"

He shrugged. "Those two aren't going to be any trouble. And the kid is so cute, how could we crush her dreams of an extended holiday?"

"Oh, so it's the little one you found cute?" Mirren raised her eyebrows. "I knew you'd like Beth."

"They both seem nice. What's the deal with the girl's dad?"

"I've no idea. He hasn't been mentioned."

Trystan hopped down from the counter. "I'm going to get changed and go for a swim."

Standing, Mirren rubbed at a dirty mark on his shoulder. "You're a right state. Where's the dust come from?"

Trystan looked at his shoulder. "It's the remains of Beth's mother."

"What?"

He explained the incident with the urn and how he'd helped Ellie clean up.

"It sounds as though she lost her mum recently," Mirren remarked. "The poor love."

"Yeah." Trystan gave a cheeky grin. "Or she didn't lose her recently and she's a weirdo who takes her dead mother everywhere. And we've invited her to stay in the house with you!"

CHAPTER FIVE

"Can we stay in Mirren's house, Mummy?" Ellie asked for about the twentieth time as they sat on the beach, eating their picnic of sandwiches and grapes.

"I'm still thinking about it." Beth was barely listening to Ellie; she was too focused on the figure cutting through the turquoise water with a perfect front crawl. She suspected it was Trystan. Presumably he'd beaten them to the water when they'd stopped at the cottage for their picnic and beach essentials.

A family occupied the other end of the beach, far enough away that Beth felt as though they had a tiny piece of paradise all to themselves.

"I want to stay," Ellie said as she chewed on a jam sandwich.

"I know you do." Beth watched the swimmer head towards the shore until he was close enough for her to see that it was definitely Trystan. As he stood up in the shallow water and strode onto the beach, she averted her gaze.

Ellie jumped to her feet when she noticed him. "Hi, Trystan!"

"Hello," he replied with a smile. "I haven't seen you for a while."

"You just saw us at Mirren's house," Ellie said, missing the joke.

"Oh, yes. I remember now." He fetched his towel from the sand nearby and rubbed it over his face and hair before patting his torso. "How was your picnic?" he asked, wandering over to them.

"Yummy," Ellie replied. "Do you want a grape?"

"Yes, please." He took the single grape that Ellie handed him and popped it in his mouth. As he chewed, he crouched beside Ellie and pointed to the horizon. "Do you see that boat?"

"Which one?" Ellie asked.

"The white one with the mast."

To avoid staring at the drips trailing down Trystan's toned torso, Beth looked out to sea too. Boats were scattered in the bay and she had no idea which one they were supposed to be looking at.

"Whereabouts?" she asked, glancing back in time to catch Trystan stealing a grape from the bunch on the blanket.

"Out on the water." He flashed a mischievous grin. "That big boat."

"Is it your boat?" Ellie asked.

"No." He popped another grape in his mouth. "It's a nice boat though, isn't it?"

Beth shuffled across the blanket to get closer to Ellie. "He's making you look at the boats so he can steal grapes without you noticing," she told her in a stage whisper.

"Are you?" Ellie asked, looking up at Trystan, who stopped chewing abruptly.

"I took three," he confessed under the scrutiny of her gaze. "I'm sorry. In my defence they're delicious and I'm very hungry."

"That's okay," Ellie told him. "You can have another. Can't he, Mummy?"

She nodded in reply.

"It's nice to share," Ellie said seriously as she plucked

another grape for him.

"Not so nice to steal," Beth remarked under her breath, then stifled a laugh at the wounded look that Trystan shot her.

"I feel as though I might not have made the best first impression." He shifted to sit on his towel. "First I steal the cottage from you and then I steal your picnic."

"You're hardly stealing the cottage," Beth argued. "If it was my house I'd want it back too. I still can't get over the view here. The colour of the water is magical."

Trystan hooked his arms around his knees as he stared out over the bay. "One of my favourite things about being back here is starting the day with a jog and a swim. Hitting the gym in London is an entirely different approach to exercise."

"I'll bet," Beth agreed.

"Do you want a sandwich?" Ellie held the small triangle out to him. "It's got jam in it."

"I haven't had a jam sandwich for a very long time." After devouring it in one mouthful, his eyes widened. "I might start eating jam sandwiches more often."

Ellie giggled and ate one herself. "Can you help me build a sandcastle?" she asked with her mouth full.

"I think Trystan probably has other things to do," Beth said quickly.

"As it happens, I'm very good at building sandcastles."

"You really don't have to," Beth insisted, but Trystan had already picked up a shovel.

"Can we build one with a moat?" Ellie asked.

"It wouldn't be a very good sandcastle if it didn't have a moat. We'll need turrets too and a drawbridge."

Ellie gazed up at him, a look of awe on her face. "I don't know how to do that."

"I can show you."

They moved a little away from the blanket and got to work, Trystan marking the outline in the sand and giving Ellie instructions.

"Should I help?" Beth asked.

Trystan quirked an eyebrow. "Considering your daughter doesn't know how to build turrets or a drawbridge, I suspect you're fairly clueless about the art of sandcastle building. It's probably better if you stay out of the way and leave it to the expert."

Beaming at his cheekiness, Beth looked to Ellie. "Can you please tell him that I'm very good at building sandcastles?"

"You're pretty good." She stepped aside when Trystan leaned in front of her to dig. "But we've never had a drawbridge."

"See!" Trystan said, without looking up. "You sound like an amateur to me."

She watched them work for a few minutes, enjoying Ellie's excitement at having Trystan to help her with the sandcastle.

"I feel a bit bad just sitting around watching you," she finally said.

Trystan paused in shovelling sand. "Feel free to go for a swim or something."

"Oh, I didn't mean … I'm fine, thanks."

Ellie nodded. "You can swim if you want, Mummy. We'll finish the sandcastle."

Looking longingly out to sea, Beth couldn't say she wasn't tempted. They'd done a lot of paddling in the shallows over the last few days, but she hadn't managed a proper swim. "I suppose a quick dip would be nice." She caught Trystan's eye. "Are you sure you don't mind keeping an eye on Ellie?"

"She seems like a handful, but I'm sure we'll be fine."

"Thank you," she said, ignoring his playful tone.

At the water's edge she turned to check on Ellie, who was deep in conversation with Trystan while they worked on their castle.

With the crystal-clear water around her thighs, Beth paused to take in the scenery. From the white sand to the turquoise water and the bright blue sky overhead, it was easy to see why Scilly had left such an impression on her mother. A wave rolled in, bringing a rush of cool water around her midriff and snapping her from her trance.

Adrenaline pumped through her veins as she dived under the water. After a couple of strokes she resurfaced with a huge smile on her face. Swimming made her feel freer than she had done in a long time. For fifteen minutes she didn't need to think about anything but the cool water on her skin and the warm rays of sunshine beating down on her.

Making her way back towards the beach, she caught snatches of Ellie's high-pitched laughter.

"We finished the castle," Ellie said, grabbing excitedly at Beth's hand as soon as she was back on the beach. "Trystan ate another sandwich and said he'd blame it on me, but it was him!"

"Hey!" Trystan called, standing proudly beside the sandcastle. "I helped you build this and now you're trying to get me into trouble!"

Hastily, Beth wrapped her towel around herself. "I got to go for a swim," she said brightly. "A couple of sandwiches and a few grapes sounds like a good trade. I can see why you like to start your day that way. It's absolute bliss."

Trystan crouched down and patted the side of the castle.

"Can we build another one?" Ellie asked.

"I think I should go and get on with some work, but maybe another day… if you decide to stay longer." There was an intensity to his piercing blue eyes as he looked up at Beth. "Do you think you will?"

"I don't know. It's very tempting. Maybe for another week." She shook her head. "I don't even know how long your mum was offering for us to stay. I'll go up and talk to her again this afternoon."

"Did you see the drawbridge?" Ellie asked, putting an end to the conversation.

"That's pretty impressive," Beth said, looking at the collection of twigs which bridged the gap over the moat.

"I should go." Standing, Trystan brushed sand from his legs.

Ellie stood too and put her hands on her hips. "Do you promise to build another castle with me another day?"

"Be careful how you answer," Beth told him. "Five-year-olds take promises very seriously."

"If you stay longer I'll definitely build another sandcastle with you." He held up a hand to high five Ellie, his eyes sparkling warmly. "So it's up to your mum really."

"Hey!" Beth called as he set off, his feet sinking into the soft sand with each step. "You realise I'm going to have no choice but to stay now. I'll never hear the end of it otherwise."

"It wouldn't be so terrible, would it?" He walked backwards for a few steps, his flirty smile making Beth's heart rate increase.

"No," she murmured, though he was too far away to hear. "I don't suppose it would be."

"Are we going to stay in Mirren's house?" Ellie asked, parking herself in Beth's lap when she sat on the blanket.

"Yes. I think that would be nice." Beth's eyes didn't leave Trystan as he walked up the beach with his towel slung over his shoulder. As though he could sense her watching, he stopped when he reached the lane and turned to wave.

Heat flooded Beth's cheeks as she waved back. Had he been flirting with her or was she imagining it? She could've sworn he had been. That couldn't be right though. He was gorgeous, and she suspected he was a lot younger than her. Probably around thirty. It was fine to check out guys ten years younger than you when you were on holiday though, wasn't it? A little bit of flirting was harmless.

"This is the best sandcastle I've ever made," Ellie announced, moving over to it. "Trystan's much better at building than you."

"Thanks!" she said, lying on her back.

With the sound of waves in her ears and the sun's rays warming her skin, it was hard to think of a reason not to extend their holiday.

CHAPTER SIX

It was a long time since a woman had affected Trystan the way Beth had. Her shy smile was magnetic and there was an elegance to her movements that was almost angelic. Building a sandcastle with her daughter had been a fairly shameless way to linger with them on the beach, but he hadn't been able to help himself. It turned out that building sandcastles was surprisingly therapeutic too. Working on moats, turrets and drawbridges had him completely absorbed.

The trouble came when he sat down with his laptop at the desk in his mum's living room and found his mind wouldn't settle on work. Mentally, he was still out on the beach, soothed by the rays of the sun and the warmth of Beth's smile. Forcing himself to focus on the task at hand, he managed a productive few hours before the sound of voices drifted from the kitchen. Ellie's high-pitched chatter brought a smile to his lips and he crept to the doorway. He fought the urge to go into the kitchen but couldn't resist listening in on the conversation between Beth and his mum.

Once he'd heard Beth accept the offer to stay longer, he moved away again. The relief he felt that she wasn't leaving the following day was crazy. As was the fact that he couldn't stop grinning to himself. When his mum wandered in ten minutes later, he schooled his features to something more appropriate for a grown man poring over the London housing market.

"Beth and Ellie were just here," Mirren told him.

He looked up from his laptop, making a show of stretching his neck. "Oh, really?" Casual as anything. He should probably have been an actor.

"They're going to stay on in the house with me from tomorrow."

"That's nice." He massaged his left shoulder as though the conversation was of little interest to him. If he had gone into acting, he'd probably have won several Oscars by now. "How long will they stay?"

"I'm not sure. I told Beth they can stay for the whole summer as far as I'm concerned. It'll be good to have some noise in the house again."

He smiled gently but refrained from commenting.

"I told Beth you'd help them with their bags tomorrow."

"Sure." He put his attention firmly back on his laptop, running his fingers over the mousepad to scroll through the property listings.

"I'll leave you to it."

Running his thumb over his bottom lip, Trystan squinted at the computer screen – his serious business face.

"Trystan?" his mum said loudly.

Slowly, he swivelled in the chair and raised a questioning eyebrow.

"Just because you're refusing to smile doesn't mean I can't tell that you're delighted about Beth staying longer."

"What?" He almost choked on a laugh at the knowing look his mum gave him. "I don't know what you're talking about. Why would I care?"

She shook her head and turned to leave. "You must think I'm a complete idiot," she muttered as she walked away.

Maybe he wasn't destined for an Oscar after all.

~

Beth had just got Ellie settled in bed when her phone rang. Smiling, she answered the call from her best friend and wandered from the kitchen to the living room.

"It feels as though you've been gone for way longer than a week and a half," Dee said. As usual, her words came out in a rush as though they might run out of time to speak. "I'm coming over to your place as soon as you're back tomorrow. We need to talk about the plan for Saturday ..."

"I don't think we need to-"

"No! You can stop that right now. I don't want to hear about how you don't want to celebrate your birthday. It can be something low-key, but we're not letting your fortieth pass without acknowledging it. There's no point in arguing with me on this."

Beth perched on the window sill, admiring the way the setting sun made the surface of the water sparkle in varying shades of red and orange. "I was going to say we don't need to plan anything because I won't be there."

"What are you talking about? You're coming home tomorrow."

"That was the plan, but Mirren offered us a guest room in her house."

"Who?"

"Mirren. The woman I'm renting the cottage from. She's letting us stay in her house so we can have a longer holiday."

Silence ensued as Dee seemed to process the information. "So how long are you staying?"

"She said we could stay for the whole summer, which seemed a bit excessive, but the more I think about it, the more appealing it is. Apart from hanging out with you and Ferne, we didn't have much planned for the school holidays."

"Wow. That's very spontaneous and doesn't sound at all like you."

"I can be spontaneous," Beth said, not sure why she felt so

offended by Dee's remark. Especially since she really did like to meticulously plan things.

"I think it's a good idea, anyway. So you'll be staying in the woman's house?"

"Yeah. I know it sounds a bit weird but she's really nice. Her whole family are lovely."

"How many of them live there?"

"Just her in the house. She has grown-up children. I'm not sure how many, but I've met three of her sons. One of them runs a tourist train, which we've been on twice now. He's really sweet with Ellie. They all are."

"Okay." Dee chuckled. "Your decision to stay for the whole summer is starting to make more sense now."

Beth laughed loudly. "They're nice guys, that's all. Kit's probably half my age. And I think they're all in relationships."

"You *think?* You don't sound too certain."

"Oddly enough, I haven't asked any of them about their relationship status." An image of Trystan on the beach popped into her head. There was no way he could be single. Then again, it probably wasn't appropriate to guess at someone's relationship status based on how good they look when they've just stepped out of the sea and have golden rays of sunshine enhancing their every delicious feature.

It wasn't just his looks that made her head swim either, but the assuredness of his posture and the glint in his eyes that hinted at a genuinely warm personality. The fact that he was incredibly good-looking was just a bonus. Not for her obviously … for his girlfriend or wife or … He could be gay for all she knew.

"I'm very jealous," Dee said, interrupting her train of thought. "A summer full of sun, sea and sexy men sounds very appealing."

Leaning close to the window pane, Beth tried to look up at Mirren's house, but the angle was wrong and it was just out of sight. "My summer isn't going to involve sexy men," she said, crossing the living room and sliding the patio door open to step out of the side of the house. From there, she glanced over the hedge and up to Mirren's place. A figure was visible in the upstairs window. She could tell it was Trystan from his confident stance as he paced in front of the window. The light illuminated him from behind as he spoke on the phone.

"Did you scatter your mum's ashes?" Dee asked, the pitch of her voice softening.

"No. Which is another reason I like the idea of staying longer. It gives me more time to psyche myself up to it. I really wish Mum had specified where exactly she wanted them scattered."

"I imagine that since she didn't specify anything, the exact spot wasn't overly important to her."

Beth sat at the table, worrying that Trystan might look over and catch her watching him. "I think she was going to show me her favourite spot on this trip. It doesn't seem fair that she didn't get to come with us." She almost laughed. "At least not alive anyway."

"It's not fair," Dee agreed. "But I'm glad you still made the trip. I'm sure it'll have done you good."

A lump swelled in Beth's throat and she caught a tear at the corner of her eye.

"So what *are* you going to do on your birthday?"

"Oh, I have big plans," Beth said, false enthusiasm in her voice. "I'm going to pretend it's not happening and try and make it through the day without crying."

"Find something nice to do," Dee said.

"I'm hoping it'll be a lovely sunny day and we can relax on a beautiful beach."

"That sounds good."

"With any luck, that will be how I spend all my days for the next few weeks."

There was noise in the background and Dee let out a sigh

that was part growl. "My little monster is refusing to go to sleep. I bet Ellie's fast asleep already, isn't she?"

"I think the sea air knocked her out."

"Yeah, right. Your child's just an angel."

Beth would argue that she was definitely no angel, but they'd had the conversation too many times to bother. To be fair, Ellie had always been easy to settle in the evenings and had slept through the night since she was three months old. It was something Beth had always been very grateful for.

"I have to go and read Ferne another story," Dee said wearily.

"Give her a kiss from me."

They promised to talk to each other in the next few days and ended the call.

Beth moved to get herself a drink, pausing at the patio doors to look over at Mirren's house. Trystan was still in the window, still on the phone. He'd stopped pacing and seemed to be looking directly at her. She smiled, though they were too far apart to be able to make out facial expressions.

Hopefully that meant he wouldn't be able to catch the way her cheeks flushed before she turned and slipped inside.

CHAPTER SEVEN

O n Wednesday morning, Beth immediately stripped the beds and put the bedding in the washing machine. Then she finished off the packing and got to work on cleaning the cottage. The doors and windows were all open to let fresh air in, which meant Ellie kept wandering outside. If Beth didn't have to constantly check what her daughter was up to, the cleaning would have been finished ages ago.

"Are you sure you don't want to watch TV for a bit?" Beth asked, backing out of the downstairs toilet in a pair of yellow rubber gloves.

"No," Ellie replied, standing just outside the front door. "I want to play outside."

"We can play later. I need to finish cleaning first." She moved back into the tiny bathroom. "Can you stay in the house, please," she shouted behind her. "Don't wander onto the lane. It might be quiet but cars still come up here sometimes …"

"Mummy?" Ellie called.

"Yeah?"

"Mummy!"

Beth's shoulders tensed as she stepped out of the bathroom again. "If you'd just let me get on, the cleaning would go much quicker and then we can …" She trailed off at the sight of Trystan filling the doorway. "Hi," she said sheepishly.

"Trystan's here," Ellie said, the sweetness of her voice contrasting with Beth's impatient tone.

"I can see that, thank you." She tried to use the back of her gloved hand to remove a strand of hair from her forehead, but all she managed was to choke on the chemical smell from the gloves. "I think I just need another half hour," she told Trystan. "Then we'll be out of your way and you can have your house back."

"I didn't mean to rush you," he said with a lazy smile. "I've just finished my run and thought I'd see if there was anything I could carry for you. Your suitcase, maybe?" He pointed at the black case just inside the door.

"That would be great." Beth pulled the bright yellow marigolds off.

"You didn't need to do a big clean," Trystan said as he stepped inside.

"It's the least I can do after you let us stay longer. I washed the bedding … should I put it back on the beds when its dry?"

"No, just leave it." He picked up the case with ease. "I'll sort it."

"That means we can go out and play," Ellie said.

"After I finish cleaning."

"I'm bored," Ellie said, looking up at Trystan. "Can you build a sandcastle with me?"

"I need to take your suitcase up to the house."

"Shall I come with you?" she asked.

"I guess you could, if you want?"

"No," Beth said, looking sternly at Ellie. "Stay here while I finish cleaning. Then we'll go up to the house together."

"She can come now," Trystan said. "It's fine with me."

"Are you sure?" She flashed him a grateful smile. "I won't be long."

"Take as long as you want." Trystan's forehead crinkled as

he frowned. "Not that you need to spend a long time cleaning. You really don't need to clean at all … I just meant that you don't need to rush on my account. I'll find something to keep Ellie entertained."

"Thank you." She switched her attention to Ellie. "Be good, okay?"

"Okay," she said as she skipped out of the door.

"I really won't be long," Beth said to Trystan, the warmth of his gaze making her wish she wasn't up to her elbows in cleaning supplies and feeling so dishevelled.

"See you in a bit." His eyes lingered on her for a couple of seconds too long before he went after Ellie.

Left alone, the last of the cleaning hardly took any time. Once she'd finished, she scraped her hair into a ponytail and inspected her face in the mirror before deciding there wasn't much she could do about her appearance. Collecting up the last of their things meant she was laden down with various tote bags and jackets and a balloon in the shape of a giraffe when she set off up the lane.

Ellie and Trystan were out in the garden playing with a kids' tennis set.

"Thanks for keeping an eye on her," Beth said.

"You're welcome." He held the ball out to Ellie as he crouched to her level. "I have to go and do some work now."

"Can we play again another time?"

"Yes." He straightened up and his eyes locked with Beth's. "I guess we'll be seeing a bit of each other, if you're staying for the whole summer."

"Let's see. Mirren might be sick of us in a few days and send us packing."

"I can't see that happening."

Mirren stepped outside, offering Beth a welcoming smile. "Me neither." She looked to Trystan. "Are you staying for a coffee?"

"No. I should get going." He held the plastic tennis racket

out to Beth. His fingers brushed hers as she took it, and she deliberately avoided catching his eye in case her cheeks were as red as she suspected they were. He ducked inside for his bags before saying goodbye to them and striding away to the cottage.

"I'll show you around, then let you get unpacked and settled," Mirren said. On the tour of the house she told them repeatedly to make themselves at home. She couldn't have been more welcoming and even entertained Ellie in the garden so Beth could unpack in peace.

They spent the day in the garden and down on the beach, then ate dinner on the patio with Mirren. Having another adult around made a welcome change, and Mirren commented that she enjoyed the company too. Once Ellie was settled in the large double bed, Beth poured herself a glass of wine and took it out onto the patio to enjoy the sunset. Mirren was tucked away in the living room, reading a book.

As Beth listened to the sound of the waves washing onto the shore, everything felt wonderfully peaceful. Occasionally, she glanced down to the row of cottages on the lane, her eyes pausing on Peswera Cottage and the gentle glow of light seeping from the living room window. As the wine relaxed her further, Beth wondered when she'd see Trystan next. His remark about seeing a lot of each other came back to her, and she found herself hoping he was right.

The only sign of him the following day was the paddling pool and sun loungers that had appeared in the garden before they even got up. Apparently, Mirren had messaged Trystan the previous day, asking him to dig the pool out of the garage and set it up. The slight pang of disappointment Beth felt at having missed him was quickly replaced by an immense amount of gratitude as she lazed on a sun-lounger and read while Ellie happily splashed away.

Late in the afternoon, she coaxed Ellie into a walk to the

town, where they made a quick trip to the supermarket so she could cook dinner that evening. Mirren had already offered, but Beth had insisted that while she'd love for them to eat together, there was no way she could let Mirren cook every evening. She glanced into Peswera Cottage as they passed it, feeling her heart quickening as she did. Sadly, she didn't catch so much as a glimpse of Trystan and chastised herself for thinking about him so much.

On Saturday morning, Beth's mind had shifted firmly away from Trystan and was somewhere else entirely. Her stomach was knotted so tightly when she woke up that she couldn't manage breakfast. When Ellie asked to go on the train, she couldn't be bothered to try to persuade her otherwise.

Down at Porthcressa Beach, Beth felt slightly relieved to find that Kit wasn't working, so she avoided the embarrassment of taking yet another train trip. Noah's girlfriend, Keira, took the tour. She was enthusiastic as she gave information about the island, and her love of the place shone through.

Despite Keira's energy, Beth struggled to concentrate on the tour and her mind wandered constantly. She felt as though she was on autopilot as she led Ellie to a cafe for lunch after the train trip. They were tucking into thick slabs of chocolate cake when Beth's phone rang.

"Happy birthday!" Dee crooned down the phone.

"Thank you."

"Are you having a nice day?"

"Yeah, it's fine." Actually, she wished she could crawl into bed and only emerge when the day was over.

"You don't sound fine," Dee said sadly.

"We've been on a train ride, and now we're stuffing our faces with cake." She managed a smile as she looked at the chocolate smeared around Ellie's face.

"I'm glad there's cake at least. What are you doing later?"

"We'll probably go to the beach."

"Are you okay?" Dee asked sympathetically.

"Yeah. I'll be fine."

"Put the phone on speaker so I can talk to Ellie."

Beth did as she was instructed, then told Ellie to say hi to Dee.

"Do you know it's Mummy's birthday today?" Dee said, while Beth silently cursed her. She hadn't bothered mentioning it to Ellie.

"Is it?" Ellie asked, looking at Beth with wide eyes.

She nodded in reply. "That's why we're eating cake."

"Can you make sure you give Mummy lots of cuddles?" Dee said. Beth cursed her again as tears formed in her eyes. "Really big cuddles, because it's a big birthday."

"Shut up," Beth said lightly, catching a tear at the corner of her eye.

"I'll give you your present when I see you."

"Thanks." Beth switched the phone off speaker and held it back to her ear.

"Try and enjoy your day. I know it's not what you'd planned, but I hope you can find something good in it."

"Cake and a beach trip aren't so bad. I just …" She trailed off, knowing that if she said too much, she'd end up bawling her eyes out. Because even though the day was perfectly acceptable in theory, she was missing her mum with an intensity that over-whelmed her. "Never mind. I better get on and finish my cake."

"I'm not doing anything tonight if you feel like a video call. We could drink wine together?"

"Thanks. I'll let you know." She suspected a video call with Dee would end up with lots of tears. An early night might be a better option.

"Love you," Dee said, then ended the call.

"Are you going to have a birthday party?" Ellie asked.

"No. I'm too old for birthday parties. I just want to eat cake with you and then play on the beach for the afternoon."

"Okay." Ellie continued shovelling cake into her mouth until it was all gone, then they set off for the beach.

When they arrived back at the house late in the afternoon, Mirren turned the sprinkler on, and Ellie happily ran back and forth through the spray while Beth sipped a glass of crisp white wine on the patio.

In the kitchen, Mirren was busy cooking dinner, and the smell of onions frying drifted outside along with the gentle hum of the radio. The view from the patio was mesmerising and the rhythm of the waves washing onto the rocky headland was hypnotic.

It wasn't how Beth had envisioned spending her birthday. If things had been different, she'd be spending the day with her mum and Ellie, and Dee and Ferne. It wouldn't have been a big flashy event, but it would have been filled with love and laughter.

Reaching for her wine, she stared into the glass and told herself that the day had been pretty good, all things considered. Apart from the odd stray tear, she'd managed not to cry, and that felt like a huge achievement. Although, if she kept drinking wine and thinking about how she should be spending the day with her mum she might not manage to keep that up for much longer.

"You're looking very serious."

Flicking her gaze up, she was surprised to find Trystan standing over her. Only then did she realise just how close to tears she was. The tightness in her chest spread up her windpipe, burning her throat.

"Are you okay?" he asked, his features crumpling in concern.

She nodded so vigorously she almost spilled her wine. "I …" Her voice was brittle as she blinked back tears. "Are you here for dinner?" she asked, turning in her chair to check on Ellie and avoid the intensity of his gaze.

"Yeah." He took a seat at the end of the table. "Mum's message was more of a summons than an invitation."

Beth tried not to be annoyed by his inference that having dinner with his mum was a chore. He'd got the one thing she longed for, and he didn't even appreciate it. That was unfair though; Trystan had been joking. And Beth had never fully appreciated her time with her mum until she didn't have it any more.

"Did you do anything fun today?" Trystan asked, his eyes on Ellie, who was laughing as she hopped over the sprinkler.

"We went for a train trip this morning and spent the afternoon on the beach."

"Is the novelty of this place wearing off already? Because you just made that sound incredibly tiresome."

"No. It was good. Sorry, I'm just miles away this afternoon. Ignore me." Her eyes swept over the garden and landed on the paddling pool. "Thank you for the pool, by the way. Ellie loves it."

"No problem." His smile was warm, but the scrutiny of his gaze made her self-conscious.

Mirren wandered out of the kitchen and greeted Trystan with a kiss on the cheek.

"What's for dinner?" he asked.

"Just pasta and salad. Nothing exciting."

Ellie skipped over, her wet hair dripping onto Trystan's khaki shorts as she leaned on him. "Can we have something different for dinner?" she asked, looking pleadingly up at Mirren.

"You love pasta." Beth leaned out of her chair to pull Ellie away from Trystan, not that he seemed bothered by her dripping all over him.

"On my birthday I always get to choose what we eat for dinner, so I thought you could choose today."

Beth winced.

"Is it your birthday?" Mirren asked.

"Yes," Beth replied hesitantly. "And I would definitely have chosen pasta, so that's perfect."

"You always say pasta is boring," Ellie announced.

Her cheeks felt as though they were on fire as she smiled weakly. "Only the way I make it."

Mirren let out a sigh. "I'd have baked a cake if I'd realised it was your birthday."

"It's a big birthday," Ellie chimed, making Beth shrink into the chair.

"Is it really?" Trystan asked with a lopsided smile.

"That's what Dee said," Ellie told him. "She's Mummy's best friend, so she would know."

"I wonder how big?" Trystan said, eyes sparkling in amusement.

"You may as well tell us," Mirren said. "Don't make me go and look up your date of birth in the guest files."

"Forty," Beth muttered with her head bent.

Mirren puffed her cheeks out. "You definitely can't eat boring old pasta on your fortieth birthday."

"Honestly, I'm just happy not to have to cook. And I was hoping to pretend it wasn't my birthday, so we really don't need to make a fuss."

"You can't let your fortieth slip by unnoticed," Mirren said. "You ought to have a treat."

"I had cake at lunchtime."

Mirren looked thoughtful. "Trystan could take you out for dinner."

"No." Beth's eyes widened. "There's really no need."

"It's your fortieth," Trystan said. "That definitely calls for a meal out." The way he looked at her with his easy smile made goosebumps ripple across the back of her neck.

She gave a subtle shake of the head. "I don't want to cause any trouble."

"It's no trouble at all," Mirren insisted, taking a seat and gesturing for Ellie to go to her. "I'll take care of this little angel. You two go out and enjoy a nice meal."

Ellie's brow wrinkled. "I'd like to go out for dinner with Trystan too."

"It'd be very boring," Mirren told her.

Trystan stretched his legs out. "Thanks a lot!"

"A meal with grown-ups is boring," Mirren clarified. "You can stay here with me, and after dinner we can watch a bit of TV and eat ice cream. Doesn't that sound fun?"

"Yes," Ellie agreed. "Will you read my bedtime story?"

"I'd love to." Mirren nodded firmly. "I'll call the Castle and get you a table in the restaurant there. They'll be full, but I'm owed a favour." Mirren pursed her lips as she ran her eyes over Trystan. "Go and put a shirt on."

He chuckled. "Are you going to tell Beth what to wear too?"

"No, just you." She turned her wrist to check her watch. "Shall I make the reservation for eight o'clock?"

"I'm really very happy to eat here," Beth said. "I feel terrible leaving you to look after Ellie."

"Why?" Mirren asked. "We're going to have a lovely girls' night. I'll enjoy it."

Trystan caught Beth's gaze. "Sometimes it's not worth arguing. Mum always gets her own way in the end."

"Are you sure you don't mind?" Beth asked him.

"I don't mind at all." His left eyebrow twitched as he smiled at her. "I'd better go and put a shirt on."

"I might have a quick shower then," Beth said, with a quiver of excitement at the thought of getting dressed up for a child-free meal out. The fact that she got to spend time alone with Trystan increased her anticipation for the evening even further.

Her birthday might not be a total washout after all.

CHAPTER EIGHT

"You look pretty, Mummy," Ellie remarked through a mouthful of pasta when Beth walked back onto the patio.

"Thank you." She'd opted for a simple green cotton sundress and sandals. Upstairs it had felt fresh and cute, but now that she was faced with Trystan in a pair of stonewashed jeans and bright white shirt she felt slightly under-dressed.

"Ready to go?" he asked, getting up from the chair.

"Yes." The twinkle in his eyes made her stomach flutter, and she wasn't sure going out with him was a good idea after all. Should she really be leaving her daughter with a woman she barely knew so she could go out for dinner with a guy she knew even less? Pulling her shoulders back, she told herself she was being silly. They might not have known Mirren long, but Beth absolutely trusted her with Ellie.

"Should I get Ellie ready for bed before we go?" she asked Mirren. "I left her pyjamas out, but I could wait and help her get ready first."

"No," Mirren said with a gentle smile. "We'll be fine. You just worry about enjoying your evening."

"Thank you. I won't be late back …"

"Be as late as you want," Mirren said. "It won't make any difference to us. We'll be all tucked up in bed."

"Thank you," she said again and kissed the top of Ellie's head, not wanting to risk being smeared with pasta sauce. "Be really good for Mirren, won't you?"

"Bye, Mummy."

"Bye, sweetheart." She took a few steps before turning back to Mirren. "Just call if there's a problem."

"I will," Mirren promised.

At the garden gate, Beth turned back once again. "I hope she won't be any trouble."

"Mum had five boys," Trystan said lightly. "I don't think looking after Ellie for an evening will be much of a challenge."

"I suppose that's true. I just feel guilty leaving her."

"She'll be fine." He held the gate for her and she wandered through, noticing how his shirt highlighted his tan.

"Where is it that we're going?"

"The restaurant at the Star Castle Hotel. It's just in Hugh Town. About a twenty-minute walk … but if you'd rather we drive …"

"No, I'd like to walk." She glanced down at her dress. She'd brought her denim jacket in case it turned cool later but carried it for now, along with her handbag. "Is it a fancy place?"

"Not really. About as fancy as it gets on Scilly, but that's still fairly casual."

"I feel a little under-dressed."

He gave her a sidelong glance. "You look beautiful."

As her heart slipped into an erratic rhythm, Beth mumbled a quiet thank you, before deftly moving the conversation on by asking him about his day. Apparently he'd spent most of it working and had been glad of the excuse to get away from the laptop when Mirren invited him for dinner.

"What is it that you do?" she asked.

"I'm a relocation specialist." He tilted his head back, watching a gull that glided on the gentle breeze. "I was an estate agent before that but got headhunted by a relocation agency. The money was better, so I thought I'd give it a go."

"And you enjoy it?"

"Yes. It's interesting to be more involved in helping people move. Not only focusing on the house, but on every aspect of the move." He cast her a half smile that made her stomach flutter. "Of course, how much I enjoy it usually depends on the clients. Some are easier than others."

"I can imagine." Beth gazed out to the boats bobbing in the bay and felt a sense of calm for the first time that day.

"How about you?" Trystan asked. "What do you do when you're not lying around on beaches all summer?"

His teasing brought a smile to her face, which faded when she realised he was expecting an answer to the question and she wasn't sure what to say. Currently, she was between jobs, but talking about it was likely to ruin her mood again.

"I'm a school photographer," she said with as much confidence as she could muster. She *would be* anyway. Wedding photography wasn't a good fit for a single mother with no support network, so she was leaving that behind and trying not to feel too sad about it. She was lucky really; her mum had left her the house that the three of them had been living in, so she only had to earn enough to cover food and bills and other expenses.

"A school photographer?" Trystan asked, a slight lilt to his voice as though he could tell she was lying. Which she wasn't – it was the job she was going to move into.

"It's not glamorous," she said. "But it fits perfectly around Ellie's school day and pays the bills."

"How long have you been doing that for?" he asked.

She pondered how to answer for a couple of steps. "I've always been a photographer. The school photography is a more recent thing."

They moved to the edge of the lane as a car approached, and

Beth took the opportunity to change the subject, asking Trystan about his childhood on St Mary's.

The walk into Hugh Town went much quicker without a five-year-old setting the pace, and they reached the harbour before she knew it. From there, they ambled up the cobbled incline to the imposing castle with the Union Jack flag flapping in the breeze.

"I'm so unfit," she declared, sucking in a deep breath at the top of the hill. "I'm used to walking at the speed of a five-year-old and stopping every thirty seconds to look at ladybirds and butterflies."

"Sorry. I can pretend to be out of breath if it'll make you feel better."

"It wouldn't be very believable. I've seen you running and swimming every morning."

A playful smile tugged at his lips. "Have you?"

Turning away from him, she bit down on her lip to stifle a smile and walked to the stone wall that bordered the castle grounds. A warm breeze lifted her hair from her shoulders as she looked out to the harbour.

"Do you work out every day when you're in London too?" she asked when Trystan stood beside her.

"Yeah, pretty much."

She admired his dedication but wasn't sure what else to say on the subject. "Do you always spend the whole summer here?" she asked instead.

"No." He cocked his head to one side and looked as though he was about to say more but stopped himself.

"Is there a story about why you're here this summer?" she asked, keeping her voice light and hoping she wasn't being too direct.

"There is," he said, eyeing her intently. "But it's a long story. We should go inside and get a drink first."

"I don't know if you're just avoiding the question," she said, falling into step with him. "But a drink sounds good."

The decor in the candle-lit restaurant was fitting for a castle; the exposed stone walls and dark timber ceiling beams gave authenticity to the historic room. Distracted by the friendly waiter and then the good wine and food and easy conversation, Beth forgot all about her earlier question until they'd polished off their main courses.

"I just remembered," she said after the waiter took their plates away. "You were going to tell me why you're spending the summer here."

He leaned back in his seat. "I thought I'd dodged that question."

"You tried." She took a sip of wine. "You don't have to tell me if you don't want to."

"No, it's fine." Sitting up straighter, he pursed his lips. "My ex-girlfriend is staying in my flat in London for the summer."

"Oh," she murmured.

"We split up a few months ago, but we owned the flat together. I'm buying her out. She asked if she could use the place for the summer."

"How long were you together?"

He grimaced slightly, his brows drawing together. "Just shy of ten years."

"Oh, my goodness." She rested her chin on her hand. "Ten years?"

"Yeah."

"Why did …" She shook her head. "Sorry, I'm being really nosy."

"It's fine. You want to know why we split up?"

"Only if you want to talk about it."

"I don't mind talking about it … but I'm not sure it makes me sound very good."

"Oh, no. Did you cheat on her?"

"No!" His features relaxed. "Definitely not. We just had different ideas about what we wanted from life."

"Such as?"

He rolled his eyes. "You're persistent aren't you?"

"Sometimes."

He inhaled deeply. "She wanted to get married and have kids … I wasn't so keen."

"You don't want kids?"

"Just not *yet,* I think. And I didn't see the point in getting married, but it became this huge issue."

"It must have been a difficult break-up after ten years."

"Yes, and no. It's pretty amicable. It's hard to completely cut someone out of your life after being together for so long. It'd be nice to think we can stay friends, at least at some point. But that might be unrealistic."

"Do you miss her?"

"Yes, and no." Shifting in his seat, he rested his forearms on the table. "Do you want another glass of wine?"

"No, thanks." Her current glass was still half full. "I take it that's your way of putting an end to the conversation?"

"Yeah. I could probably have been more subtle." His eyes sparkled in the flickering candlelight. "How did you choose St Mary's for your holiday destination?"

A heaviness in her chest made her shift in the seat. She could definitely use his tactic of changing the subject or make up some generic reason for their trip. Talking about it with Trystan felt oddly natural though.

"My mum used to come here for family holidays when she was a kid. She always talked about coming back but never got around to it, so we planned this trip for my birthday treat. It was supposed to be the three of us. Me, Mum and Ellie." She paused, focusing on breathing evenly. "Mum passed away three months ago. I thought about cancelling the trip but …" Her bottom lip quivered as she shrugged. "I decided to come anyway."

Trystan moved his water glass aside and slipped his hand across the table to cover hers. "I'm so sorry. Was she ill?"

"No. Perfectly fit and healthy. My dad has Alzheimer's and she'd been to visit him at the care home. She liked to walk there.

Always said the fresh air and exercise kept her healthy." She frowned at the irony. "She was on the pedestrian crossing. The sun was in the driver's eyes and he didn't see her." Her chest felt as though it was being squeezed, but her words continued to tumble out. "He stopped and stayed with her. Held her hand while they waited for the ambulance, but she died before it got to them. I met him afterwards. He was distraught. Nice man. I felt sorry for him."

"That's awful," Trystan whispered, his hand tightening around hers.

"When we planned to come to Scilly, Mum was so excited to show me all the places she remembered." She sniffed. "I had no idea until she died, but in her will it stated that she wanted her ashes scattered on her favourite beach on St Mary's. I guess she'd planned on showing me when we were here, but I don't know which beach it is." Her words were coming out garbled, but she couldn't seem to stop. "I thought I'd just pick a nice spot somewhere. I was actually glad when it rained all week so I didn't have to deal with it … and now … I don't think I can do it."

A hand on her arm made her turn to her right, and she blinked back tears to focus on the older lady on the next table, who was holding out a packet of tissues.

"Thank you." Pulling her hand from Trystan's she fumbled with the packet, only realising how much she was crying when the tissue was soaked through within seconds of touching it to her cheeks. And the tears wouldn't stop.

She sniffed loudly and felt a pang of embarrassment that she was making a scene in the middle of the restaurant. "I'm so sorry."

"It's okay." He reached out to her again, but she was already out of her seat.

"I'll be back in a minute," she said and made a dash for the bathroom.

CHAPTER NINE

"P oor thing," the woman on the next table said after Beth rushed out of the room.

Trystan smiled weakly in reply, then took a sip of his water. Tapping on the table, he kept an eye on the door until he couldn't take the waiting any longer and got out of his seat.

In the hallway, he paused before tentatively pushing the door to the ladies' and softly calling out to Beth.

"I'll just be a minute," she said in reply.

He ventured further, catching sight of her blotchy face in the mirror above the sink. "Is there anyone else in here?"

"No." She shook her head and their eyes met in the mirror. "I'm so sorry. I'll be out in a minute."

"Are you all right?" It was a stupid question; clearly she wasn't all right. He was torn between giving her privacy and wanting to comfort her.

"I can't seem to stop crying," she said, losing her composure and raising a tissue to her cheeks.

He rested his hand in the centre of her back and rubbed lightly between her shoulder blades. "You need to stop trying."

She lifted her chin. "What?"

"The more you try to stop crying, the harder it makes it. You just need to let it out."

"I'm so embarrassed. I was having such a nice evening. I don't want to be crying in the toilets. I'm such a mess."

"You're a bit of a mess," he agreed with a sad smile. "But there's no need to be embarrassed about it. Of course you're upset after what happened with your mum. Today must have been difficult."

She dabbed furiously at her cheeks, but her eyes continued to fill with tears. "I spend so much time pretending I'm fine for Ellie … you'd think I could pretend in a restaurant full of people."

"It's okay."

"I thought I'd be spending today with Mum." Her chest heaved as she fought for breath. "But I'll never spend another day with her again and it hurts so much."

"I know." Gently, he collected her in his arms while blinking back his own tears and wishing he didn't know just how much it hurt.

"I miss her," she sobbed, her voice muffled by grief and by his shoulder.

He held her tighter, pressing his cheek against her hair so the sweet scent of flowery shampoo tickled his nostrils. It took a couple of minutes for her to calm down, and then a few more tissues to dry her cheeks, but her tear ducts finally called it a day.

"Better?" he asked, rubbing her back again while she tried to remove the mascara smudges from under her eyes.

"Yes. Thank you." She straightened her spine. "I don't think I can face going back into the restaurant. I made such a show of myself."

"You didn't, but if you want, you can wait outside while I get our stuff and pay the bill."

"Do you mind?"

"Of course not." He rocked forwards, intent on kissing the

side of her head before realising he barely knew her. When someone spent five minutes crying on your shoulder, the lines blurred quickly. "I'll meet you out the front."

Five minutes later, he caught up to her outside the main entrance. She had her arms wrapped around her waist and he held out her jacket for her to put her arms into.

"Thank you." She took her handbag from him. "I'd actually intended to pay for dinner."

"It's your birthday," he said, offering her his arm, "so that was never going to happen."

"Thanks." She held his arm tighter on the cobblestones. "You don't really go in for street lights around here, do you?"

"No, it's part of the charm of island life."

"Are broken ankles considered charming?" she asked, watching her footing.

"The moon is pretty full tonight, there's plenty of light."

Her laugh cut through the silence. "It's pitch black."

"I know the island like the back of my hand. Stick with me and you'll be fine." His over-the-top fake stumble drew more laughter from her, the sound wonderfully melodic.

Walking through the town, she continued to cling to his arm. The warmth of her body against his felt completely natural. As did the silence between them. The emotional evening left Trystan thinking about his dad, and he was lost in thought when Beth spoke again.

"Could we walk along the beach?"

He blinked a couple of times, not having noticed that they were already reaching Old Town Bay. Veering off the lane, they carefully navigated the couple of wooden steps onto the sand, where Beth used his arm to balance while she slipped her sandals off.

"Have you been to any islands other than St Mary's?" he asked as they ambled along.

"No. Mum had talked about going to Tresco and Bryher, but I haven't been able to face much exploring without her. It felt easier to stay around here." She pushed her hair behind her ear. "I'm sorry I'm so depressing this evening."

He shook his head, gazing at the moonlight flickering on the surface of the water. "My dad drowned." The words were out before he knew he was going to say them.

She pulled on his arm to stop him and the moonlight reflected in her eyes as she looked up at him.

"It was a couple of years ago," he continued. "He was fit and healthy too. Went out sailing one morning and didn't come back."

"God, that's awful."

He nodded and shoved his hands into his pockets. "His boat was found, and a couple of days later his body was found washed up. We don't know for sure what happened. The theories are that he either had a heart attack and fell in the water, or that the boom swung over and knocked him out. They couldn't tell from the body since it had been in the water so long and had been beaten up by the rocks." His ribcage tightened and a lump formed in his throat.

"I'm so sorry. That's horrendous. Life can be so shit."

"I don't know why I told you that," he said, shifting his weight. "I guess I wanted you to know that I know how you feel. I wish I could tell you it gets easier, but I'm not sure that's true." His shoulders hitched. "It's better now than it was. The first weeks and months were awful. Now it's more of a chronic dull pain."

Shaking her head, she stepped towards him. Expecting a hug, he was taken aback when she laid her hand on his cheek and lightly touched her lips to his.

The shock in her features mirrored his own as she pulled away.

"Sympathy kiss?" he asked, swallowing the lump in his throat.

"No!" She put a hand over her mouth. "God, no. That's not

what that was. I don't know what that was. Apart from completely inappropriate. I'm really sorry."

"It's fine," he said, feeling his shoulders relax.

"It's not fine! Imagine if you'd have come into the bathroom earlier and kissed me. It would've been so out of line. How is me kissing you when you're upset an appropriate reaction? What is wrong with me tonight?"

"To be fair, it wasn't a terrible reaction. I'm not complaining. Just took me by surprise, that's all."

"Me too! I really am sorry." She ran her hands down her face. "I hope you've at least learned a lesson tonight … the next time your mum tries to set you up with an unstable forty-year-old woman on her birthday, just say no. Run, if you need to, but get away as fast as possible."

"I don't think you give yourself enough credit." He took a tentative step towards her. "I had a really nice night." Which was actually a massive understatement. He'd been happy when his mum had suggested the two of them go out for dinner, but he'd enjoyed it even more than he'd anticipated.

"I did too," she said, her hands grazing over the front of his shirt as she ventured nearer to him. "Obviously you shouldn't take the fact that I ended up bawling my eyes out in the ladies' bathroom as any indicator as to what a good night I had."

He slipped his hands over her hips and beamed at her. "I'll be honest, I don't consider it a good night *unless* I end up in the ladies' bathrooms, so you don't need to feel bad about that."

Her dainty laugh sent a frisson of breath dancing teasingly over his lips. The warmth of her fingertips on his neck sent a shiver through his whole body, and his arms tightened around her until there was no space left between them. With a tilt of his head their lips met again, causing an ache of desire deep in his gut. Their noses touched as the kiss deepened, and he tasted a hint of wine as his tongue flicked into her mouth.

Just when he was about to pull away, she pushed her fingers

into his hair and held him in place. The gentle sigh that escaped her lips made him desperate for more.

Dragging his hands up, he held her face and continued to kiss her until they were both breathing heavily.

"As far as sympathy kisses go, that one was way better," he murmured with his face still close to hers.

"It wasn't a sympathy kiss," she said indignantly.

"What then? An *it's my birthday and I've had a couple of glasses of wine* kind of kiss?"

"No." Her smile was adorably bashful. "It was an *I've had a really lovely evening* kiss … and …"

"And what?"

"And I find you very attractive." She winced. "And maybe also something to do with wine and my birthday."

"Thought so!"

"Just so long as you know it wasn't a sympathy kiss. There's no such thing. Or there shouldn't be."

"Maybe it should be a thing," he said, amused. "Sympathy snogs could really help take the edge of the grieving process."

She gave him a playful shove as she backed out of his arms, then bent to retrieve her shoes.

Taking her hand, he entwined his fingers with hers as they walked up the beach. Outside the cottage he paused, wondering whether he should invite her in. Sleeping with the guest staying in his mum's place for the summer might not be his greatest idea. God, he wanted to though.

"Thank you for a lovely evening," she said.

"I can walk you to your door."

"You don't need to. I'm fine."

"I was actually wondering whether it'd be appropriate to invite you in to my place …"

"For a nightcap?" she asked hesitantly.

"Yeah," he said slowly. "Except I don't drink so there's no alcohol in my place."

"I wondered about that at dinner. I didn't know if you were on a detox or something, but I didn't like to ask."

"It's a very boring story."

"So maybe you could tell it to me inside? Over a glass of water?"

"Sure." He set off down the path with her hand still enclosed in his. "But I mean it when I say it's a boring story. Not even a story really, just a boring bit of information. It'd probably be better if I told you a different story." Or better yet, skip the stories completely. Flicking the second light switch, the two lamps came on, bathing the living room in a warm glow.

"It's strange being back here," Beth said, setting her shoes by the door.

Trystan bit his lip as he remembered that Beth had stayed in his cottage – and specifically the incident when he'd met Ellie. "I have to tell you something."

"Why do I get the feeling you're trying to dodge the question about alcohol?"

"I am, because it's genuinely uninteresting. But I also need to tell you something else. It's kind of a funny story … or maybe it's not. Now I've set it up as an entertaining anecdote and you might not find it funny at all." He screwed his features up, wishing he could stop waffling. "It's more of a confession."

"Okay. Tell me then."

They sat close together on the couch and he ran his arm along the back of it as he turned to face her. "The day we met … that morning … I was about to go for a jog and Ellie came out of the cottage in floods of tears."

"Really?" She looked suspicious and slightly nervous. "Where was I?"

"In the shower." He winced. "Ellie told me her granny had fallen in the kitchen."

"What?" Beth gave a small shake of the head before her eyes widened in comprehension. "Oh my god!"

"Yeah. I guess she wanted to look at the ashes but knocked

them off the shelf."

Beth paled as she put a hand over her mouth. "She was curious so I tried to explain what the ashes are, but that only led to more questions. In the end I put them up high and brushed her questions aside. That probably made her more curious. Had they spilled?"

He nodded. "They were all over the counter and the floor and the chair. I collected them all up and managed to put them back but …"

"But what?" she asked, her brow wrinkled.

"While I was tipping them back into the urn, Ellie sneezed."

The confusion in Beth's features was quickly replaced with understanding. "She sneezed in the ashes?"

"Mmhm." He braved a smile. "I was engulfed in a cloud of ash."

"No," she whispered, the corners of her mouth twitching upwards.

"I was covered," he told her, smiling as he thought about it. "But we cleaned everything up and I intended to hang around and explain everything to you, but Ellie marched me to the door and shoved me back outside." He chewed the edge of his lip. "I should've told you later that day, but I didn't know you and I had no idea how you'd react."

"I'm so sorry. You must have thought you had some nutter staying in your house who took their dead mother's ashes on holiday with her."

"It did cross my mind to wonder if it was sensible to invite you to stay in my mum's house with her."

Beth tipped her head back and grinned. "That's hilarious. I just wish I could tell Mum. She'd laugh so much."

"I'm glad you find it funny," he said, inching his fingers along to caress the back of her neck.

She leaned into his hand. "Are you going to tell me the other story now? The teetotal thing?"

He let out a breath. "I just don't drink. That's all really."

"As a health thing?"

"Sort of … I like starting the day with exercise, and I can't do that if I've been drinking the night before. Hangovers really do me in. Always have done. I always felt as though I got all the negatives of alcohol with none of the positives."

"So you're not a fun drunk person?"

"I'd argue I am," he said, more focused on the feel of her skin under his fingertips than the conversation. "But I'm also fun sober. I feel like all the reasons people drink don't apply to me. I don't care about the taste, it doesn't particularly relax me, I'm very social anyway … and I'm always happy to talk to random people. I'm also pretty good at making an idiot of myself without alcohol, so I've got that covered too."

She smiled lightly. "And you never drink? It seems extreme."

"I used to drink quite a lot. When I wanted to cut down, I realised it was easier not to drink at all." He leaned his head on the back of the couch as he moved his fingers into her silky hair. "Not because I'm one of those people who can't stop at one, but because if you have one drink, people tend to give you more drinks … or top you up … or bring you a shot. Whereas, if you don't drink anything, people assume you have some sort of problem and wouldn't dare put a drink in front of you."

"Being around you makes me feel pretty unhealthy," she told him.

"Speaking of health, it's important to stay hydrated. Do you want a glass of water or something?"

"Maybe I could go for an *or something,*" she said with a flirty smile. "Depending on what that might be …"

His heart hammered against his ribcage as he leaned closer to her. She closed her eyes when their lips met, and the intensity of the kiss was immediate. Dipping his head, Trystan kissed her neck, then pushed her jacket aside to access the delicate skin over her collar bone and shoulder. Wriggling her arms free, she slung the jacket aside then began to undo the buttons of his shirt.

The feel of her hands on his chest made him long for more skin contact, and he drew down the zip at the back of her dress and lifted it over her head. He shifted on top of her as she sank back onto the couch. Wrapping her legs around his waist, she kissed him tantalisingly slowly.

Trying to figure out whether to suggest they move things upstairs was difficult when his brain felt like mush. He also didn't want to say anything to risk breaking the moment.

"I can't stay over," she mumbled against his lips.

"What?"

"Because of Ellie. I can't stay."

"Okay." Breathing hard, he gave her a final kiss, before forcing himself to sit up. "Sorry. I got a bit carried away."

She stared at him for a moment, her lips a deep shade of red and her cheeks pleasantly flushed. "I didn't mean …" Swallowing hard, she sat up, her bare legs remaining tangled around his waist.

"I wanted to suggest we go to your bedroom, but I can't stay all night and I didn't want it to be weird when I have to get up and leave." She squeezed her eyes closed. "Maybe this is all too weird. I wouldn't normally … I mean this is very out of character. But I'm on holiday and I have a babysitter. I really never do stuff like this, but I also never get a chance to do stuff like this." She trailed her fingers over his chest. "I'm waffling, aren't I?"

"Yes." His lips curled to a smile. "But what I'm hearing is that you don't want to leave just yet?"

Her eyes sparkled as she gazed up at him. "No. Not just yet."

"Good." He untangled himself from her then took her hand to lead her to the stairs.

"Hang on." She tugged on his arm. "I need my dress."

He kept a firm hold of her. "Unless I've seriously misread the situation, you're not going to need your dress."

"I meant for later," she said, laughing as she hurried up the stairs after him.

"I know what you meant, but let's worry about clothes later."

CHAPTER TEN

With an immense amount of willpower, Beth forced herself up from Trystan's chest and swung her legs off the edge of the bed. "I really have to go."

"You said that half an hour ago." Sitting up beside her, he rested his chin on her shoulder. "But then you started kissing me again."

"You're very kissable." She gave him a quick peck before reaching for her underwear.

"So it's my fault?"

"Definitely." Her smile widened as he hampered her efforts to put her bra on by nuzzling her neck. "I really need to go," she said, gently nudging him away. "It's one o'clock in the morning and I have to sneak into your mother's house without waking anyone." Standing, she untwisted the strap of her bra. "Oh god. What if your mum wakes up?"

"She won't. Even if she does, the last thing she's going to do is quiz you about why you're back so late." Standing, he slipped his arms around her waist. "Mostly because the pub closed ages ago and there's nowhere else to go, so she'll know exactly what kept you out so late."

She laughed at the amusement in his eyes. "You're not making me feel any better."

"I'm just saying it's not something she'll want to have a conversation about."

Hooking her arms around his neck, she kissed him again, feeling slightly stunned at having slept with a guy she barely knew, but also utterly unremorseful. She only wished she didn't have to leave. "I told you I should have brought my dress upstairs," she said, forcing herself away from him.

"That was a tactical move so I get to watch you walk back through the house in your underwear."

At the top of the stairs, she glanced back and snorted a laugh. "Aren't you going to put any clothes on?"

"I'm not cold," he said, eyebrows waggling cheekily.

Grinning, she descended the stairs. "I'm starting to see what you meant about not needing alcohol. It certainly doesn't seem as though you have any inhibitions to get rid of."

"Exactly," he said, pinching her bum at the bottom of the stairs.

Once she was dressed and had her shoes on, she lingered by the door.

"Sure you don't want me to walk you back?" he asked.

"I think it's probably better if you don't." She leaned into his chest, trying hard to keep her eyes at face level. "I can't believe you're just wandering around naked."

"There was no point in putting clothes on to walk you down-stairs. I'd only have to take them off again five minutes later. It's not like you haven't already seen it all."

"Do you sleep naked?"

"Yeah. When it's warm enough."

She pressed her lips against his, then opened the door.

"Shall I give you a tip?" He leaned against the doorframe, his playful smile making the skin around his eyes crinkle. "When sneaking into my mum's house, there's a creaky floorboard on the third step. Avoid that one. Also, stick to the edge of the hallway upstairs."

Glaring at him, she jabbed at his ribs. "Stop teasing me. I don't know if you're joking or not, but I'm going to be creeping through the house like an amateur ninja."

"I'll see you tomorrow," he said, resting his head on the doorframe as he watched her go.

When she was almost at the house she turned to see his naked form illuminated by the faint glow of the lights behind him. Laughter bubbled out of her as she raised her hand to wave.

Inside, she crept straight upstairs, managing to avoid any creaky floorboards. Ellie was fast asleep in the middle of the bed and Beth shuffled her over when she climbed in beside her.

With a flurry of endorphins buzzing in her system, it was difficult to settle down to sleep. After tossing and turning for a while, she reached for her phone, intent on messaging Dee. It was highly unlikely she'd be awake to exchange messages but it was worth checking.

The screen lit up in the darkness, showing a missed call from Dee from several hours ago, and a message asking what it was like being so old. The teasing jibe made Beth's smile stretch even wider and she tapped out a reply.

It's bloody brilliant!

The following morning Beth was still struggling to stop her incessant smiling when her phone rang.

"You sound far too happy," Dee said when Beth greeted her. "What's going on?"

She stretched her legs out in the sun, causing a couple of friendly sparrows to hop out of the way and continue pecking around at the edge of the patio. "What's not to be happy about? I have the sun on my face and a coffee in my hand. My child is having the time of her life splashing around in a paddling pool. The sky's the brightest blue you've ever seen; the sea is calm and turquoise and beautiful. There are palm trees, and birds so tame they'll eat from my hand. I can hear gulls squawking and waves rolling onto the shore …"

"All right! I get the picture. No need to rub it in. It's grey and windy here."

"I'm keeping all the sun for myself."

"What the hell is going on with you, Little Miss Sunshine? Why were you sending me messages in the middle of the night telling me how great your life is? I'd been worried you were going to be miserable all day."

"There were a few moments of misery," she admitted, remembering how she'd sobbed in the ladies' bathrooms at the restaurant. "But overall I had a fantastic birthday. And one o'clock is hardly the middle of the night."

"Since when? You're a single mother in your thirties – of course one o'clock is the middle of the night. Oh, sorry. You're in your forties now. Did your circadian clock reset for your birthday? Because that's not something I'd look forward to. I like my ten o'clock bedtime."

Beth beamed. "What if you had something really fun to do after ten o'clock?"

"What's better than sleeping?" Silence fell for a moment, before the penny dropped and she shrieked down the phone. "You were having sex? Who with? Where? What the hell? Start talking!"

"It was all so random." Beth had her gaze fixed on Ellie who was happily hopping in and out of the paddling pool. "Ellie blurted out it was my birthday to Mirren—"

"The woman you're staying with?"

"Yes. She insisted on looking after Ellie while her son took me out for dinner. We went to this lovely restaurant in the castle."

"Sounds fancy."

"It was perfect. At least until I started talking about Mum and ended up a blubbering wreck."

"Oh, dear." Dee sighed heavily.

"It was pretty embarrassing, but Trystan was lovely. He lost his dad a couple of years ago and he was so understanding and sweet."

"Interesting chat-up technique!"

"It wasn't like that. If anything it was me who came onto him. I couldn't help myself. We just clicked. And he's bloody gorgeous."

"Really?"

"Yes. Why do you sound as though you don't believe me?"

"I just wonder if you've hit forty and your standards have dropped."

"No." She laughed. "My standards are through the roof after last night."

"This really doesn't sound like you," Dee said, amused.

"It's not. Maybe my forties are going to be full of fabulous one-night stands."

"As opposed to your thirties which were full of dull and dreary one-night stands?"

"I've never had a one-night stand before," she protested.

"Um … what about Ellie's teacher?"

"He wasn't Ellie's teacher! He was a teacher at Ellie's school. There's a big difference. And I didn't have a one-night stand with him, I was dating him. I only slept with him once because it was awful. That's not a one-night stand."

"So last night was a one-time thing?"

"I've no idea what last night was. Trystan lives next door, so I guess I'll see him later." She'd been glancing at the cottage for the last hour but there'd been no sign of him.

"Have you got a photo? I want to see if he's as hot as you say he is."

"No, I haven't."

"How old is he?"

She dragged her teeth over her bottom lip. "I'm not entirely sure. I'd say at least thirty, probably early thirties."

A sharp intake of breath made a whooshing sound in her ear. "You don't sound sure. Like maybe he's in his twenties!"

"I suppose there's a remote possibility he could be twenty-nine. I'm sure he's not younger than that. But I really think early thirties, maybe mid-thirties."

"Being forty sounds more fun by the second. Will you find me a hot twenty-something when I turn forty?"

"He's not twenty-something. I don't think. And you're married."

"Separated, remember?"

Beth's shoulders sank. "How is everything?"

"Don't change the subject to my wreck of a marriage. It's boring. And we definitely don't need to talk about that when you can tell me all about your hot birthday sex!"

"It was very hot," she said coyly.

"Are you blushing just thinking about it?"

"Maybe a little bit."

"I'm so jealous." Dee's voice went muffled while she shouted for Ferne to hurry up and get ready for dance class. "I'm really pleased you're having a good time. You deserve loads of hot sex."

"I don't think it'll happen again. It can't really. Nice memories to have though."

"Have a summer fling. You can tell me all about it and I'll live vicariously through you."

"It's a bit difficult with a five-year-old in the mix."

"True. Ship my little sweetie back to me. I'll look after her while you have your holiday fling." There was a clatter in the background, then more muffled shouting. "I have to go. All hell is breaking lose over a lost tutu."

"Good luck with that. I'll talk to you later." Beth ended the call, then picked up the bottle of sunscreen from the patio table and rubbed some into her face.

"Mummy!" Ellie called. "There's Trystan."

Her head shot up in an instant and her heart rate increased at the sight of him jogging shirtless along the lane, his abandoned T-shirt in his hand. After waving at them, he disappeared into his cottage, then reappeared a few minutes later in his swim shorts with a towel slung over his shoulder.

Keeping her eyes off the water while he swam turned out to be a difficult task. Beth had to force herself to only glance over there occasionally. When he started back towards the beach, she slipped into the kitchen to avoid him thinking she was just sitting out there ogling him. Hopefully he couldn't see her standing at the kitchen window.

"I wonder how old you are?" she muttered as he walked up the beach.

"Who?"

Startled, she looked down at Ellie. "No one. I mean, I just saw Trystan and I wondered how old he is." Maybe Ellie knew. It was the sort of blunt question she asked. "Do you know how old he is?"

She looked thoughtful. "Maybe eleven."

Beth smiled. "I think he's older than eleven."

"Eleven is pretty old."

"Eleven is a kid. Trystan's not a kid."

"Why don't you ask him?"

Good question. "Sometimes it's rude for adults to ask people how old they are … you could ask him. Then you could tell me and we'd both know."

"You said it's rude to ask people how old they are."

"It's rude for adults to ask. For kids it's fine. It doesn't matter though. You probably shouldn't ask him."

"Don't you want to know any more?"

"Not really. It doesn't matter how old people are."

"No. And it doesn't matter if they have holes in their socks. It only matters how kind they are."

"That's very true," Beth said, stifling a grin at the random comments Ellie came out with.

They'd moved outside again when Trystan came up to the house. Beth had clocked him the moment he stepped out of the cottage, and her heart was galloping by the time he reached the patio.

"Morning!"

"Hi." She felt like a teenager when their eyes locked.

"Trystan!" Ellie called, running over to him with a skipping rope trailing behind her, which Mirren had found in the garage along with a bunch of other outdoor toys.

"How are you this morning?" he asked her, taking a seat.

"Fine, thank you," Ellie replied sweetly.

"How was your run?" Beth asked.

"Great."

Ellie sidled over to him, leaning against his leg. "How old are you?"

Inwardly Beth cringed but managed to keep her smile fixed. Had she really expected her daughter might have developed some awareness of the concept of subtlety? Their earlier conversation suddenly felt like a very bad idea.

"Why do you want to know?" Trystan asked her.

"Mummy wants to know."

Openly cringing now, Beth decided there might be something fascinating near her feet and cast her eyes down there.

"It's strange that Mummy didn't ask me herself," Trystan said, his voice oozing amusement.

"It's rude for adults to ask," Ellie explained matter-of-factly. "But it's fine for kids."

"I'm thirty-two," he mock-whispered.

"He's thirty-two," Ellie echoed loudly.

Beth forced herself to look up. "I feel as though I might actually be on fire," she said, touching her cheek.

"You do look as though you might spontaneously combust."

"Mirren's here!" Ellie called, then ran off down to the gate to wait for her.

Watching the golf cart trundle along the lane gave Beth a moment of respite from her embarrassment.

"How old did you think I was?" Trystan asked.

"I didn't know. And now I'm really embarrassed."

"I can see that."

"There's no need to look quite so amused by my discomfort."

"I'm not. I'm just smiling because it's such a beautiful day."

"Yeah, right." Stretching her leg out, she gave his foot a gentle kick.

"Morning!" Mirren called as she approached them with shopping bags in her hands.

"Need some help?" Trystan asked.

"No. This is everything." She took the bags inside and came straight back out to them. "Did you two have a nice evening last night?"

While they both told her they did, images of the end of the evening flicked through Beth's mind and she avoided eye contact with Trystan.

"Thank you for looking after Ellie," she said.

Mirren waved a hand dismissively. "It was my pleasure. We had a lovely time, didn't we?"

"Yes." Ellie wedged herself between Beth's legs but kept her eyes on Mirren. "How old are you?"

A snort of laughter erupted from Trystan.

"You can't ask that," Beth told Ellie in a rush. "It's rude."

Ellie's bottom lip twitched manically. "You said it's just rude for adults to ask."

"I know." She pushed a curl from Ellie's face. "It's okay. It was my fault; I didn't explain properly. Sometimes it's okay and sometimes it's not."

"It's quite confusing," Mirren said, stroking Ellie's hair.

"You're not supposed to ask really old people. Because they usually don't want people to know how ancient they are."

"You're not *really* old," Ellie said.

"You might be my new best friend." Mirren held out a hand to her. "Come inside with me and I'll tell you how old I am. You'll have to keep it a secret though."

"I will." The smile lit up Ellie's face.

"I got you a little treat from the shop as well."

Beth watched the two of them disappear inside. "Ellie's never going to want to leave."

"Mum's never going to want her to leave." Trystan slouched in his chair, stretching his legs out so they rested against hers. "What have you got planned for today?"

"I'm not sure yet. How about you?"

"Unfortunately, I have a ton of work to do." He looked at her intently. "I was thinking—"

"Mummy! Mirren got me a colouring book."

"That was very kind." Beth shifted her leg away from Trystan's and took the book that Ellie held out to her. "Did you say thank you?"

"Yes." She took the book back and moved to show Trystan. "I got new crayons too." She set them on the table and opened the book to show him. "Which picture do you think I should colour first?"

"The first one?" he suggested.

"That's not my favourite."

"I don't know then." Lifting her onto his lap, they looked through the pictures together until Ellie decided on one.

"Can you move closer to the table?" she asked him.

"There's another chair there." Beth pointed. "Sit on that one."

"No. I want to sit on Trystan's knee."

"I'm afraid I have to go," Trystan said, lifting her as he stood and setting her back in his vacated seat.

"We're going on Kit's train later," Ellie told him.

Beth raised an eyebrow. "Are we?"

"Yes." Ellie smiled up at Trystan. "Do you want to come with us?"

"I'd love to but I have to work today. Maybe I can do something fun with you another day." He flashed Beth a smile before calling to his mum that he was leaving.

"I'm just about to make sandwiches," she called back. "Why don't you stay for lunch?"

"I have to work," he told her, then turned to Beth. "I'll see you later."

Her disappointment at his leaving was ridiculous. She was forty years old and getting butterflies over a guy she barely knew.

CHAPTER ELEVEN

I f overthinking was an Olympic sport, Beth would be in line
for a gold medal. She couldn't stop thinking about the situation with Trystan – wondering if their night together had been a
one off, or if there was more to it. The connection she felt to him
was intense and she suspected he felt the same.

While she and Ellie rode the train around the island that
afternoon her mind kept flicking to the previous evening. It
made her stomach flip just remembering their evening together –
and not just the time spent in his bedroom, but the entire night,
from their conversations over dinner, to walking home arm in
arm, to their kisses on the beach.

After the train trip, Beth and Ellie spent a couple of hours on
Porthcressa Beach, then bought ice creams to eat on the walk
back to the house. There was no sign of Trystan when they
passed his cottage, and Beth felt slightly on edge for the rest of
the afternoon, wondering if he might come over to the house and
pondering the fact that he'd said he'd see them later and what
that might mean.

By the time she'd put Ellie to bed she'd just about given up
on seeing him again that day. As per her usual routine, she
poured herself a glass of wine and took it onto the patio with her

book, wondering if she'd even be able to concentrate on the words.

She hadn't even bothered to open it when she caught sight of the figure walking up to the house in the fading daylight.

"I'd intended to come over earlier," Trystan said, pulling a chair close to hers. "I got caught up in work and lost track of time."

"Did you get everything done?"

"Yes." Tentatively, he reached for her hand. "Took me way longer than it should have done. I was pretty distracted all day."

"Really?" she asked, trying her best to temper her smile.

"Yeah." He glanced furtively at the back door. "My mind kept replaying last night. It was difficult to focus on work."

"I hope you're not expecting an apology," she said lightly. Goosebumps rippled up her arm as his fingers traced a pattern on the back of her hand.

"Definitely not." His left eyebrow twitched. "I wanted to ask you something earlier … I'm pretty slammed with work for the next couple of days, but after that I can take some time off. Since you said you haven't seen much of the other islands, I thought maybe I could show you around a bit."

"That sounds nice." She interlinked her fingers with his, enjoying how tactile he was.

"We could go over to Tresco one day. I think Ellie would like to see the gardens there. And there are good beaches too."

"I'd like that." Tresco had been on her mum's itinerary. Going alone hadn't been appealing, but it'd be fun to go with Trystan.

"How about Wednesday?" His brows pulled together and his eyes darkened. "Or Thursday?"

"What's better for you?"

"Either. I just remembered I was planning to go over to Bryher on Wednesday, but I can do that another time."

"We could also go to Tresco on Thursday. Then you don't have to change your plans."

"Yeah, okay. That would probably be better."

"Good. I'm looking forward to it already."

"Me too." When he leaned in to kiss her, it felt surprisingly natural, and also wonderfully thrilling. Their lips had only just touched when a clatter from the kitchen made them jump apart.

"Any chance I can tempt you to a walk or something?" Trystan asked, craning his neck to peer in the kitchen window.

"Or something?" she asked with a grin.

He licked his bottom lip. "I really enjoyed the *or something* yesterday. It was a good choice."

"I can't leave Ellie," she said in reply to his questioning look.

"Ask Mum to keep an ear out for her. She won't mind."

"It's not that I don't want to. I just feel uncomfortable asking your mum to look after Ellie while I … you know … With you."

"Would it make you feel better if we actually went for a walk?"

"Not really." She bit her lip, feeling terrible because she wanted nothing more than to sneak off with him for the evening. "Sorry."

"I understand." He stood up and Beth's stomach plummeted at the thought of him leaving. "Do you mind if I hang out here for a bit?"

"No," she said, confused.

He rested a hand on her shoulder and gave it a gentle squeeze. "I'm going to raid the sweet cupboard."

"Nice to know you've at least got one vice."

His fingers trailed over her shoulder, moving her hair from her neck. "I've got a few," he murmured in her ear, then laid a soft kiss just below her earlobe.

Beth only remembered to breathe again when he'd gone inside. It crossed her mind to abandon her child and take him up on his offer to go back to his place.

Instead, she settled for spending an hour on the patio with

him, the conversation as easy as it had been the previous evening, but with fewer tears and more laughter.

When he wished her goodnight, he gave her a lingering kiss that made her insides fizz with desire. Spending a whole day with him on Thursday would be bliss. It couldn't come soon enough.

∾

Fresh from the shower on Monday morning, Beth found her mobile ringing in the bedroom and answered the call from an unknown number with a quizzical hello.

Through the window, she watched Trystan arriving back from his jog, too focused on him to pay much attention to the woman from the leisure centre in Plymouth, who she presumed was about to try and sell her something.

"We were expecting Ellie for the swimming course this morning," the woman said, the use of Ellie's name getting Beth's full attention. "I wanted to check if she'll be here for the rest of the week?"

Beth's mouth hung open. How had she forgotten about the one thing on the calendar for the whole summer holiday?

"Is she ill?" the woman asked in a clipped tone. "If it's that stomach bug that's going around, she might have to skip the week altogether."

"No, she's not ill. We're away."

"Excuse me?" The woman's tone was impatient and Beth inwardly cursed. Why hadn't she said it was the stomach bug?

"Sorry. I forgot." Honesty was the best policy, after all.

"You forgot? You do realise we have a waiting list for the classes?"

"Yes. I'm so sorry. We extended our holiday and …"

"It's all right for some," the woman huffed. "A phone call would have been nice. We'd easily have been able to fill the space if you'd warned us."

"I'm so sorry."

"I hope you're not expecting a refund. We can't give you your money back when you didn't cancel."

"It's fine." Annoying, but she wouldn't have expected a refund.

"I'd advise you not to underestimate the importance of swimming lessons. It's a matter of safety; the sooner kids learn, the better. Especially if you're spending so much time on holiday."

The condescending tone almost left Beth speechless.

"I understand the importance of swimming lessons," she said through gritted teeth. "Which is why I signed Ellie up for them. We just have a lot going on at the moment. When we're back home I'll rebook for later in the year. Thank you for calling." With her jaw clenched, she jabbed at the button to end the call.

Immediately, she messaged Dee to vent. The phone rang straight away.

"The woman on reception at the leisure centre is such a cow," Dee said. "I bet it was her who called you."

"I don't know how I managed to forget to call them."

"You've had a lot on your mind." Her voice was laced with mirth. "All the hot sex probably clouded your thinking."

Dropping onto the edge of the bed, Beth looked out of the window towards the cottage. "I think you're right."

"I was joking. You forgot to cancel the swimming lessons. So what? It's not so bad."

"The woman made me feel like a terrible mother. She gave me a lecture on how kids need to learn to swim for safety."

"Well, duh! That's why we send them to swimming lessons. But I don't think it matters whether she learns this month or next."

"I did spend all day yesterday thinking about Trystan." Beth chewed the edge of her thumbnail.

"So?"

"So, maybe if I hadn't been so busy thinking about him I'd

have remembered the swimming lessons. He's on my mind all the time. I'm like a pathetic schoolgirl with a crush."

"Um … no. You're like a fully grown woman with a crush. Which is awesome. There's nothing pathetic about it."

"It feels pathetic."

"Did you see him yesterday?"

"Yes. Briefly at lunchtime. Then he came over in the evening and we had a drink on the patio while the sun went down. It was lovely. And he's taking us out for a day trip on Thursday."

"Wow. This is turning into a proper holiday romance."

"Yeah." She grimaced. "Which might not be a good thing."

"Why not?"

"Because I'm a single mother. I should be focusing on Ellie, not chasing after some young guy. He's thirty-two, by the way. Ellie asked him on my behalf, with the subtlety of an elephant wearing clogs. It was completely embarrassing but he was very sweet about it."

"Thirty-two's respectable. Have you got a photo for me yet?"

"No."

"Take your camera when you go out on Thursday and get some good ones."

"Maybe." She shook her head. "Of the scenery and wildlife, I mean. Not of him."

"At least get *one* of him!"

"I'll try. How's everything with you?"

"Same old. I'm missing you. I could do with an evening of drinking wine and slagging off Hugh."

"Has he been around much?"

"Unfortunately, yes. Acting the model father and begging me to take him back. He's such a prick."

Beth rolled her eyes, knowing it was only a matter of time until they got back together. He wasn't a bad guy in Beth's opinion, but the pair of them had fiery personalities and the relationship was inevitably similar to a volcano: all calm until things exploded. She suspected Dee enjoyed the drama but would never say so.

"At least he's making the effort with Ferne."

"I guess so. And while I'm not saying being a single parent is easy for you, there are times I'm envious of you not having a fella interfering in your life."

"I think the grass is always greener on the other side. I'd quite like having someone to share the responsibility with."

"Can I interest you in Hugh?"

Beth's shoulders shook as she laughed. "Not really, no."

"Not when you've got some hunky thirty-two-year-old chasing after you."

"I should go and see what Ellie's up to. Check she's not getting under Mirren's feet."

Dee told her to have a good day and they ended the call.

The kitchen was filled with the sweet scent of baking, and Beth inhaled deeply as she walked in.

"I helped Mirren," Ellie said, twirling on the stone tiles to the music drifting from the radio.

"What did you make?"

"Flapjack," Mirren said, her cheeks flushed as she sliced it up. "I should have made it yesterday so it had time to cool. The Tupperware will get all steamed up now. And I'm a mess." She dusted off her jeans, then pushed her hair from her face. "Maybe I should get changed. I don't really have time though."

"Are you all right? Ellie hasn't been getting in your way, has she?"

"No. Sorry, I'm just waffling on. Ignore me." She rifled through a cupboard for a Tupperware container. "I'll be out for most of the day, so you'll have the place to yourselves."

"Where are you going?" Ellie asked, continuing to twirl until Beth put her hands on her shoulders to stop her.

"I'm getting the boat over to Bryher," Mirren said.

Beth didn't like to pry but her curiosity was piqued; Trystan had mentioned needing to go to Bryher too, and she wondered if the two were connected.

"I've a friend who owns the hotel there," Mirren said, placing slices of flapjack in the container. "I'll have lunch with her. And call in and see Lowen too. The flapjack's for him. It's his favourite. Though he'll no doubt tell me it was his favourite when he was eight and claim he's not bothered now that he's almost forty."

Beth was confused as to who they were talking about, and also by Mirren's nervous energy. She'd never known her waffle on so much. "Who's Lowen?"

"My eldest!" she said, swinging round and raising her eyebrows. "I must have told you about Lowen. He has the pottery studio on Bryher."

"I don't think you've mentioned him."

"I must have done. It's just hard to keep track with me having so many boys."

"You have five sons, right?"

"Yes. Jago lives in New York. Then Lowen's over on Bryher. You've met the others; they all live on St Mary's. Well, Trystan lives in London, really, but he's here a lot."

"Does Lowen come over to St Mary's much?" Beth asked.

"Not if he can help it," Mirren said on a sigh. "Just for special occasions these days." After pulling her cardigan on, she picked up her handbag and the flapjack. "You two have a lovely day. If any of the guests from the cottages come up for anything, tell them to call me or point them towards Trystan or Noah. I won't be late, but don't wait for me for dinner if I'm not back. Just sort yourselves out."

"We will. Have a nice time."

She waved at Ellie as she backed out of the door.

"What are we going to do today, Mummy?"

"What would you like to do?"

"Go on the train."

She shook her head as she chuckled. "We can't go on the train every day."

"Kit said I'm very important, remember? And he said I can go on the train with him whenever I want."

"Not every day though. It's not fair on the other people who want to ride. I think we'll go to the beach today."

"Can we ask Trystan to build sandcastles with us again?"

"He has to work today, but I'm sure he'll build one with you another day."

After spending a couple of hours at the beach, they walked into Hugh Town for lunch in a cafe.

They hadn't been back at the house for long when Beth's mobile rang, vibrating around the patio table. If it was another unknown number she was ignoring it. Her heart rate increased when she saw it was a call from her dad's care home.

"Is everything all right?" she asked after the manager greeted her.

"Yes," Maureen said brightly. "Geoff's very well. I just wanted to check in with you as you've not been to visit for a while."

"I sent an email," she said, with the vague feeling that she'd done something wrong. "About extending my holiday. I got a reply to say it was fine …"

"We got the email. Of course it's fine. Are you still away?"

"Yes." Beth's chest felt suddenly tight. When she'd decided to stay away for longer, she hadn't given her dad much thought. She tended to visit him once a week, sometimes every two weeks. Since he never had any clue who she was or why she was sitting there chatting to him, she didn't really think it made any difference whether she visited or not. Her mum had always let her off the hook, telling her she needn't bother.

"We might be away until school starts again. I'm not quite sure of our plans yet."

"Oh," Maureen said flatly.

"We're just on the Isles of Scilly," Beth told her, feeling

suddenly guilty. "If there was anything urgent I could get back quickly."

"Right. That's good to know. I'm sure everything will be fine until you're home again. Did you get the invitation to the family day? Our little summer fete?"

"No." Presumably they sent it to the house, which reminded Beth that she needed to ask Dee to go around and check through the post.

"It's a week on Sunday. If you did end up being home by then, it would be great if you and your daughter could make it. The residents get such a boost from being around family."

Beth pursed her lips, not sure if that was entirely true since her dad wasn't even aware she *was* family. "Ellie doesn't like to visit," she said. It was a strange atmosphere and Beth could understand why she didn't like it.

"There'll be games and face painting for the kids. It'll be a lovely, joyful event."

"I guess we'll still be on holiday, so we won't be able to."

"The only other thing is that we need to arrange for the doctor to visit to review your father's medications. But it's best if you're here for that, so I guess we'd need to hold off on that for now."

"Do I really need to be there in person? I'm happy to speak to the doctor over the phone."

"It's possible, but if the doctor needs to change any of the medicines we really need you here to discuss that and sign off on it."

"Would a video call suffice?" she asked, pacing the patio.

"Not if changes are needed to his medications. Then you'd need to be here in person. That's the protocol. There are safe-guarding measures we need to adhere to. I'm sure you understand."

"Yes. Sure." Beth's voice was strained as she spoke through gritted teeth. "Why don't you arrange for the doctor to visit, and if anything needs to be changed, *then* we can discuss a time for me to be there. Would that work?"

"Yes. We can do that," the woman said, her voice surprisingly calm considering Beth's hostile tone. "I appreciate this is a difficult situation, and I know it's been a difficult time for you. You have my sympathies."

"I needed a break," she said, sinking onto the nearest chair and feeling like the worst daughter in the world. "Is it so bad for me to want a holiday?"

"Of course not," Maureen said. "Let me set up the doctor's visit and we'll go from there."

"Thank you," she whispered before ending the call.

Ellie called out to her, wanting her to look at the bubbles she was blowing with the bubble mixture Mirren had given her. Forcing a smile, Beth watched her jumping to pop them as they floated around her, spilling bubble mixture from the tube in the process.

The phone call played on her mind. It was difficult to relax and enjoy the scenery now, when all she could think about was what a terrible daughter she was. Whether her dad knew who Beth was or not was irrelevant; he was her responsibility. She'd left him so she could indulge in some extended holiday which she'd convinced herself she was owed.

She was forty years old and acting like a carefree teenager. Staring out to sea, she realised she needed to start acting like the responsible adult she was supposed to be.

CHAPTER TWELVE

B eth hadn't seen Trystan approach. Startled, she jerked her head up from her phone to be met by his smiling face.

"What are you engrossed in?" he asked, tipping his head towards her phone.

She set it face down on the patio table. "Nothing." Actually, she'd been checking her options for getting back to Plymouth and trying to decide on the best course of action.

"Is my mum here?"

"No …" It took her a moment to remember where Mirren was. "She went to Bryher for the day."

"I'd have come over earlier if I'd realised." He quirked an eyebrow and pulled a chair over to sit beside Beth. After glancing at Ellie at the other side of the garden, he put a hand on top of Beth's in her lap. "I was thinking maybe we could do something this evening. There's a quiz at the pub. Noah and Keira are going, so I thought we could join them if you fancy it?"

"I can't ask your mum to look after Ellie," she said, her whole body tensing.

"You won't need to. I'll just mention it in front of her and she'll insist you come too."

Pulling her hand away from his, she sat up straighter. "I can't go to the pub with you."

"Okay. We don't need to go to the pub. We can go for a walk … or hang out at my place?"

She rubbed at her forehead. "I can't leave my daughter to sneak off and have sex with you."

His brow wrinkled. "That's not what I—"

"I think I gave you the wrong idea. The other night I'd had some wine and I was feeling vulnerable …"

His hand rested on her knee as he looked at her in confusion. "That's not what happened."

"Please stop," she hissed through gritted teeth.

"Stop what?"

"Touching me." She pushed his hand away. "Stop all of this. I barely even know you. I'm on holiday with my daughter and you're ..."

"I'm what?" he asked weakly.

"You're crowding me. I can't do this. I need you to back off." Even as she tried not to look at him, she was aware of the hurt in his eyes. He started to speak and she cut him off. "Please leave me alone."

"I'm sorry," he muttered as he rose from his chair.

By the time Beth braved looking, he was already at the gate. Even from that distance, the set of his shoulders radiated anger. Not that she could blame him. Taking a deep breath through her nose, she contemplated chasing after him to apologise. Where would that get her though? Her words might have been harsh, but putting an end to whatever was going on between them was the right thing to do.

"Mummy!" Ellie called running over to her. "Where's Trystan gone?"

"He had some work to do."

Ellie looked over to the cottage where he was walking inside. "Is he coming back later?"

"I don't think so." At least she couldn't imagine him

returning any time soon after the way she'd spoken to him. Oh god, she'd been awful.

Shaking her head, she told herself it didn't matter anyway. There was space on a flight on Thursday, so she'd soon be a distant memory to him. And vice versa. She picked up her phone again, intent on booking the flight.

"Can you play with me, Mummy?" Ellie asked.

"I just need to—"

"Please, Mummy. Let's play chase. It's really fun."

"Okay." Booking the flight could wait until later.

"I'm so excited," Keira said when Trystan joined her and Noah at the round table in the back corner of the pub. "I've been wanting to do the quiz ever since I moved here, but Noah always says it's lame."

Noah screwed his face up. "I don't like the quiz because I'm not allowed to win it. Charlie thinks it would be inappropriate for the staff to win."

Kit arrived, taking the stool beside Trystan. "Otherwise you'd win it every week, wouldn't you?"

"I'm pretty good actually," Noah retorted.

"Who invited you?" Trystan asked Kit.

"What do you mean who invited me? I thought we were having a Treneary family quiz team."

"No. That's not what we were doing. It was supposed to be a double date vibe."

"Who's your date?" Kit asked. "And why did you choose Noah and Keira over me and Seren?"

"Because Seren's working." Trystan managed a smile, hoping his baby brother didn't quiz him further on that one. Seren *was* working. He just hadn't known that at the time he'd hatched his double date plan.

"So who's your date?" Keira asked.

Before he could answer, Seren appeared beside him and slid a tray of drinks onto the table. "Have you got a date?" she asked.

Trystan frowned as he took his glass of water. "Maybe I should drink tequila this evening … No, please remind me that I don't drink. I might need reminding."

"What's going on?" Seren said, perching on Kit's lap and looking at Trystan intently.

"Do you think I'm creepy?"

She gave him a puzzled smile. "No. Why?"

"Because I thought I had a flirty, charming kind of vibe and now I'm worried I'm actually a creep." He wiped condensation from his glass while they all stared at him, clearly waiting for further explanation. "I wanted to bring Beth out tonight."

"Beth who's staying with your mum?" Keira asked.

"Yeah." He winced. "I took her out for dinner the other night for her birthday and …" He tapped the table, debating how much to say. "We ended up back at my place."

"You slept with Beth?" Kit asked, nodding his head approvingly. "Nice!"

"Kit!" Seren slapped his leg.

"What? She's very attractive for an older woman."

Trystan choked on a laugh. "Older woman?"

"Yeah." Kit shrugged. "I guess she's like twice my age."

"Not far off actually," Trystan conceded. "This is why I wasn't going to involve you in my double date."

"Right! A minute ago it was because Seren was working!"

"Get over it," Noah said. "I want to hear the rest of the Beth story."

"I'm not entirely sure what happened." Trystan shifted in his seat. "I really like her and I thought we had this connection … but when I saw her today she flipped out and told me to back off. It was as though she thought I was harassing her or something."

"Seriously?" Seren said.

He nodded. "I feel as though I missed something. I'd been

flirting with her and being a bit suggestive … but I thought she was enjoying it."

"Women are very strange creatures," Kit remarked, earning himself another slap from Seren.

"That does sound weird," Keira said. "I haven't known you very long, but I can't imagine you harassing someone."

"It really wasn't how I thought I was coming across. When I saw her today it was as though she'd had a personality transplant."

"Maybe there's something going on with her," Keira suggested.

"She lost her mum recently," Trystan mused. "I think that's partly why we clicked. I ended up talking to her about Dad." He blew out a long breath. "Anyway, I don't know what to do now. It's going to be awkward with her staying with Mum all summer."

"What did you say when she told you to back off?" Noah asked.

"I apologised. She wouldn't let me say any more, so I just got out of there quick."

"Maybe go and try and talk to her about it," Kit said. "Clear the air at least."

"I can't." He'd wanted to go back there all afternoon and explain that he'd never intended to make her uncomfortable, but he was sure it would only make things worse. "If I go near her now, it'll just look like I'm hassling her even more."

"That's true," Seren agreed. "If she asked you to back off, you really should back off."

He dragged his hands through his hair and let out a frustrated sigh. "I just want to go and talk to her."

Noah raised an eyebrow. "You really like her?"

"Yeah." And he couldn't shake the feeling that there'd been more going on when she'd snapped at him. The desire to go back and check on her was hard to quell.

"What's the deal with Ellie's father?" Kit asked. "Is he on

the scene? I've spent a bit of time with them on the train, but I've never heard him mentioned."

"I've got no idea. I almost asked the other night." He'd felt as though he could've veered into the topic when Beth had been asking about his ex, but he'd decided not to pry. "It feels weird asking. I suppose it's probably a sensitive subject one way or another."

"Presumably he's not on the scene or you'd have heard Ellie mentioning her dad," Keira said.

"True."

"I better get back to work," Seren said, glancing at her watch. "The quiz starts in five minutes. Shall I sign you up?"

Trystan shook his head. "I'm going home in a minute."

"No, you're not," Keira said. "The quiz was your idea so you have to stay and help us. I suspect Noah's going to be rubbish at it."

"Hey!" Noah gave her a friendly shove.

"You have a point." Trystan looked from Noah to Kit. "It would be really mean of me to leave you with these two." Staying for the quiz didn't appeal at all, but it seemed like a marginally better option than going home to mope.

The way Beth had spoken to Trystan left her with a knot in her stomach that refused to budge. By the time she'd put Ellie to bed and taken her usual spot on the patio she was tempted to go and apologise. He was definitely owed that. Except if she really was going home that week, it might be easier to leave things as they were with Trystan. Not that she'd got around to booking the flight. If she was honest, the idea of leaving so soon was becoming less and less appealing.

Pulling her phone out, she pressed dial on Dee's number.

"If you're calling to tell me about what a fantastic day you've had lounging around in paradise and flirting with hunky guys, I think I might pack my bags and come and join you. I've just got Ferne to bed and poured myself a massive gin and tonic."

"It sounds as though you didn't have a great day?"

"No. Mum's ill and can't look after Ferne this week, so I've taken extra holiday time from work. I'd thought we could make the most of it and do some fun days out but the child's on a mission to drive me crazy. It's one tantrum after the other, no matter what I do."

"Is she missing Hugh?" Beth tried to focus on her friend's problems, but her gaze drifted to Trystan's cottage. As the daylight faded, the place remained in darkness, making her think he might not be at home even if she did decide to talk to him. Which she probably shouldn't.

"I guess so," Dee said. "I'm trying to be patient with her but … well, thank goodness for gin! How was your day? Try not to make it sound too great."

"No fear of that, I'm afraid. It's been awful." She filled Dee in on the phone call from the care home and how guilt-ridden she was at not taking her dad into account while she'd been making her plans for the summer.

"He doesn't even know who you are." Dee sounded outraged by the situation. "What does it matter if you visit or not? You pay an absolute fortune for him to be looked after. I think it's bloody cheeky of them to give you a guilt trip about going on holiday."

"It's not my money. It's Dad's." It had probably been a mistake to mention to Dee how much the care home cost.

"That might be so, but you have power of attorney, right? If I were you I'd find him a cheaper place and take the extra money for yourself."

"I'm not going to do that. He's well looked after. And they weren't guilt-tripping me… I just felt guilt. That's my issue."

"Even so, you're a better daughter than me keeping him in such a fancy place."

"Anyway …" Beth shook her head, wanting to get the conversation back on track. "I'm thinking that staying away for the whole summer is pretty self-indulgent and we should probably come home."

"No!" Dee shrieked. "No bloody way. Don't you dare."

"But spending the entire summer away is very extravagant."

"Not really. Lots of people do it. People who deserve a break far less than you do. I can't believe you'd even contemplate coming home … what about your holiday romance?"

Beth grimaced and automatically glanced at the cottage again, where there were still no signs of life. "I messed that up. It's another reason that leaving seems like a good idea."

Dee made sympathetic noises while Beth told her about how she'd snapped at Trystan.

"I'm sure if you explain the situation, he'd understand," she said softly.

"I don't even know if I want him to understand. I shouldn't be chasing after some guy. Spending so much time thinking about him has meant I've been neglecting my daughter and my dad."

"Oh shut up!" Dee snapped. "No one could ever accuse you of neglecting Ellie. You're an amazing mum. You always put her first, and it's probably not healthy. It's perfectly fine to make time for yourself too. As for your dad … well that's a difficult situation, but I really don't think you should come rushing home just to visit him. From what you've told me, I could go along and claim to be you and he wouldn't know any different." She gasped loudly. "Oh my god, that's a great idea, isn't it?"

"No." Beth couldn't help but laugh. "You need to slow down on the gin. It's a terrible idea. You can't do that."

She let out a cackle of a laugh. "You're right. That's an insane idea even for me. But I could go and visit him."

"What?"

"I could go and see him. Check he's being fed and looked

after and that he's happy. Maybe that would put your mind at ease. Or is that a bad idea too?"

"No." A lump formed in Beth's throat at her friend's generosity. "It's a lovely idea. I'd just feel terrible for you …"

"I'm totally up for it. I've never been in an old people's home, but I watched a sitcom about one once and it was hilarious."

"You might be disappointed in that case."

"I'm really happy to go, if it'll make you feel better."

"Are you sure you don't mind?"

"Not at all. Especially if it means you'll stay there and carry out a sordid holiday romance and give me all the juicy details."

"I don't know." Beth's emotions were all over the place and she couldn't decide on the best course of action. "Maybe it would be better if I come home and check on Dad. That seems like the responsible thing to do."

"I suppose in the end you have to do what feels right for you," Dee said kindly. "But can you do me one favour?"

"What is it?" Beth asked when Dee went quiet.

"I'm probably about to upset you …"

"Just say whatever you want to say," Beth said, already feeling a tightening in her chest.

"When you're considering your options," she began quietly, "can you think about what your mum would tell you to do?"

Big fat tears welled in Beth's eyes, then dripped down her cheeks.

"I've made you cry, haven't I? I'm sorry."

"It's okay," Beth sniffed. "It's a good point."

Through her tears, Beth managed to smile. Because she knew exactly what her mum would say – she'd tell her to stay where she was and have a fantastic summer exploring all that Scilly had to offer.

And that would definitely involve a fling, if possible.

CHAPTER THIRTEEN

Almost as soon as she'd got off the phone, Beth marched determinedly over to Trystan's cottage and rang the door-bell. As she'd suspected from the darkness inside, there was no answer. Going back to the patio, she staked out the cottage for an hour, then gave up and went to bed.

The following day Trystan was just as elusive. There was no sign of him out for his usual morning exercise. Likewise when Beth surreptitiously looked in the windows when she and Ellie had been passing. If he was avoiding her, it was understandable, but also annoying when she wanted to apologise.

"Want me to pour you a wine?" Mirren offered when Beth came down from putting Ellie to bed that evening.

"You must think I've got a drinking problem, sitting out drinking wine every evening."

"Not at all. I was the same when the kids were young. Wine was always my treat once I'd got them into bed."

Beth glanced out of the window, where she could see lights on at Trystan's place. "I was wondering if I could ask you a favour … if you're not going out, would you mind if I go for a quick walk? It doesn't matter if not …"

"Of course. You get out. Why not have a wander into town?

It's a good bet that either Noah or Seren are working. You could prop up the bar and they'd keep you company."

"I just thought I might have a wander along the beach. I won't be long."

"Whatever you want, hun. I'm here for the evening and even if Ellie wakes up she's never any bother."

"Thank you." The minute she stepped outside, Beth's heart began to pound. Trystan might not even hear her out. There was a good chance he had her pegged as neurotic and was thinking he'd had a lucky escape.

A faint glow illuminated the front window and she was in full panic mode when she reached the door. After pressing the bell she focused on her breathing and tried to quash her nerves. Time seemed to slow but eventually it became clear that he wasn't going to answer. Stepping back, she craned her neck to look at the upstairs window, thinking he might have looked out and decided to ignore her. Instinctively, she moved to the down-stairs window and peeked inside. A light was on in the living room but she couldn't see Trystan. She tried to placate herself with the idea that he could be in the shower, but in reality it was much more likely that he was ignoring her.

All set to give up, she had one last idea and went to look around the side of the house. The sight of him on the patio star-tled her. He had his laptop open on the table and didn't appear to have noticed her. The patio door was open though so she was certain he'd have heard the doorbell.

She was about to back away when she spotted his earphones. He didn't react when she said his name, but waving got his attention.

"Hi," she said anxiously.

He pulled his earphones out and flashed a brief smile.

"I rang the doorbell ..."

"I didn't hear it." He held up his earphones before depositing them on the table. "Everything okay?"

"Yes. Well, sort of. Not really." She took a few steps towards him. "Is it okay if I join you for a minute?"

"Yeah." He closed the lid of the laptop. "I was just doing some work."

"Sorry." She hovered behind the chair nearest to him. "I wanted to apologise. I came over yesterday evening but you weren't here."

"I was at the pub with my brothers."

She nodded. "The quiz?"

"Yeah."

"I just wanted to say … I'm sorry for snapping at you. I really shouldn't have."

His brow creased. "I'm sorry if I made you feel uncomfortable. I never intended that."

"You didn't. Honestly, it wasn't anything you did. You just caught me at a bad moment." She opened her mouth to explain exactly what had been going on but thought better of it. "I was having a bad day and I took it out on you. I'm sorry. You probably think I'm completely neurotic, but I swear I'm not usually like this."

Looking at the situation from his point of view, she couldn't see how he'd want anything more to do with her, but if she could at least clear the air it would be something. "I'll leave you to get on with your work, but I didn't want you to feel uncomfortable about coming up to your mum's or anything."

"Okay."

"I really am sorry." She forced a smile and took a couple of steps backwards. "Goodnight."

"Beth?" The sound of her name from his lips made a tingle shoot up her spine. She turned back and looked at him questioningly. "Do you want to talk about it?"

"About what?"

"Your bad day yesterday." He pushed the chair out from the table and gestured for her to sit down.

"Do you really want to hear? Because I wouldn't blame you if you didn't want anything to do with me."

"I want to hear," he said solemnly.

"My life must seem like such a mess." She sighed when she sat down. "Right before I saw you yesterday I had a call from my dad's care home, and to cut a long story short, by the time I got off the phone I felt like a terrible daughter for not considering him when I decided to stay here for the summer."

"He has Alzheimer's?"

"Yes. He has no idea who I am, but the staff at the care home think it's important for him to have visitors."

"I can see why that would put you in a bad mood."

"It wasn't just that. I'd also forgotten to cancel Ellie's swimming course and had an angry call about that, along with a lecture about the importance of kids being able to swim. I felt as though I was neglecting Ellie by not having her in lessons this week. Which I realise sounds ridiculous. I think the other thing was that …" She put her hands up to her face. "This is so embarrassing, but the other night when we went out, I had such a great night. I don't remember the last time I enjoyed myself that much. So when I got those phone calls it almost felt like the universe telling me not to be so selfish, and that I should be thinking of my responsibilities instead of spending my time daydreaming about you." She winced in humiliation as she finally stopped talking.

"I was daydreaming about you a lot too," he said, looking at her intently. "After you told me to back off, I kept wanting to come and check you were okay …"

"You're far too nice. When you didn't answer the door tonight I thought it was because you were hiding from me, and I really couldn't blame you."

"I wasn't hiding. I had to force myself to stay out of the way today." He gave a crooked smile. "When someone accuses you of crowding them, you kind of feel as though you shouldn't go near them again."

"I'm so sorry. I shouldn't have said all that stuff. I didn't mean any of it."

He tilted his head. "I was being a bit intense."

"No, you weren't." She thought back on it. "Okay, maybe you were, but I encouraged it."

His gaze landed on the laptop.

"Did I interrupt you? I can go and leave you to work."

"I was just trying to get some stuff out of the way so I can take a couple of days off. Do you still want to go to Tresco on Thursday?"

"I'd love to." She forced herself to stand, desperate to stay but not wanting to make a nuisance of herself. "Are you going to Bryher tomorrow?" she asked when he walked around the front of the house with her.

"Yes."

"To visit your brother?"

"Yeah." He looked puzzled.

"Your mum went yesterday. She was telling me about him."

He stopped at the gate, pushing the toe of his shoe into the gravel. "I'd invite you along but Lowen can be a bit ..." He dragged his teeth along his lower lip. "He's not always the most sociable."

"I wasn't angling for an invite," she said, not entirely sure that was true. Now that she'd decided to stay, she was desperate to spend more time with Trystan.

"Well, I would invite you ... it's just a bit tense with Lowen sometimes."

"Don't you get on?"

"Um ..." His gaze shifted behind her, to the water which had turned a soft pink with the setting sun. "It's complicated."

"I'm being nosey. Sorry."

He grinned. "Has anyone ever told you that you apologise a lot?"

"Not really. But you might be right. Or I just have a lot to apologise for around you."

"You don't." He licked his lip and her heart fluttered as she anticipated kissing him. "Thanks for coming over."

"You're welcome." She felt like an idiot, grinning up at him, hoping he'd kiss her.

"So, I'll see you on Thursday, if not before."

"Yes." She took a step backwards. "Great. Have a good day tomorrow."

"Goodnight," he called and headed back to his laptop.

Wandering back along the lane and through the garden, Beth was left feeling slightly deflated. It had gone well, she supposed. Trystan had been lovely and understanding so she should be grateful for that. It was the lack of physical contact that bothered her. Of course it was completely her own fault. What did she expect after the way she'd snapped at him?

He might be understanding, but he probably wasn't going to forget that in a hurry.

CHAPTER FOURTEEN

Trystan told himself he was calling over to his mum's place to let her know he was visiting Lowen and check if she needed him to take anything over there, but realistically he just couldn't resist the opportunity to see Beth.

Ellie was playing outside and skipped over to him when she saw him walking towards the house.

"Good morning, Trystan," she said in her adorably sweet voice.

"Morning," he replied.

"I'm going to have breakfast outside." She took his hand and they walked together.

"That's the best way to eat breakfast. What are you having?"

"Toast," she said, as Beth stepped outside with two plates in her hands.

The way she smiled when she saw him made him glad he'd called over before heading to Bryher. Visiting Lowen could be stressful, and spending time with Beth first felt like balancing things out.

"Do you want me to put some toast in for you?" she asked as she slid the plates on the table.

"No, I'm fine, thanks."

"Coffee?" she asked, heading back inside.

"Coffee sounds good." He helped Ellie push her chair closer to the table then sat beside her.

"I didn't think we'd be seeing you this morning," Beth said when she returned.

"Can't stay away from you," he said with a flirty smile, then wondered if he was coming on too strong again. Maybe he should try playing it cool.

"Do you want some of my toast?" Ellie asked. "I'm very good at sharing."

"That's very kind of you, but I already had my breakfast."

"I bet it was something healthy," Beth teased.

"Was it?" Ellie asked when he didn't respond.

"I had a smoothie before my jog," he said, smiling bashfully. "Then avocado on toast with a poached egg."

"He's much healthier than we are," Beth told Ellie.

Trystan picked up his coffee. "Toast isn't exactly unhealthy."

"It is when you put this much butter and jam on it." Beth raised her eyebrows and took a bite. "We're on holiday though, so it doesn't really count."

Ellie held her toast out to him and he took a bite, not feeling he could refuse.

"That is a lot of jam," he teased.

"We like jam," Ellie said.

His mum stepped out of the back door. "I thought I heard your voice."

"I'm going over to see Lowen in a bit. Is there anything you want me to take over there?"

"No. I was there on Monday. He'll be happy to see you, though."

Trystan would argue otherwise but smiled benignly and sipped his coffee. "I'll take the boat."

"Check the tides," his mum said, and he bit his tongue to stop himself from telling her that of course he'd checked the tide. "Why don't you take Beth and Ellie with you?" She looked at Beth. "It's beautiful on Bryher. You've not been yet, have you?"

"No. But I'd hate to intrude. We'll go over another time."

"I'd like to go on a boat," Ellie said, looking pleadingly at Beth.

"Trystan's going to visit his brother today, but we'll go another day."

"Is it Kit?" she asked, looking at him with big eyes.

"No, my older brother, Lowen."

"Does he have a train too?"

"No," he said, chuckling. "No train, I'm afraid."

She looked thoughtful. "I'd like to go anyway. Even though he doesn't have a train."

"Take them with you," his mum said. "They'll enjoy it. And it'll be nice for you to have the company."

Maybe she had a point. He'd been worried it might be awkward for Beth to come along with him, but it might have the effect of making it less awkward for Trystan. And it's not as though he ever stayed long with Lowen.

"Do you want to?" he asked Beth.

"Yes, we do!" Ellie said excitedly.

"It seems as though we're keen," Beth said. "If you're sure it's okay?"

"We can get lunch over there," he said, warming to the idea. "And do some exploring, go to the beach …"

"Who's going to drive the boat?" Ellie asked, slipping off her chair to stand by Trystan's legs.

"Can you drive a boat?" he asked her.

"No."

"I guess I will then."

"Can I help? When I go on the train, Kit lets me sit on his knee to help him drive."

"Does he now?" Mirren shook her head. "I'll have to have a word with him about that."

"You can help me drive the boat," Trystan told Ellie, who looked delighted.

"Make sure there are life-jackets for all of you," his mum said.

His smile was tight. "I will."

"If there isn't one that fits Ellie properly, call Kit and he'll be able to borrow one from the lifesaving club."

"Can we go *now?*" Ellie asked.

"As soon as we've finished our coffees," he said. "We need to pack our beach things too."

Half an hour later, the three of them were bouncing gently over the waves as they headed away from St Mary's on a northerly course. The noise of the engine had unsettled Ellie at first, and she sat timidly on Beth's lap in the middle of the boat, having put aside her notions of helping skipper the boat. After a while she relaxed and Trystan offered her his hand and asked if she wanted to help steer. Perched on his lap, her hair blew in his face and he leaned to the side, pulling strands from his mouth.

Beth moved to take a photo of the two of them and he dutifully smiled alongside Ellie. He slowed the boat to let her take photos of the scenery and she seemed totally absorbed as she held the camera to her face.

They were rounding Samson when Ellie thrust her arm out, pointing towards a rocky outcrop. "Penguins!" she squealed. "Mummy, look at the penguins."

"Puffins," Trystan corrected her, turning the tiller to get them a little closer, then cutting the motor to bob quietly on the listless waves.

"I've never seen puffins before," Beth whispered, staring out at the pair standing proudly on the rocks. She lifted her camera to her face and pressed the shutter button repeatedly. "Can you get any closer?" she asked, without looking at him.

He surveyed the water before shaking his head. "I'd rather not risk it."

"That's fine." She squinted into the lens, adjusting the zoom before taking more photos. Then she lowered the camera and stared at the striking birds.

"I like puffins," Ellie said. "They're my favourite."

Beth moved over, showing them the crystal-clear photos on the camera, then zooming in to show Ellie the distinctive bill with its triangle of blue beside the vibrant orange that perfectly matched its webbed feet.

They watched them for a while, before leaving them in peace to continue to Bryher. Soon, they reached Anneka's Quay and Trystan killed the engine to drift alongside the stone boat ramp.

"You must be old enough to remember *Challenge Anneka*?" he asked Beth as he tied up the boat. "The TV show with Anneka Rice?"

"I loved that programme," she said, looking slightly wistful.

He reached out for Ellie to help her off the boat, then gave Beth his hand as she stepped off. "She made this," he said, gesturing the ramp. "Anneka's Quay."

"No way? That was one of her challenges? I probably watched it."

"They originally built a wooden jetty. It was replaced about ten years ago. She even came back to officially open the new one. She always causes quite a buzz on the islands."

"I'll bet. I'd be excited." They set off walking and Beth gave him a sidelong glance. "When you asked if I was old enough to remember … do *you* remember her coming here?"

"Which time?"

"The first time!"

"God, no. I'm not that old."

She scowled in response to his teasing grin.

"I was joking. Kind of. It wasn't quite before my time, but I was too young to remember it."

Ellie took his hand and swung on his arm as they wandered up the boat ramp. "Are we nearly at your brother's house yet?"

"Not really. We're not even off the jetty."

"How far is it?" Beth asked.

"About a fifteen-minute walk. Maybe a bit more."

In fact it was about double that thanks to Ellie's snail-like pace.

"Is it a shop as well?" Beth asked when they arrived at the lone building on the western side of the island.

"Yeah." The pottery studio and shop were housed in a converted boat shed, and a weather-beaten cottage stood just over the sand dunes. Lowen's plan had been to renovate the house, but as far as Trystan could tell he'd done precisely nothing to the place.

"Mostly he sells his pottery in a shop on St Mary's, so I don't think he puts a lot of effort into attracting customers here." He suspected it was the opposite and he'd rather discourage customers. It definitely didn't have a welcoming air. Until you got to the door with the list of opening times, it was difficult to tell if it was open to the public or not.

"We don't need to stay long," he said, pushing at the door.

"Don't touch anything," Beth whispered to Ellie as they stepped inside.

There was no sign of Lowen, which was normal.

"These are amazing," Beth murmured as she wandered along the shelves, admiring Lowen's collection.

"I like the cups, Mummy," Ellie said. "That one's got a puffin on it like we saw."

"They're gorgeous," Beth replied. "Just don't touch them."

Focused on finding his brother, Trystan wandered towards the workshop. Surprise flashed in Lowen's features when he walked out from the back. He tipped his chin at Beth before returning his attention to Trystan.

"I didn't know you were coming over today."

"I messaged you."

"You said you *might* come. I didn't know it was definite."

Trystan shook his head, annoyed. "I messaged you this morning to say I was about to set off."

"I didn't see that." He glanced around as though looking for his phone. "I've got loads of work on at the moment."

"You always have," Trystan said, not managing to disguise his bitterness and worrying that bringing Beth and Ellie along had been a bad idea.

"Jenny emailed me, asking for a set of dishes for her new place. You two are definitely over then?"

"Yeah. I told you that months ago."

"I didn't know if you'd finally get around to proposing and everything would be fixed."

"Obviously not," he said in a low growl, then turned to Beth, who was lingering behind him. When he introduced her, Lowen's eyebrows rose.

"Sorry. I didn't realise you were together." He winced. "Together in the shop, I mean."

"Mummy," Ellie said. "Can I have this cup with the puffin on it?"

She had it in her hands as she walked over to them, and Beth lurched for it when it slipped through her fingers. It had no chance against the stone floor and broke into two large pieces and several smaller ones.

"I told you not to touch!" Beth hissed, which immediately brought tears to Ellie's eyes.

"It's okay," Lowen said, but was drowned out by Ellie's crying.

Beth glanced up at him apologetically. "I'll pay for it."

"It's broken," Ellie wailed.

"It's okay," Beth soothed. "It was an accident."

"But it's broken."

"Choose another one," Trystan told her.

"I'm so sorry," Beth said, picking up the pieces.

Lowen shrugged. "It's fine. It's only a mug; there are plenty more."

"I'll pay for it," Beth said again, as she wiped tears from Ellie's cheeks. "You can choose another one too."

"You don't need to pay for it," Lowen said as they went to look for another one.

Ellie's crying got louder as Beth suggested other mugs she might like. It seemed the one she'd broken was the only one she wanted. Since they were handmade, they were all slightly different, and that was the only one with a puffin on it. The crying showed no signs of abating and nothing Beth or Trystan said helped.

Eventually, Lowen appeared and crouched beside Ellie. She stared at him for a moment then cried even more. "Sorry, I broke the cup," she said with a loud sniff.

"It doesn't matter," he said softly. "I can make another one."

"Did you make it?" Ellie asked, the crying dialling down a notch.

"Yes." He looked at the shelves beside them. "I made everything here."

"How?" Ellie asked through a shuddering hiccup.

"In my workshop." He tipped his head in that direction. "I can show you, if you want. But you'll have to stop crying. There's no crying allowed in the workshop."

"Okay." Her chest heaved as she dragged in a deep breath. Beth took out a tissue and wiped away the line of snot beneath Ellie's nose.

"Come on then," Lowen said, straightening up and offering Ellie his hand. She walked with him into the back room and Trystan exchanged a look with Beth before following them. They hovered in the archway while Lowen showed Ellie around the messy workshop. Beth hung back with Trystan, only speaking to tell Ellie to be careful a couple of times.

Ignoring Beth's obvious tension, Ellie asked Lowen a string of questions which he patiently answered.

"If you give me those …" Lowen reached out to take the broken pieces of the cup from Beth. "I can make another one like it, with a puffin on it."

"You can make it for me again?" Ellie asked.

"Yes."

"Can I help you?"

He looked at his pottery wheel and shrugged. "I guess so … If you're not in a hurry?" he said, directing the question at Beth.

"We're not in a hurry," she replied. "But don't feel you have to …"

"It's fine." He patted the stool by the wheel for Ellie, then pulled up another and sat beside her. "Is it okay if you get a bit messy?" he asked her.

"Yes. I like getting messy. It's okay, isn't it, Mummy?"

"It's fine," she said, smiling at Lowen. "Thank you."

"No problem. You can put the kettle on if you want …" The remark seemed to be aimed at Trystan, but it was hard to tell since he didn't look at him. He moved to the sink in the corner and filled the kettle.

"That was nice of him," Beth whispered, creeping up beside him.

"Yes." He looked over at Lowen and Ellie who were focused on the lump of clay in the centre of the wheel. Lowen directed Ellie to press the foot pedal and her face lit up as the wheel began to rotate.

The atmosphere in the workshop was unusually relaxed thanks to Ellie's giggles, which filled the room for the next twenty minutes. Beth peppered Lowen with questions about his business and how he'd come to make pottery for a living. Conversation flowed easily, not that it would have mattered if it hadn't since they were all mesmerised by Ellie's enthusiasm over the pottery wheel.

"I think that looks like a great mug," Lowen finally said of Ellie's third attempt, which had come about with a lot of help.

"It doesn't have a handle," Ellie said. "And it doesn't have the birds and the colours."

"I'll have to let it dry a little. I can put the handle on later and paint it. It needs to go in the big oven too and that takes a while."

"How long?"

"A few days." He looked to Beth. "How long are you on holiday for?"

"A few more weeks, I think."

Trystan didn't like the uncertainty in her voice and reminded himself that he'd just come out of a long-term relationship and this was only destined to be a short-term thing.

"I can get it to you before you leave," Lowen told them.

"Thank you." Beth directed Ellie to wash her hands at the sink in the corner but hovered around the wheel herself. "I was wondering …"

"You want a turn?" Lowen asked, a hint of a smile pulling at his lips.

"Could I? I've never done it before and it looks like fun."

"It's a lot of fun, Mummy." Ellie said, as she struggled to reach the taps in the deep stainless-steel sink.

Trystan lifted her up while Lowen set Beth up at the pottery wheel. She was just as entertaining to watch as Ellie had been.

"Thank you so much," she said to Lowen when she'd thrown a mug that she was adorably proud of. "Can you say thank you?" she prompted Ellie.

"Thank you." Ellie took Lowen's hand and swung on his arm. "Can we come back and visit you again another day?"

"Maybe," he said, looking uncertainly down at her, as though remembering that he didn't like visitors. "You might have lots of other things to do."

"I'm going to go on Kit's train again," Ellie told him.

"That sounds like a great idea."

"I've been on it four times."

He smiled down at her. "That's a lot."

"I'm sure Kit's sick of having us along," Beth said. "But Ellie loves it."

Together, they all wandered back through the shop and out of the front door.

"I hope the weather stays nice for your holiday," Lowen said, lingering in the doorway.

"Thanks again." Beth gave him a quick hug and Trystan did the same.

"Nice to see you," Trystan said, which earned him a curt nod before Lowen disappeared inside.

"He seems lovely," Beth commented as they set off along the beach. "Definitely not as outgoing as the rest of the Trenearys, but he has a quiet charm about him. You and he look quite alike."

"No, we don't!" Trystan scoffed, slightly offended by the comparison. A few years ago they'd had a similar build and features, but Lowen had let himself go and looked more like he was approaching fifty than forty.

"You do," Beth insisted. "It's the eyes. You have the same eyes."

"Maybe. Anyway, who's hungry?"

"I am," Ellie shouted. "Are we having a picnic?"

"No." Trystan felt her delicate fingers curl around his. "We'll eat at the hotel. It's not far away."

"I've got very little legs," Ellie huffed. "You're making me walk too much."

"It's not far, I promise. Look, you can see it up there on the hill. And the faster you walk, the quicker we'll be there."

"Walking faster will make me more tired," she told him adamantly.

"How about a shoulder ride?"

"What's that?"

He couldn't help but smile. "I can carry you on my shoulders."

"Okay," she said, looking slightly dubious.

"Ready?" he said as he hoisted her up.

"I'm as big as a giant," she said, clinging to his head a little too tightly as he set off across the sand.

After a few steps, he turned to look back at Beth, who was staring at the two of them.

"You okay?" he asked.

She nodded a couple of times and hurried to catch up.

CHAPTER FIFTEEN

When they were settled on the terrace at Hell's Bay Hotel, Beth couldn't resist getting her camera out and snapping a few photos of the scenery while they waited for the waitress to come and take their food order. Turning away from the beautiful expanse of blue-green water, she brought the camera to her face again to take a photo of Trystan and Ellie peering at a ladybird walking across the table.

"Can you take a photo of the ladybird too?" Ellie asked.

"Sure." She moved closer and clicked the shutter, then glanced inside, hoping the service would be fast. Ellie was prone to tantrums if she had to wait too long for food. After the earlier scene with the broken mug, she'd rather avoid any more drama for the day.

Her stomach was also beginning to complain of hunger and she was hoping for quick service for her own benefit too. It made choosing a dish difficult, since she was now torn between ordering a burger and chips, like she really wanted, and the salad which seemed more fitting around Trystan.

She was still dithering when the owner came over and made a fuss of Trystan before asking what they wanted to eat.

"We'll have the sausage and chips from the kids' menu and

…" Beth scanned the menu and frowned. "Just a sec … You order first." She waved a hand in Trystan's direction.

He snapped his menu shut. "I'll have my usual: burger and fries."

"Oh, thank goodness." Beth closed her menu. "I thought you were going to choose something healthy and I'd have to follow suit. But I'll have the same. The burger sounds great."

"Okay." The woman scribbled on her pad with an amused grin. "Coming right up."

"You seem to have me down as some sort of health nut," Trystan said as she walked away.

"Not a nut, no. Just very healthy. Which I usually am too, but not while we're on holiday, obviously."

"Obviously," he said, glancing at Ellie, who'd slipped off the chair to follow the ladybird down the table leg and onto the ground. "How did you get into the school photo business?" he asked when Beth went to pack her camera back into its case.

She looked at him in surprise. "Oh god. That's not really what I do … I mean … I forgot I told you that."

"What do you mean that's not what you do?"

She grimaced. "I wasn't lying, more like just trying it out to see how it sounded. I didn't know we'd end up being …" She winced, completely flustered. "Friends or … I just didn't think it mattered what I told you I did for a living. I probably *am* a school photographer … I haven't quite figured it out yet."

"Right … that's confusing."

"I specialise in wedding photography," she told him. "At least I did. Mum used to look after Ellie while I was at work because it was mostly at the weekends. I had to cancel the jobs I had lined up for the summer holidays. Partly because I just couldn't face it. I still have a couple of weddings lined up in the autumn. My friend will look after Ellie then. After that, I need to find something that fits around Ellie better. I've done a bit of school photography before. It's not my dream job, but it's money." She grinned. "And it's a lot less pressure, considering very few parents expect school photos to come out well. The same can't be said for people's weddings."

Ellie came back to them and casually climbed up onto Trystan's lap. It felt a little petty to be jealous of her daughter, but it highlighted how little physical contact Beth had had with Trystan since she'd had a go at him. She missed how tactile he'd been prior to her outburst.

"You've got big hands," Ellie said, taking Trystan's hand and holding it against her own.

"Thank you," he replied. "I grew them myself."

It took Ellie a moment to laugh, but when she did it was a proper belly laugh. "I'm growing my hands too. Will they get as big as yours?"

"Probably not as big as mine," he said, raising an eyebrow. "Maybe as big as your mum's."

Ellie reached out to Beth and they compared hand sizes. The conversation jumped from one random subject to the next until the food arrived.

"Sausage and chips," the young waitress announced, setting Ellie's food down. "And your vegan burgers and sweet potato fries will just be a minute."

"Thank you!" Trystan positively beamed as the waitress nipped back inside.

"Was that a joke?" Beth asked, nudging Trystan when he began to chuckle. "Please don't tell me you've tricked me into a healthy lunch. I was looking forward to a big juicy piece of meat!"

"I don't think I tricked you. I just didn't mention that my usual was a vegan burger."

"You're not vegan, are you?" She thought back to their meal together and shook her head. "You ate meat the other night."

"I just like the vegan burger here."

Beth reached across to help Ellie open the ketchup sachet. "I can't believe you'd do this to me. I keep telling you I'm on holiday. I'm supposed to eat nothing but junk. It's the law."

"You'll like the vegan burger. If not, I promise to find you a hamburger later."

When the food came out, Beth had to admit it was tasty. If she hadn't had her heart set on a regular burger, she'd have enjoyed it even more.

As soon as Ellie had wolfed down her food, she announced she was bored and wanted to go to the beach. Thankfully, Trystan was happy to go along with the demands of a five-year-old and they hastily paid the bill and set off again.

"I'd like to build two sandcastles," Ellie told Trystan once they were on the nearby beach with towels laid out and all of them having stripped down to swimwear.

The sight of Trystan with no top on made Beth crave physical contact even more. With Ellie around it would be inappropriate, but just a brush of hands would suffice at this stage.

"Two castles isn't a bad idea," Trystan agreed. "It's nice to have neighbours." His eyes lit up. "Maybe there could be an underground tunnel connecting them."

"That's a good idea." Ellie nodded her approval. "Then the people can sneak into the other castle."

"Yes! They can move over and hide in the next castle if they come under attack."

"Who would attack a princess castle?" Ellie asked, deadly serious.

"It's a princess castle?"

"Yes." She stared at him as though it was obvious. "The princess in the pink dress will live in one castle, and the princess in the yellow dress will live in the other castle."

Trystan grinned at Beth. "I was picturing an entirely different kind of castle. They can be princess castles though," he said, redirecting his attention to Ellie.

"I hate to put a dampener on your plans," Beth said. "But we don't have buckets and spades."

Looking at Ellie, Trystan rolled his eyes dramatically. "Your mum really doesn't know much about sandcastles, does she?"

Ellie propped her hands on her hips, giving Beth a glimpse of what she was in for in her teenage years. "No, she doesn't know much at all."

"If you're going to be mean, I might just leave you and take myself off for a swim." Beth tilted her head and switched to a more serious tone. "Would you mind?"

"No." Trystan moved to stand beside Ellie. "Go for it. We've got a lot of work to do anyway."

As she walked away, Beth listened to Ellie and Trystan discussing the particulars of the castles. It kept her smiling as she swam in the blissfully cool waves. When she re-joined them twenty minutes later, two sandcastles stood a little apart from each other. Without buckets and spades the constructions were much rougher, but still impressive.

"I collected the shells to decorate the castles," Ellie told her as she pointed them out.

"I'm impressed." Beth smiled at Trystan, who sat beside the castles with a sheen of sweat on his forehead and a fair amount of sand sticking to his arms and torso.

"We haven't even built the tunnel yet. That will be the really impressive part."

"Do you know how to build a real tunnel?" Ellie asked him. "Or will it just be pretend?"

"I know exactly how to build it. But it's a two-person job. You're going to have to help me."

Ellie nodded excitedly while Beth flopped onto her towel.

"I'd offer to help," she said. "But we all know I'm a bit clueless, so I'll just lie over here and watch the experts."

"That's a good idea, Mummy," Ellie said, making Trystan snort with laughter.

Beth glared at him. "I feel as though you're turning my daughter against me."

"Maybe you should brush up on your sandcastle-building skills."

"I'd rather not," she said, closing her eyes. "I think it's something I prefer to observe."

When he didn't reply, she opened her eyes and caught him looking at her intently. Her stomach flipped as their eyes locked.

"Are we making the tunnel now?" Ellie asked, breaking the moment.

"Yes. We are. I'll start it. I'll need you to help in a minute."

Ellie waited patiently while Trystan dug down from one of the castles, then did the same from the other.

"You take this sandcastle business very seriously," Beth told him, shielding her eyes from the sun.

"I grew up with a beach on the doorstep. Of course I take sandcastle building seriously." He sat back on his heels. "Okay. I think it's almost done," he told Ellie. "I'm going to put my arm in this hole and dig around a bit further. You do the same from the other side and we should meet in the middle."

Ellie looked sceptical as she reached into the hole. "There might be crabs hiding under the sand."

"Maybe," Trystan said, causing Ellie to whip her arm out again. "Probably not though," he added quickly. "Put your hand back in the tunnel and try and find my hand. Otherwise the way is blocked in the middle and the princesses can't get through."

"Can't you finish the tunnel on your own?" Ellie asked, sitting back on her bum.

"It's a two-person job."

"Can you do it, Mummy?"

"I have no idea how to build sand tunnels," Beth said, walking over to them. "I'm an amateur, remember?"

Trystan chuckled. "Put your hand in the hole and dig around until you find my hand."

"I suppose I can try." She lowered herself to her knees and delved into the hole, the damp sand coarse against her skin.

"You have to dig around," Trystan said, beaming at her. "You must be really close to my fingers."

After scratching around in the sand, she finally brushed

against something warm and fleshy. Her squeal came automatically and she snatched her hand back.

"Is it a crab?" Ellie asked.

"No!" Trystan said. "It was my finger. Dig around some more and the tunnel will be finished."

Beth did as she was told, pushing the sand aside until their hands met under the sand. She was about to withdraw when his fingers wrapped around hers, trapping her in place.

"What's wrong?" Ellie asked.

"I'm stuck." Beth laughed. "Trystan's got me. Go and tickle him until he lets go."

Ellie didn't hesitate in throwing herself on Trystan and tickling his bare torso. The feel of his hand clutching hers, made Beth's heart beat clumsily and her eyes locked with his for one breathtaking moment before he released her and fell back onto the sand with Ellie climbing all over him.

"I got him for you, Mummy," Ellie said proudly after Trystan had tickled her until she screamed.

"You did. Thank you."

Trystan brushed sand from his hands, then raked his fingers through his hair as he sat on the sand. "Is anyone going to mention how amazing my tunnel is?"

"It's pretty cool," Beth admitted.

"Can the princesses really go all the way through it?" Ellie asked, looking at the holes in the sand with suspicion.

"Yes," Beth said. "Put your hand in and you can feel my hand in the middle."

Hesitantly, Ellie stuck her hand into the hole, then laughed loudly when her fingers found Beth's. It was impossible to resist grabbing onto her hand and trapping her in place, as Trystan had done to her.

"I'm stuck!" Ellie shouted at Trystan.

Mischief flashed in his eyes. "I can help."

"Don't you dare tickle me!"

"Oh, I dare." He dropped to his knees and tickled Beth's ribs.

Laughing, she released Ellie's hand and fell back, landing against Trystan's solid chest. The warmth of his bare skin against hers felt wonderful, and the moment before they moved apart was gone too soon.

"What do you think of my tunnel?" Trystan asked Ellie when she walked over and casually slung her arms around his neck.

"Can we pour water in it?"

He laughed. "You want to flood the tunnel? How would the princesses get through?"

"The princesses aren't real," she said, resting her head on his shoulder. "I was only pretending."

"Okay. Let's flood it then." He peeled her off him as he stood. After drinking from his water bottle, he instructed her to fill it with sea water.

"That should keep her occupied for a little while," Beth remarked, moving to lie on her towel again, while Trystan did the same.

He watched Ellie running back up from the shore. "She has so much energy."

"Yep. It's annoying sometimes."

"You never get a break, do you?"

A lump formed in Beth's throat and she was thankful that Trystan didn't look at her. Since her mum died it certainly felt as though she didn't get a break … and having someone notice it made her overwhelmingly emotional.

All she wanted to do was reach over and kiss him, but with Ellie around she really couldn't. Besides, she wasn't sure how things stood between them now.

"Do you still want to go to Tresco tomorrow?" she asked, changing the subject to something more neutral.

"I'd like to," he said. "If you're not sick of me yet."

"Definitely not," she said, smiling widely.

CHAPTER SIXTEEN

B eth had her camera at her face almost constantly as they walked through Tresco Abbey Gardens. Each time she lowered it, another stunning sight begged for a snapshot. A stone archway from the ruined priory in the centre of the gardens was a fascinating sight – with plant life growing through the cracks between the stones. After photographing it from a distance, she moved closer, twisting the zoom ring then waiting a beat for the autofocus to kick in for a close-up of the stunning pink flowers at the base of the archway. The pungent scent of them was over-whelming and the buzz of hovering bees filled the air.

Straightening up, she marvelled at the dense vegetation around her, then finally dropped her gaze to the space beside her leg. She turned in a quick circle.

"Ellie?" she called, her heart rate kicking up a notch. "Ellie?"

Upping her pace, she slipped through the archway and pushed fronds of a young Nikau palm aside as she turned on the path. Rounding the next corner, she heard whispered voices and remembered Trystan was with them. She wasn't used to someone else keeping an eye on Ellie.

"What are you doing?" she asked, spotting Ellie lying on her tummy across the path, peering under a hedge with Trystan crouched beside her.

"Shhh," they both hissed.

Ellie scowled as she stood up. "You scared it away, Mummy."

"What was it?"

"A Golden Pheasant," Ellie said, clearly reciting what Trystan had told her. "But that's a funny name because the feathers are lots of different colours, like a rainbow. It's very pretty. If you can be quiet you might see one as well. You shouldn't shout or you'll scare them away."

"I'll bear that in mind. I just thought I'd lost you for a minute."

"I won't get lost with Trystan," Ellie said. "You can take pictures and Trystan and me will look for pheasants."

"I could come with you," Beth said.

Trystan turned back as Ellie tugged on his arm. "It's fine. We'll find you in a bit."

When they met up half an hour later, Ellie's cheeks were flushed and she was in high spirits as she ran around the flowerbeds. Trystan and Beth settled themselves on a wooden bench beneath a tall palm tree. Setting her camera beside her, Beth took out her phone which was buzzing repeatedly.

She smiled as she read the influx of messages. "My friend Dee is messaging me," she told Trystan. "She's been to visit my dad today to help put my mind at ease that he's okay."

"And is he?"

"Yes. It sounds as though Dee had a great time. They invited her to stay for lunch and she's raving about the quality of the food." She chuckled as she read the message. "She also got a bunch of the residents involved in a game of bingo … that's so typical of Dee."

"It was good of her to check on him."

"Yes." She fired off a quick reply, then put her phone away

and picked up her camera to look through the photos she'd taken.

Trystan peered over her shoulder as she scrolled through. "They look amazing."

"It's hard to take bad photos when everything is so beautiful." Stretching her neck, she felt the warmth of the sun on her face, making her skin tingle.

"How did you get into wedding photography?"

She slouched back on the bench. "I've always loved weddings. There's something so magical about them. My dad was into photography, so my interest developed from him."

"Were you close?"

"Not really. Photography was our only common ground." She closed her eyes for a moment as a gentle breeze blew across her face. "I'm really going to miss the weddings. It always felt like such a privilege to be a part of."

"Were you ..." he trailed off. "Never mind."

"Was I what?"

"You can tell me to mind my own business ... but were you married to Ellie's dad?"

"No." She stared at him, wondering what he'd been imagining. "I've never been married."

"Is he involved in Ellie's life at all? Sorry ... it's none of my business ... you don't need to talk about it if you don't want to."

"It's fine. There's not much to talk about though." She set her camera back in its case and cast a quick glance at Ellie, who was happily ambling around the plants. "I wanted to have a baby since I was about twenty. After a few dead-end relationships in my twenties I started to get desperate. In my early thirties I was going on dates and immediately trying to suss out if the guy was someone I'd want to have kids with. It makes dating slightly awkward if you're dropping not-so-subtle hints to figure out if the other person would be interested in settling down and having babies with you. I didn't want to waste my time with guys who didn't want to have kids—" She stopped abruptly. "Oh, wow. Sorry. That came out wrong, but you know what I mean…"

"I know what you mean," he said with his usual relaxed smile.

She cleared her throat. "In the end I realised I wanted a baby more than I wanted some perfect nuclear family, and I didn't need a man for that."

His eyebrows shot up. "So …?"

"I used a sperm donor."

"Wow." Trystan looked slightly awed. "You did it all alone?"

"Yes." She pressed her lips together. "Except I always had my mum. She was there with me every step of the way, so I never really felt alone." Not until recently anyway. She focused on the red squirrel scampering up a nearby tree while she fought to get her emotions under control.

Trystan didn't speak, but his hand gently covered hers and she turned her hand over to interlock her fingers with his, the contact sending goosebumps prickling at the back of her neck.

"I was thinking I should get your number," Trystan said when he appeared on the patio shortly after Beth had put Ellie to bed that evening. "It'd be easier than always coming over here any time I want to ask you something."

She took his phone and programmed the number in before calling herself. "What did you want to ask?"

"How do you mean?"

"You said you wanted to ask me something …"

"Oh! No, I only wanted to ask for your number … and that was just an excuse to come over here. I guess I've kind of blown that now."

"I guess you have. In future, we can just have messaging conversations from one patio to another."

"I might just delete your number," he joked.

Beth glanced behind her. "Do you want to go to the pub if I ask your mum to babysit?"

"I'd love to."

Mirren made it easy for her by offering to look after Ellie before Beth had even got the words out.

As usual, the conversation flowed easily while she and Trystan walked to the Mermaid Inn. Noah was working and kept coming over to chat to them. By the time they walked home, the lack of physical contact was driving Beth crazy, and she felt self-conscious as she slipped her arm into his. She'd suggested they leave after a couple of drinks in the hope that they might go back to his place, but his previous flirty energy had all but disappeared.

"Can I ask you a question?" she said when they were almost at the cottage.

"Yep."

"The other day when I had a go at you …" She paused, not quite sure where she was headed with the sentence. "I think maybe I seriously offended you. You've been a little standoffish since then."

"Was there a question in that?" he asked playfully.

"No. I suppose there wasn't. I meant to ask if I'm imagining it, or if you're being standoffish?"

They'd stopped at his cottage and he moved to perch on the stone wall. "Maybe," he said on a sigh.

"Maybe? So I did irrevocable damage with my comment about you crowding me?"

"No." He smiled lightly and crossed his legs at the ankles. "But it made me realise that I'm pretty intense. And I have no idea if that's just the way I am, or if it's because I've spent ten years in a relationship and that's all I know. I don't think I know how to date."

"I'm not sure if that makes me feel better or not." She moved closer. "I'm not exactly a pro at dating myself … but I kind of preferred it the way you were before."

"Really?" He straightened up and slipped his arms around her waist.

"Yes."

The lightness of his lips against hers made her insides quiver. He pulled back too soon. "I'm also never sure how affectionate I can be when Ellie's around."

"It's probably better to keep it toned down."

"Good to know." His lips met hers again and he kissed her in earnest.

"Maybe we should go inside," she murmured.

He took her hand and led the way, a smile playing at his lips. "No one could accuse you of being standoffish."

CHAPTER SEVENTEEN

With Trystan working the following day, Beth and Ellie spent a relaxed morning in the garden, then set off for a walk into town.

"Can I have an ice cream?" Ellie asked, tugging on Beth's arm.

"Maybe. If you're good while we do the shopping."

"Can we go on the train?"

"No, we have to go shopping. Besides, the train will already have left." She'd timed it that way, since she was now slightly embarrassed by how often they'd been on the train. "Look! Here it comes. We can wave!"

"Maybe Kit will stop and let us on," Ellie suggested excitedly.

"He can't do that. And we have to go shopping, remember?"

"But I want to go on the train." As she waved at Kit, she hopped up and down in excitement.

"Just a quick stop here," Kit announced to the passengers as he slowed the train. He pulled his headset off so he was no longer broadcasting. "Do you want to hop on?" He leaned over and opened the door, then patted the seat beside him.

"We were just on our way to the supermarket …" Beth

trailed off as Ellie climbed aboard. Maybe they were going for a ride after all, since she'd now have to deal with a massive tantrum in front of a train full of people if they didn't.

"I can take the little lady, if you want?" Kit said. "That way you can do your shopping in peace."

"Oh, thank you, but it's fine. You need to concentrate. She'd be in your way."

"No, she won't." He grinned at Ellie. "We don't need Mummy, do we?"

"No."

"See you back at the beach in an hour?" Kit said, leaning across Ellie to close the door while Beth did an impressive imitation of a goldfish.

"Are you sure?" she asked, to which Kit replied with a smile and a nod. The train was already setting off again, and Ellie leaned out to wave enthusiastically until Kit pulled her back onto the seat.

"We'll see you later!" he called out.

"Thank you …" It took Beth a couple of minutes to process what had just happened, and the fact that she had an hour to herself. When she came to her senses, she realised she was wasting precious time. She had one hour and there was no way she was going shopping.

When Beth stood at the little train stop by Porthcressa Beach an hour later she felt utterly refreshed. She pulled out her phone to message Dee and gush about her surprise hour alone, then remembered she had Trystan's number and opened a messaging chat with him instead.

I think I might be a little bit in love with your brother, she typed out quickly and pressed send. As she read the message back she slapped a hand over her mouth. Surely he'd read it as a joke. In her head it had been very jokey, but written down the humour could be missed. The ticks turned blue to say the message had been read and she held her breath as dots ran across the screen to show he was writing a reply.

Which brother? he asked.

She smiled as she tapped on the phone. *Kit.*

Fair enough, he replied immediately. *He has youth on his side.*

Her phone rang a second later and she answered the call from Trystan with a wide smile on her face.

"I feel as though I should warn you that this is a very gossipy island," he said without preamble. "There'll be whispers about the age difference between you and Kit. You do realise you're old enough to be—"

"Stop! Please don't say it. Oh my god. You're right, though. I'm ancient."

She could hear the amusement in his voice. "What's Kit done to win your affections?"

"He took Ellie on the train. Without me! I've had an hour to myself and it was absolute bliss."

"What did you do with your hour to yourself?"

"I sat in a cafe and drank a coffee and ate cake without having to share it. I watched the world go by and didn't have to answer incessant questions. I just sat in peace and did nothing."

"You're very easily pleased."

"I really am." The train rounded the corner and she waved at Ellie, who was beaming and waving enthusiastically. "They just got back. I have to go, but are you coming up to your mum's for dinner? I'll cook."

"I thought I'd come up and get the barbecue going."

"I was going to go to the shop. Should I buy stuff to grill?"

"No, it's fine. I'll sort it. See you later." He ended the call before she could protest. Between him and Mirren, it was starting to feel like a luxury holiday. She should probably just enjoy it while it lasted. They were already three weeks into the school holidays and time was going far too quickly. Before she knew it they'd be back home again.

Ellie charged at her legs, breaking the unpleasant thought.

"How was the ride?" Beth asked, scooping Ellie up and holding her on her hip.

"I helped drive! But only after we went past the police station. Because last time we did that Kit got arrested."

"Not arrested!" Kit said in a mock whisper as he came over to them. "I told you if you help drive the train, you have to keep it a secret."

"Oh yeah." Ellie put a finger against her lips. "It's a secret."

Beth shifted her to the opposite hip before deciding she was too heavy and setting her down again. "What was that about the police?" she asked Kit.

"Oh, it was nothing." He waved a dismissive hand in front of his face. "The police here aren't exactly swamped in work, so I got a lecture after the last time they saw me driving past with Ellie on my lap. And since they have nothing better to do it was quite a long lecture. Not a big deal; I just waited until we were away from civilisation this time."

"Was she well behaved?" Beth asked.

"Of course. She's a little angel. Did you get your shopping done?"

"No. I decided there were much better options for my alone time, so I treated myself to coffee and cake."

"She's welcome to come on the train with me anytime. I only take afternoon rides at the moment, though. Keira does the morning rides." He glanced behind him at the bustle of people lingering beside the train. "I promised balloon animals, so I better get back to them. Enjoy your shopping."

"Trystan said he's going to barbecue so we don't even need to go shopping any more."

"Tonight?" he asked as he backed away.

"Yes."

"Sounds good. I'll message him ... might see you for dinner!"

"What are we going to do next?" Ellie asked, taking Beth's hand.

She sighed. An hour to herself wasn't nearly long enough.

Every effort Beth made to help with the barbecue preparations was scuppered. She wanted to make salad but Mirren managed to get there first. Then Keira arrived and made frozen margaritas and made sure everyone had drinks while Noah brought more chairs from the garage to the patio. Beth managed to take the ketchup and condiments to the patio table but that was about all. When Keira handed her a margarita, she gave up and sat down with it. The smell of smoke in the air was wonderful and she cast a discreet glance at Trystan, who was busy turning meat on the barbecue.

"The paddling pool's out!" Kit exclaimed loudly when he and Seren arrived. "Someone forgot to mention swimwear on my invite."

"It's too little for you," Ellie said, staring up at him with her hands on her hips. "You can't fit."

"That sounds like a challenge."

"Don't you dare!" Seren said, pulling him away by his elbow.

"Spoilsport," he muttered, before getting himself a beer and sitting beside Beth.

"Thanks again for taking Ellie on the train today. It was so good of you."

"No problem. I can also offer swimming lessons."

Her brow creased in confusion. "What?"

"I volunteer at the lifesaving club. There's a summer camp during August in the mornings. We have swimming classes and teach water safety and do some sailing and various other activities. It's for island kids really, but I managed to pull some strings and get Ellie in for next week, if you want. I'm not sure about the week after yet. She'd be one of the youngest, but I think she'd really enjoy it."

Emotions bubbled up in Beth's chest until it felt as though she might choke. "I'm sure she would," she said, her voice brittle.

"It's 9.30 to 1.30 Monday to Friday," Kit went on. "They have lunch there. I'd be with her the whole time and I'm sure she'd make friends quickly. Do you think she'd be up for it?"

"I … um …" She put a hand over her mouth as her lip trembled and tears pooled on her lower lids. "Sorry. I'll be back in a minute." Keeping her head down, she scurried inside. She sank onto the couch in the living room and heaved in deep breaths.

"Did I say something wrong?" Kit asked, appearing in the doorway.

"No." She smiled through her tears. "You're all so kind. I just got a bit overwhelmed." Sniffing loudly, she ran her fingers under her eyes to catch the tears. "Just ignore me. It'd be great if Ellie could join the kids' club. Thank you."

"You're welcome." He sat beside her and put an arm around her shoulders, pulling her into a side hug that she happily leaned into.

They were interrupted by Trystan clearing his throat.

"I thought you were joking when you said you had a thing for my brother," he said, his eyes sparkling with mischief.

"I never said that," she said to Kit, who only grinned before walking away, giving Trystan a friendly punch on the arm as he passed him.

"Are you okay?" Trystan asked.

"Yes." She crossed the room to stand squarely in front of him, resting her hands at his waist. "I just got a bit emotional. Kit said Ellie can go to the kids' club next week … although I guess you already know about that."

He shrugged. "I'm not sure what you're talking about."

148

"I don't believe you. You knew I was worrying about swimming lessons. You also knew how grateful I was to get an hour to myself this afternoon." She leaned into him, inhaling his scent at his neck. "Thank you."

"It was nothing." He clasped his arms behind her back. "I mean, barely a day goes by that I don't put Kit in a headlock and threaten him about something, so there was really nothing to it."

"You better not have!" She pulled back and gave him a mock stern look.

"No. I asked him nicely and he was very happy to help."

"I feel as though I'm being spoiled rotten by you Trenearys." Pushing onto her toes, she kissed him softly.

He flashed a playful smile. "Wait until we hand you the invoice at the end of your stay."

CHAPTER EIGHTEEN

F our hours to herself felt like such a gift for Beth, but after
two hours alone on Monday morning the novelty of it
faded. Not that she hadn't enjoyed her swim, or that reading a
book while sunbathing on the beach wasn't bliss. It *was* bliss but
when she found herself reading the same page for the third time
she put the book aside and picked up her phone. After scrolling
through the recent messages between her and Trystan, she chastised herself for being insecure enough to search for some
hidden meaning in the words when he probably meant exactly
what he'd said in his message that morning. She'd asked what he
was doing and he'd told her he was snowed under with work.

It wasn't as though she'd specifically invited him to do
something and he'd turned her down. But he knew Ellie was at
the kids' club and Beth had assumed that she and Trystan would
spend the time together. And, if she was completely honest,
she'd imagined some of that time might be spent in his bedroom.

But he had to work, and she shouldn't be spending her time
overthinking everything and feeling rejected. Packing up her
beach things, she pulled her tote bag onto her shoulder and set
off for a walk along the coastal path. The stunning views were a
nice distraction, and she stopped regularly to take photos.

As happy as she was to have the child-free time, she was also happy to see Ellie again at pick-up time at the lifesaving club.

"Mummy!" she squealed, running over to her and crashing into her.

"Did you have a nice time?" Beth asked, crouching to her level.

"I had to kick my legs like a frog to swim. And we had sandwiches and ice cream. And I've got a new friend." She turned around and waved furiously at a little girl with brown curls who waved back just as enthusiastically. "That's Steph. She's my best friend."

"That's nice."

"Hi!" Kit called, making his way through the throng.

"It seems as though she enjoyed it," Beth said. "Was she good?"

"Yes." He high-fived Ellie. "She was great. No problem at all."

"Thank you so much."

"You're welcome. I've got to run to the train, but I'll see you both tomorrow."

"Can we go on the train?" Ellie asked.

"No!" Beth said quickly. "Let's leave Kit alone for a bit."

He grinned and told them to have a good afternoon before dashing away.

"Am I going to the kids' club tomorrow too?" Ellie asked as they set off along the road.

"Yes. You can go all week if you want to?"

"I do want to. My friend Steph will be there and she said sometimes they have a party."

"That sounds fun."

They ambled back towards home, with Ellie keeping up a steady stream of chatter along the way.

"Can we see Trystan today?" she asked when they were approaching the row of cottages.

"I think he's busy with work."

"I'll ask him." Before Beth could intervene, Ellie had set off at a run, turning onto the path at Peswera Cottage and standing on her toes to reach the bell.

"Sorry," Beth said when Trystan answered. "I told her you were working but she took off before I could stop her."

He barely seemed to register her words and bent to Ellie instead. "How was the kids' club? Can you swim yet?"

"Not yet, but Kit showed me how to do froggie arms and legs."

"That's a good start. How about we get our swim things on and go down to the beach so you can show me what you learned?"

She beamed at him, then turned back to Beth. "Trystan and me are going swimming. You can come too if you want?"

"Thanks for the invite," she said mockingly, then smiled at Trystan. "Are you sure you have time?"

"For this little lady, I'll make time." He tickled Ellie's tummy until she ran away from him, giggling loudly.

Beth, meanwhile, was torn between being touched by how sweet he was with Ellie and feeling jealous that he'd make time for her but hadn't made time for Beth that morning.

Half an hour later she was sitting on the sand at the shore, enjoying the feel of gentle waves sweeping up her legs with hypnotic regularity. Trystan was further out with Ellie, holding her tummy while she frowned in concentration as she swept her arms and legs through the water.

Instead of being soothed by the surroundings and the company, Beth's stomach was tied in knots. She liked Trystan too much, she realised with a bolt of clarity about the constant buzz of anxiety that refused to leave her. It wasn't a feeling she was used to, and while it should have been thrilling to meet someone who set her heart racing and induced butterflies in her stomach every time he looked at her, it actually made her question everything. Did he feel the same? Why hadn't he made time for her that morning? Would she get some time alone with him

153

that evening? And what exactly was it between them anyway – just a holiday romance or something more?

"Mummy!" Ellie shouted, breaking her thoughts. She was standing on Trystan's shoulders. "Watch me!"

"I'm watching," she called back, then laughed when Ellie jumped into the water. Trystan immediately reached out to her, holding her afloat while Ellie's arms and legs kicked furiously under the water.

"Be careful," Beth called, then was immediately annoyed with herself. She drove herself crazy with how much she worried about everything.

"You look very serious this afternoon," Trystan said when he came and sat beside Beth, so close that their legs touched. Ellie ran up the beach and parked herself by the bag of beach toys.

"I know I'm being irrational." Idly, she scooped up a handful of wet sand and rubbed it through her fingers. "But now that Ellie's having swimming lessons I'm worried she'll be over-confident. Her healthy fear of the water was quite reassuring to me. What if she suddenly thinks she's a strong swimmer and gets into trouble?" Too late, she remembered how Trystan had lost his dad. "I'm sorry. That was insensitive."

He gave a dismissive shake of the head. "Growing up on an island, we were taught water safety the way other kids are taught road safety. It's drummed into island kids and it's taken seri-ously. At the kids' club they teach the kids how to stay safe. They know not to go in the water alone. Usually the kids take the rules more seriously than adults. I can see why you'd worry though."

"Thank you."

"What for?"

"Not dismissing me as a neurotic mother."

He leaned a little closer, dropping a kiss on her shoulder. "Kit got really involved at the lifesaving club right after Dad died," he told her. "He already volunteered there, but he really threw himself into it after that. His way of coping I think. Trying to make sure the same thing doesn't happen to anyone else."

"How old is Kit? He's got such a baby face, but he must be older than he looks."

"He's twenty-two."

"Okay, so he's not older than he looks. It must have been so hard for him, being so young when your dad died. Hard for you all, obviously, but even more so for him being so young."

"Kit really has his head screwed on right. He's coped with everything amazingly well."

"He has a great family around him," Beth said. "That makes a difference."

Trystan glanced over at Ellie before pressing a soft kiss to Beth's lips.

After spending the following morning obsessively checking her phone, Beth decided she couldn't take it any more. Hastily, she made enough sandwiches for two and set off to Peswera Cottage.

"I thought you might have time for a lunch break," she said, holding up the plate of sandwiches when Trystan opened the door. Realising he had his phone to his ear, she grimaced. "Sorry," she whispered.

Smiling, he ushered her inside and mouthed that he'd just be a minute before sitting at the kitchen island and scrolling on his laptop while continuing to talk business on the phone. Beth put the plate down and quietly poured them each a glass of water.

"I can go again," she whispered to Trystan, pointing at the door.

He shook his head, not breaking the flow of his phone conversation.

"Sorry about that," he said, when he'd wrapped up the call a couple of minutes later.

"I thought you might be ready for a lunch break, but I can just leave the sandwiches if you're busy?"

"Don't do that," he said, slipping his fingers into the waistband of her shorts and pulling her between his legs to kiss her. When he pulled away, she looked at him seriously.

"I'm going to sound horribly needy," she said, her fingers stroking the fine hairs at the back of his neck. "But I'd hoped we could spend some time together while Ellie's in the kids' club. Is there any chance of you taking a morning off this week or do you have too much to do?"

"I can take a morning off."

"Are you sure? Don't feel you have to."

"I'm sure."

She should probably leave it at that, but she knew she'd drive herself crazy if she didn't tell him what was on her mind. "I kind of got the feeling that you might be using work as an excuse not to see me … I don't know why. Maybe I'm being paranoid, and I really don't want to seem clingy but I just had this feeling that maybe you were avoiding me …"

His eyebrows twitched together. "You weren't being paranoid."

"So you *were* using work to avoid hanging out with me? Am I being too full on? You can just say if I am, it's fine." Actually, it wasn't fine at all. If he said she was being too intense, she'd struggle to keep her emotions in check. She wanted to spend every minute of the day with him and that made her vulnerable in a way that terrified her.

"I wanted to spend time with you … I just …" He paused and dragged his hands through his hair. "After I got Kit to sign Ellie up for the kids' club, I panicked that you'd think I was trying to get her out of the way so I could get you to myself."

"That never crossed my mind."

"Good, because I love spending time with Ellie. I wasn't scheming to get her out of the way."

Her heart suddenly felt like it was taking up more space in

her chest. She touched her forehead to Trystan's. "I honestly didn't think that, but with Ellie in the kids' club I was excited about spending more time with you."

"Really?" He sounded unsure of himself.

"Yes."

"You said you never get any time to yourself, so I also didn't want to assume you'd want to hang out with me."

"I do want to hang out with you. Whenever you have time."

"Be careful what you wish for," he said, quirking an eyebrow. "Because I can make time every morning this week."

She brushed her lips against his. "I'd like that a lot."

CHAPTER NINETEEN

Beth and Trystan spent the following morning walking the coast and sunbathing and swimming. All while acting like a pair of lovesick teenagers who couldn't get enough of each other. When Beth needed to collect Ellie from the kids' club, Trystan couldn't bring himself to part from her so tagged along too.

"Would you like to go for a coffee?" he asked Ellie as they walked away from the lifesaving club.

She looked at him incredulously. "I don't drink coffee – I'm just a kid!"

"Oh, yes. I remember now. I guess you could have a chocolate milk or a lemonade or something while me and your mum drink coffee."

"Okay." She took his hand, then laughed when he lifted her off the ground before lowering her back down.

Beth veered away from them when they approached the harbour, taking her camera from its case to snap a few photos. The look of concentration on her face while she peered into the viewfinder had Trystan enthralled. At least until Ellie tugged on his arm, demanding to be lifted up and down as he'd done before. He smiled at her, then shifted his attention back to Beth as he continued the action of lifting her repeatedly off the ground.

"Sorry," Beth said when she came back to them. "I love taking photos of boats."

"I noticed." He set Ellie down as his bicep began to burn with the effort.

Beth gave him a quick peck on the lips, the automatic gesture seeming to take her by surprise as much as him. They both glanced at Ellie, who either hadn't noticed or didn't register it was anything out of the ordinary.

"Have you ever been to the Pottery Cafe?" he asked her.

"No." She took Ellie's free hand and they ambled along in a row. "I think we've been to every cafe in Hugh Town except for that one."

"How come?"

"Because it's full of beautiful pottery and it doesn't feel like a good place to take Ellie."

"It's Lowen's pottery," Trystan said. "The woman who owns the cafe sells it for him on commission."

"I know you said he sells his stuff over here, but I never twigged it was in the cafe."

"Let's go and grab a coffee. Ellie will be fine."

It was busy in the cosy cafe and they only just managed to get a table.

"It's really cute in here," Beth said, then turned in her seat to look across the room to where Lowen's handiwork was neatly arranged on shelves and sideboards.

"The crockery for the cafe was all made by him too."

"I love how proud you are of your brother," Beth said, twisting back to face him.

"Am I?"

"Why else did you bring us here?" she asked. "And you sounded a bit braggy then when you said he made everything."

"Maybe I did," he admitted.

The conversation was interrupted by the owner coming over.

Pippa must have been in her late thirties – a petite woman with wavy brown hair. Patting Trystan on the shoulder, she smiled warmly and asked how he was. When he introduced her to Beth and Ellie, she tilted her head.

"Are you staying with Mirren?"

"Yes," Beth replied with a puzzled smile.

"I have something for you," Pippa said. "I'll be back in a second."

Beth squinted at Trystan. "That was strange."

He didn't have a chance to tell her that he often found Pippa a bit strange since she reappeared so quickly. Strange was the wrong word though; she actually seemed pretty normal, there was an air of negativity to her and he wasn't overly fond of her. Not that he knew her well.

"Here you go." Pippa set two small cardboard boxes on the table in front of Beth, then looked at Trystan. "That grumpy brother of yours put those in my delivery today with a note asking me to take them up to the guests at your mum's house. I don't know why he couldn't take them himself." She clicked her tongue and took their drink order before leaving them alone again.

Trystan took a deep breath through his nose, ignoring the anger that niggled in his gut. As much as he didn't like the way Pippa grumbled about Lowen, he had to admit that she had a point: he could have delivered the mugs in person.

"Is that our cups?" Ellie asked, wriggling in her seat.

Beth pulled at the lid of one the boxes. "I guess so. Oh my goodness." She lifted the mug out and turned it in her hand. "Isn't that gorgeous?"

"It's got the puffin," Ellie said, shuffling off her chair and moving close to Beth to look.

"Look at the handle. It's got your name on it." Setting it aside, Beth took out the matching mug from the other box. "This one has my name on it." Her eyes lit up as she showed Ellie. "That's so lovely of him."

Trystan was staring at the mug in her hand, barely registering what she was saying until she waved a hand in front of his face.

"What?" he said, snapping his head up.

"You went into a trance. Are you okay?"

"Yes."

"There's no wonder you're so proud of Lowen," she said, beaming. "These are beautiful. It was so kind of him to go to all that effort."

"Yeah." Trystan nodded vaguely. "It was nice of him."

Pippa arrived with their drinks and Trystan was thankful for the distraction. A dull ache had attached itself to his chest and he couldn't concentrate on anything other than the fog of melancholy that seemed to engulf him. He felt as though he was somewhere else entirely as he sipped his coffee to the sound of Ellie's incessant chatter. At least her running commentary meant that his lack of input into the conversation wasn't so noticeable.

Although he suspected from the way Beth kept glancing at him that she'd noticed his change in mood. His fake smile became hard to maintain.

"Are you okay?" Beth asked him when they reached the bottom of their drinks.

"Yeah." He swallowed hard. "I might need to head home. I have a bit of work I should be getting on with."

"I thought you were taking the day off."

"Yeah … I was … but I just remembered I have a couple of emails that I should have responded to. I might go and take care of it so it doesn't play on my mind." He pulled his wallet from his pocket as he stood up.

"I can get it," Beth said. "Just go if you need to."

"Thanks. I'll see you later." He managed an uncomfortable smile before making a hasty exit.

Shoving his hands into his pockets, he set off for home at a brisk pace, keeping his head down as he went. His breathing was unnatural by the time he reached the cottage and he burst inside as though breaking the surface of water after a long dive.

His long inhale brought tears to his eyes. As he dropped to the couch, he cradled his head in his hands and focused on taking steady breaths. Unlocking his phone with shaking hands, he scrolled to Lowen's number, then flopped back on the couch as he held the phone to his ear. If his brother answered he wouldn't be able to speak through the lump in his throat. Not that it mattered, since he knew there was no way he'd answer. These days, the only times Trystan called Lowen was to torture himself. Maybe if he felt bad enough about what he'd done, Lowen might finally forgive him and they could get back to being friends again.

Bored of listening to the phone beeps, he tossed it aside and lay down on the couch, draping a hand over his eyes as though he could block it all out.

It didn't work. His mind raced, rehashing the past and imagining how different everything might be if he could just go back and change things.

CHAPTER TWENTY

Almost an hour had passed when the doorbell rang. Trystan stayed still, hoping whoever it was didn't peer in the window. They'd clearly be able to see him. Listening for the sound of retreating footsteps, his heart sank when he heard the click of the door being opened.

After wiping his hands over his face, he pasted on a smile and sat up.

"Hi," Beth said, sympathy flashing in her features. "I left Ellie with your mum."

"Miss me already?" he said, forcing cheer into his voice. "I think I'd just nodded off."

"Don't do that," she said, closing the door behind her and venturing further into the room.

"Do what?"

"Pretend to be cheerful when you're obviously upset. I knew there was something wrong in the cafe. If you want to be left alone, I'll go again. I'm worried about you though. Whatever's going on, you can talk to me about it if you want."

He was torn between not wanting her to see him when he was such a mess and wanting to tell her everything. When he didn't say anything she sat beside him and tenderly kissed his cheek before wrapping her arms around him.

"Do you want me to leave you?" she asked, pulling back a couple of minutes later.

"No."

"Do you want to tell me what's going on?"

He pressed his palm against his forehead. "Kind of. But you probably don't want to hear all my family drama."

"I would like to hear whatever you want to tell me," she said softly.

It was difficult to even know where to start, so he took a deep breath and blurted out the first thing that came to mind.

"Lowen hates me." He realised he sounded dramatic and that it probably wasn't quite the truth, but it wasn't far off. "That's why he sent your mugs to the cafe instead of bringing them here."

"He said he was busy with work. Maybe he just didn't have time."

"That's not the reason. He won't come anywhere near here. If there's a special occasion – one of the family has a birthday or something – he'll come over to St Mary's but he'll only meet us in the pub or a cafe or somewhere neutral. I keep going to visit him and hoping things will get better between us, but I think he might just hate me forever."

"Why would he hate you?"

Standing, Trystan paced the room before stopping at the fire-place and resting a hand on the mantel. "We used to be really close. Lowen's a fair bit older than me, but when we were kids I idolised him. As we got older and the age difference didn't matter so much we were best friends. We lived together in London for a while before I moved in with Jenny. Even after that we were on the phone most days. Anytime I had a problem or there was anything going on in my life, he was the person I called."

"What happened?" Beth asked when he stopped talking.

"When Dad went missing I was back here for the weekend. I'd had the cottage for a couple of years and was spending the odd weekend here. Lowen had bought the pottery studio, but he was still working in London. He spent a lot of time here and was talking about moving back. He was in London that weekend. Dad went out on the boat on the Friday morning …"

Trystan clenched his fists as the emotions of that day flooded back. "There were search parties out looking for him but by the afternoon I kind of knew he was gone." Tears filled his eyes and fell down his cheeks when he blinked. "Mum was convinced he'd be found safe and sound on one of the smaller islands. She said there was no point in worrying Lowen unnecessarily and that we could tell him all about it once Dad was home."

Pausing, he pushed his hands across his damp cheeks. "I thought someone should call him, but there was so much going on … we were all out searching and the whole day was frantic."

"When did you finally call him?"

"We didn't," he said, tears stinging his eyes. "He called me that evening. He was excited about a date he was going on. I couldn't bring myself to say anything. Part of me wanted to believe Mum was right and Dad would come wandering back home with some crazy story to tell. So I just got off the phone as soon as possible. Then I spent all night feeling terrible and called Lowen back first thing in the morning … or tried to. He didn't answer the phone." He chewed on his lower lip. "He's never answered the phone to me since."

"What do you mean?" Beth asked, sympathy shining in her eyes.

"One of his old school friends had messaged him, assuming he already knew what was going on with Dad."

Beth sighed. "Oh god."

"I was so angry with myself for letting him hear it from someone else. He got on a flight that afternoon and had just got back here when we got the news that Dad's body had been found. Lowen's never forgiven us. He moved to Bryher and is practically a hermit."

"That must be so hard. For all of you. I can't imagine what it was like."

"I should have called him as soon as we knew Dad was missing."

"It must have been such a difficult time. I can't imagine any of you were thinking clearly."

"That's no excuse." Trystan sat back beside Beth. "To make matters worse, Mum had called Jago in New York to let him know what was going on. Lowen took it personally … he thought …"

"What?" Beth slipped her hand into his, the feel of her soft skin soothing him immediately.

"Lowen is Dad's son from a previous marriage. His biological mother died shortly after giving birth to him. He always had a bit of a chip on his shoulder about the fact that our mum isn't his biological mother. I could never really figure out why, since he was two when Mum and Dad got together. He doesn't remember a time when Mum wasn't in his life and she always treated him the same as us." He smiled lightly. "Actually, I sometimes thought she favoured him … I kind of got the impression she over-compensated for not being his birth mum. He seemed to get away with everything. Mum was stricter with the rest of us …" He looked at Beth and took a breath. "Sorry, I'm rambling on."

"It's fine."

"I've kind of got used to Lowen being distant with me, but sometimes it hits me how much I miss him. I miss the way things used to be between us. I get angry with him for not letting it go … and then I get angry with myself. I should have called him the minute I heard Dad was missing. If it was the other way around I'd have wanted to know."

"Does he really never answer your calls?"

"No. We haven't spoken on the phone since that night. He'll

reply to my messages, though it usually takes him a day or two. And if there's anything pressing he'll email or message me, but most of the time it seems as though he doesn't want anything to do with me."

"I'm sorry."

"It's like he's not the same person that he was. But when you and Ellie were there last week, it felt like I got a glimpse of who he used to be. He was so relaxed with you and Ellie. I remembered why he'd always been my best friend. He's the sort of person who'd patiently let a little girl play around on the pottery wheel to cheer her up after she broke a mug." He let out a low growl as he flopped back onto the couch. "He's making a whole dinner set for my ex-girlfriend."

Beth frowned. "Do you think he's doing that to try and annoy you?"

"No. That wasn't my point. My point is he's a nice guy. The sort of person who'd make a dinner set for his brother's ex, which I doubt he'll charge her for." He pinched the bridge of his nose. "I really miss him."

"Things will get better. I know it's a cliche but time is a great healer. I'm sure he's hurt and grieving. I really don't think he hates you."

"I don't either really. I just want things to be how they were before."

"Be patient," she said, stroking his cheek. "Maybe one day they will be."

Pulling her closer, he kissed her slowly. "Thank you for coming over."

"You're welcome. Ellie was going to do some baking with your mum, but I should go back and check she isn't terrorising her too much. Do you want to come up and have dinner with us?"

After being adamant he wanted to be alone, it wasn't very appealing any more. "That sounds good," he said, but didn't move to get up. "Can we just stay here for a few more minutes."

"Yes," she said, settling against his chest.

They stayed that way for a good ten minutes before they finally dragged themselves up. Somehow, Beth managed to get him laughing on the short walk up to his mum's house, and he was struck once again by how easy she was to be around and was amazed by how she'd managed to completely change his mood.

They'd just reached the back door when Beth's phone rang. Creases wrinkled her forehead as she looked at the display.

"I need to take this," she said, already moving away from him. "I'll just be a minute."

In the kitchen the sweet smell of freshly baked biscuits filled the air. He smiled at the chatter from his mum and Ellie, but hovered by the window, glancing frequently out at Beth, who paced the length of the patio with the phone to her ear and a serious expression on her face.

"What's wrong?" he asked when she walked into the kitchen.

"That was the manager at my dad's care home." The tension was evident in the set of her shoulders. "His doctor wants to change one of his medications and they need me to go in and sign paperwork for it."

"Can't they send you the paperwork?" Mirren asked.

"No. They have a policy of the paperwork being done in person."

"When do they need it by?" Trystan asked.

She slumped against the sideboard. "They said preferably by the end of this week."

"So soon?" his mum asked.

"Yes. I'll get my laptop and look at flights."

While she nipped upstairs, Trystan felt a vague sense of unease at the thought of them going back home. Surely it wouldn't be for long though.

"There are Smarties in the biscuits," Ellie told him, breaking his thoughts and holding one out to him. "Do you want to try?"

"Thank you." He smiled and popped it in his mouth.

"I'm hoping we can manage the trip in one day," Beth said, reappearing and sitting at the kitchen table with her laptop. "It'll depend on the flight times. It'd be nice if we could leave on Friday morning and be back on Friday evening."

Trystan breathed a sigh of relief that she wasn't keen to be gone for long.

"Where are you going, Mummy?" Ellie asked.

"We're going back home. Just for a quick trip on Friday." Her brow furrowed as she scanned the website. "At least I hope so."

"I can't go on Friday," Ellie said firmly. "I have the kids' club and it's a party on Friday."

"Sorry," Beth said, not paying Ellie much attention. "We have to go and see Grandad."

"I don't like going to see Grandad. He forgets my name and he smells funny."

"He'll enjoy seeing you though," Beth said with a smile that was clearly forced. She looked back at the computer screen. "Okay. There's availability on the flight on Friday morning ... But only one seat coming back in the evening." She concentrated on the website. "We'll have to come back on Saturday."

"I can't go, Mummy," Ellie insisted. "Steph will be very sad if I'm not at the party. All my new friends will be. And I'll be sad too."

"I'm sorry sweetheart." Beth turned to face her, taking her hands. "We have to go. There's no choice."

"Ellie could stay with us," Trystan said without a lot of thought.

Beth's gaze flicked to him. "Leave her here? With you?"

"Yeah." He shrugged. "That way you could just go for the day. Ellie would be in the kids' club in the morning. Then I can pick her up and keep her entertained until you get back."

"That's a good idea," Mirren agreed. "It'll be much easier for you. You'll be able to focus on your dad."

"I couldn't possibly. It's too much, and I'd feel terrible

leaving her." She smiled at Ellie. "I'm sorry you'll miss kids' club but I promise we'll have a good time. It's fun to go on a plane."

"I don't want to go," Ellie told her flatly. "I'll stay here with Trystan and Mirren."

Beth took her hand and looked her right in the eyes. "I don't want you to stay here without me."

"Why not?"

"Well … because …"

As she struggled to come up with a reason, Trystan had the feeling he'd said the wrong thing by offering to look after Ellie; it would have at least been better to discuss it when Ellie wasn't around.

Beth sighed heavily, then caught his eye. "Are you sure it's okay?"

"Yes. No problem at all."

"I don't know." She bit her lip and looked to his mum.

"She'll be absolutely fine," Mirren told her. "I promise."

"Okay." Beth still didn't look overly convinced by the idea. "If you're sure."

Ellie passed Trystan another biscuit, looking thoroughly pleased with herself.

CHAPTER TWENTY-ONE

B eth spent Wednesday evening and the whole of Thursday in a mild panic about leaving Ellie while she went back home. No matter how much she told herself that Ellie would be fine, she couldn't silence the voice in her head that told her she was being irresponsible.

On the short plane ride on Friday, the feeling only intensified. She forced herself to think of the look on Ellie's face that morning when she and Trystan had waved her off at the airport. It certainly wasn't the face of a child who was upset about being left. If anything, Ellie was excited about the time without Beth. She'd no doubt be spoiled rotten by the Trenearys.

During the hour she spent chatting to the manager of the care home, Beth was thankful for not having Ellie there. It gave her the space to concentrate on the conversation. Not that there seemed to be anything new with her dad, except for the slight change to his medication.

Beth had long since given up any hope of her dad recognising her, but the usual pang of sadness hit her when she sat with him in the communal lounge. The first few minutes of conversation were always the worst; she'd learned to tell him that she knew him from years ago and was just calling in to see how he was doing. It was easier than trying to explain. Polite as ever, he smiled and told her it was kind of her to visit, and how nice it was to see her. Conversation flowed much more easily when she mentioned her holiday on the Scillies. He asked her questions and she enthusiastically told him how beautiful it was and described all the places she'd visited.

At lunchtime she declined the offer to eat with them and instead used it as her cue to leave. Walking out of the rather grand red-brick building on the outskirts of Plymouth, she felt a mixture of relief at having the task out of the way – and guilt at thinking of her dad as a burden.

Driving the familiar route back home in the car she'd rented at the airport, she made the usual detour to avoid passing the place where her mum had been killed.

The stale smell of the house was unwelcoming as she shoved at the door, pushing the collection of mail out of the way with the action. Dee had been over earlier in the week to go through the post but the junk mail had built up quickly.

Walking through the house, she opened windows, hoping the fresh air would make the place less depressing.

With no supplies in the kitchen, her only options were black tea or coffee, so she opted for the bottle of iced tea she'd bought at the airport.

The stillness of the house unsettled her and she was happy to hear the doorbell chime half an hour after she'd arrived. Dee had said she'd bring lunch over and Beth couldn't have been more grateful.

"I missed you so much!" Dee said, barrelling into a tight embrace.

"You too," Beth replied. "It's good to see you."

Taking a step back, Dee's gaze travelled over Beth. "You look fab. All that sunshine and sex has obviously been doing you good."

"Dee!" she hissed, rolling her eyes before bending to hug

six-year-old Ferne. "How are you, sweetie? I think you've grown."

"I'm still six," Ferne told her, going ahead of them into the kitchen.

"How did it go at the care home?" Dee asked.

"Fine. It was all very straightforward."

"I'll go and visit again next week."

"You don't need to." Beth was slightly put out that Dee actually seemed to enjoy visiting.

"I love old people. I was talking to the manager about volunteering there."

"Don't you have enough going on?"

"Yes. But I find it a very soothing place. I get chatting with the old people and forget everything else for a while."

"I wish I felt like that. Whenever I'm there I end up stressed."

"It's different for you." She laid a hand on Beth's arm. "It's your dad. Of course it's difficult."

"Where's Ellie?" Ferne asked loudly.

"She's still on holiday," Beth told her.

She stared up at Beth. "You left her there?"

"I'm going back again later." A pang of guilt hit her. Even a six-year-old could see it was an irresponsible thing to do.

"I still can't believe you left her there," Dee said.

"Don't start! I feel bad enough as it is."

"I wasn't intending to make you feel bad." Dee set a shopping bag on the counter, then raised a hand in the air. "I was going to high-five you. I think it's great. I'm very proud of you."

Beth's hand tingled from slapping it against Dee's. "What are you talking about?"

"You're usually such a control freak about who looks after Ellie. You're even uptight about me looking after her."

"No, I'm not!" She paused the conversation while Ferne asked if she could go upstairs and play with Ellie's things. Her footsteps banged on the stairs as she ran up there.

"You're a total control freak." Dee picked up the conversation when they were alone again, taking plates from the cupboard at the same time.

"I'm not a control freak, I just don't like to inconvenience people."

"So it's not because you think no one can take care of Ellie as well as you can?"

"No." She pulled her phone from her back pocket and felt a flutter of anticipation when she saw she had a message from Trystan. "I'm not worried about Ellie at all, I'm more worried about how Trystan will cope. He already told me he doesn't want kids – a day with Ellie will probably only confirm that decision." Clicking into the message, she was met with a photo of Trystan and Ellie with their heads together as they ate ice creams.

"I have so much to say, I'm not sure where to start. But first of all I'd like to know why you're grinning at your phone." When Beth turned the screen, Dee gasped and snatched it from her. "Bloody hell. I cannot believe this was your birthday present to yourself. Please tell me you're getting me something similar for my birthday?"

"Stop objectifying him," Beth complained half-heartedly.

"I can't. He's too hot."

"He's also sweet and kind and lovely." She thought back to how upset he'd been about the situation with Lowen. "He's sensitive."

"Now you're just showing off! He sounds perfect."

"He kind of is." It wasn't as though she thought he was flawless, just that he was pretty perfect even with his flaws.

"What were you saying about him not wanting kids?" Dee went back to the task of putting pre-packed sandwiches on the plates and took them to the table. "That sounds as though you've been having some fairly deep conversations."

"We have. He split up with his girlfriend because she wanted to get married and have kids, but he didn't."

"He's good with Ellie, though?"

"What do you think?" Beth brought up the photo of the two of them again, partly as proof and partly because she wanted to look at it again. "I wouldn't have left her with him if he wasn't good with her, would I?"

"So why doesn't he want kids?"

"I don't know. I didn't ask."

"Maybe it's babies he has an issue with. I can understand that. Babies are a nightmare." For a moment, it seemed as though Dee might rehash Ferne's first year and her intense battle with croup. Thankfully, she moved the conversation on quickly. "Ellie's such a little angel though. Maybe Trystan will spend a day with her and change his mind about kids."

"I know you don't believe me, but Ellie's hard work too. She might be pretty calm most of the time, but I think all kids are tiring."

"It's different when it's not your own kid though. I bet Trystan will enjoy spending the day with Ellie."

"She was in the kids' club this morning with Kit, and Mirren will be around this afternoon, so I'm sure they'll be fine."

"Of course they will."

Beth took a bite of her sandwich and leaned back in the chair as she chewed slowly. "It's so strange to think that I've only known them for a matter of weeks. They feel like family." Beth vaguely registered the worry lines on Dee's brow but ploughed on regardless. "Trystan and I have such a connection – we talk about everything. I've never been with a guy who I felt I could be completely myself with." She smiled widely, but Dee's features were fixed in concern.

"What's going to happen at the end of the summer?"

"I don't know." As her smile fell away, Beth reached for her sandwich then set it back on the plate, realising she no longer had an appetite.

"Do you think you'll keep seeing him?"

Her lungs felt tight and she sat up straighter. "It'd be difficult considering he lives in London and we live in Devon."

"Not impossible, though. Lots of people have long-distance relationships. Or he could move to Plymouth."

"That's not going to happen."

"Why not?"

"Because I've only known him a few weeks." She shook her head. "It's a holiday fling, that's all. Which is exactly what I needed."

"So at the end of the summer you'll go your separate ways?"

"I would imagine so." She took a bite of her sandwich, chewing slowly. "You've depressed me now. In two weeks we'll be back home." The thought of not seeing Trystan every day made her bones feel heavy. "It's going to be a shock to the system settling back to real life. It'll be hard for Ellie – she's got used to being surrounded by people. Being here will no doubt feel lonely in comparison to being surrounded by the Treneary family."

"Can I put something out there?" Dee smiled sympathetically. "Do you think you've latched onto this family to help you cope with losing your mum?"

Looking at the situation objectively, Beth couldn't deny it was a possibility. "Does it matter?" she asked, wiping a tear from the corner of her eye. "I've been feeling so much more positive."

"That's great, and I'm not trying to burst your bubble. Maybe you should talk to Trystan, see what he's thinking. He might be keen to keep seeing you after the holiday."

Beth shook her head again. "I really don't think that's where things are headed. He's just got out of a ten-year relationship. My life is kind of a mess – I don't even know what I'm going to do for a job. I think a fling was something we both needed. I can't imagine it being anything more than that, given our circumstances."

"You obviously like him a lot though."

"Of course I like him a lot. What's your point?"

"I'm just worried that it's going to be a difficult adjustment when you come back home."

"I'm already aware of that," Beth said, rolling her eyes. "Up until now I've been avoiding thinking about it."

"Sorry." Dee's features relaxed. "Avoidance is the kind of strategy I'd opt for too. Feel free to ignore me. Maybe you should just enjoy the rest of your holiday and worry about getting back to reality when you really have to."

That was exactly what Beth wanted to do. It would be slightly more difficult to do now that Dee had put thoughts of the future in her head.

CHAPTER TWENTY-TWO

Trystan had been convinced that looking after Ellie for the afternoon would be a breeze. His mum had asked him to pick up milk when he collected Ellie from kids' club. Without thinking, he picked her up first and took her for an ice cream before nipping into the shop. It soon became clear that it would have been a better idea to do the shopping before he'd picked up Ellie. She insisted on walking along every aisle even though he only needed milk. And she wanted to buy *everything*. When she got to the cosmetics section and begged him for nail varnish, he caved and they finally made it out of the shop.

She then proceeded to ask him a string of endless questions on the walk home, from why the leaves on the trees move, to why birds fly, to why the man they passed had no hair. She asked that one embarrassingly loudly. She also had a habit of pointing at pretty much everything she saw and asking, "What's that?"

By the time they got back to his mum's place he was mentally exhausted.

Then his mum had asked Ellie if she was allowed to wear nail polish, making him wonder if he'd been duped into buying her something illicit. It hadn't even occurred to him that Beth might not allow it. Ellie said it was fine. Although he supposed she would say that.

"Are you sure your mum is okay with you wearing nail varnish?" he asked for about the fifth time as they sat together at the patio table. There wasn't actually much point to the question now that he'd already painted her nails.

"Yes," she said confidently while she slopped polish over his fingernail.

"You know you're just supposed to paint the nails, not my fingers as well?"

Her tongue was poking out in concentration. "I just went a bit wobbly."

"Are you sure pink is my colour?" he asked, holding up his left hand to inspect the damage.

"Pink can be for boys too."

"I know. I just think a nice blue might have brought out my eyes."

Stopping abruptly, she looked him in the eyes for long enough to make him uncomfortable. "If your eyes came out, you wouldn't be able to see."

"I meant … never mind."

"We don't have any blue anyway."

"If I'd have realised you were going to give me a makeover I'd have picked out a different colour in the shop."

"Don't you like this one?" She finished the final nail and put the brush back in the pot. "I think it's nice."

"I suppose it makes a change."

"Next time we can get blue if you want."

"Thanks."

"Can we go to the beach later and build sandcastles?"

"Isn't that going to ruin our nails?"

"I think it will be okay." She blew on his nails to dry the polish. "We could look for nice shells as well."

"Okay."

"I'd like to play hide and seek later too, and maybe we can draw pictures for a surprise for Mummy."

"That's a good idea."

With Ellie's non-stop activities, the afternoon went by in a blink. Mirren made dinner for the three of them, then got Ellie ready for bed before letting her watch TV.

"I don't know which one of you looks more tired," Mirren said, when the episode of Peppa Pig came to an end.

Trystan had been struggling to keep his eyes open while Ellie was curled up with her head resting on the arm of the couch.

"I think you might need to go up to bed," he told her.

"I thought Mummy would be back to read me a bedtime story."

"She'll be back soon," Mirren said. "Why don't I take you up and read your story? Mummy will come up to see you as soon as she's back."

Trystan had offered to pick Beth up from the airport, but she'd insisted she could walk.

"Can Trystan read the story?" Ellie asked without lifting her head from the arm of the couch.

"I suppose so." He yawned as he stood, then held a hand out to her, but she only stared up at him. "Shall I carry you?"

"Yes, please." She said goodnight to Mirren as he carried her out of the living room. Halfway up the stairs she snuggled into his neck and quietly asked if he'd read two stories.

"Maybe." He yawned again. "If I can stay awake that long."

The house was quiet when Beth arrived back, except for the low hum of the TV drifting from the living room. Sticking her head around the door, she greeted Mirren.

"How was Ellie?" she asked.

"I've hardly seen her. She had Trystan running around after her all afternoon. It seemed as though the two of them enjoyed themselves. He took her up to read her a story not long ago. She might still be awake. I said I'd send you straight up to see her."

Beth slipped out of the room again and up the stairs. In the bedroom, the lamp was on and both Trystan and Ellie were fast asleep. Perching on the edge of the bed, Beth felt a surge of love as she looked down at them. Her conversation with Dee about what would happen at the end of the holiday came back to her and she banished it to the back corner of her mind. Carefully, she removed the book from Trystan's lap and nudged him awake.

"Hi." His voice was croaky as he forced his eyes open.

She whispered hello and tipped her head towards the door. They walked downstairs in silence except for the sound of Trystan yawning loudly.

"It seems as though my daughter wore you out," she said when they reached the kitchen.

"Yes." He groaned as he stretched, raising his arms so his T-shirt rose up, exposing his toned midriff and sending a bolt of desire coursing through her. "She's exhausting. How do you do that every day?"

"You get used to it." She slipped her arms around his waist, satisfying her need for physical contact.

His arms locked behind her back as he kissed her. "How was your day?"

"It felt like a bit of a waste of time, as I'd suspected, but I don't feel like such a terrible daughter now that I've seen Dad." Her chin twitched and she turned her head to the side. Trystan held her tighter, which only served to intensify her emotions.

"You're not a terrible daughter. It's a difficult situation, that's all."

"I know." Burying her face in his neck, she was over-whelmed by the heady scent of him. "It's always so emotional seeing him. I'm not sure I'll ever get used to him not knowing who I am."

"I can't imagine it."

Pulling back, she forced a smile. "It was good to see Dee and

Ferne. That was nice. And it was all so much easier without having to drag Ellie around with me. Thanks so much for looking after her."

"You're welcome." He moved his hands up to cup her face.

Snatching at his right hand, she turned it over. "What happened?"

"Your daughter happened. Is she allowed to wear nail polish? She swore it was okay, but given the way my mum questioned it I was worried I might be in trouble."

"It's fine." She couldn't help but smile – both at his nervousness and at his bright pink nails. "You look ridiculous."

"I actually quite like it."

"Really?"

"Please don't say that boys can't wear pink, because even Ellie knows better than that. We discussed it at length this afternoon."

"Maybe it's just a shock to see you with pink nails. It might take some getting used to."

"I wasn't sure to start with either." He hooked her hair behind her ear. "I missed you today."

"I missed you too."

She really had missed him, and it'd only been a day. She refused to let herself think how much she was going to miss him when she was back in Plymouth permanently.

CHAPTER TWENTY-THREE

Trystan generally spent at least part of the weekend working. He could barely remember the last time he'd gone a day without opening his laptop, never mind a full weekend. Previously, he'd never begrudged the extra hours he'd put in. But now all he wanted to do was spend his time with Beth and Ellie. The weekend had been spent lazing on beaches and exploring rock pools. They'd walked miles too, mostly with Ellie perched on his shoulders, which seemed to be her preferred way to get anywhere now.

On Monday, he was up at the crack of dawn and forced himself back into work mode. He and Beth had been out for dinner the previous evening, then back to his place for some alone time, so he hadn't slept much. Not that he was complaining.

After not having done any work over the weekend, the tasks were mounting. He stopped for a quick lunch with Beth, then settled back down to work solidly for the afternoon so he could close the laptop in time for dinner.

The bright sunshine was dazzling as he ate with his mum and Beth and Ellie on the patio. While Beth took Ellie up to bed, he helped his mum clean the kitchen before she slunk away to the living room to call a friend and he returned to the patio. A barrage of messages from Kit kept him amused while he waited for Beth.

"What's so funny?" she asked, pushing her fingers into his hair when she reappeared and stood over him.

"My little brother. He's in the pub with Keira for the quiz. Any chance you feel like joining them? Noah and Seren are down there too, but they're both working."

Beth glanced towards the house. "Your mum looked after Ellie last night. I can't ask her again."

"She won't mind."

"I know she won't, but I'll still feel bad asking. You should go though."

"I'm not going anywhere without you," he said, pulling her onto his lap to kiss her.

When the sound of his mum clearing her throat interrupted them, Beth shot up and into her own chair, her cheeks flaming red.

"I just wondered if you two are going to the pub tonight?" Mirren asked, her amusement at Beth's reaction evident in her smiling eyes.

"We weren't planning on it," Trystan said. "Why?"

"Because I've had Kit on the phone insisting I get you to hurry up. He reckons Keira's terrible at trivia and he needs help. Then I had a call from Keira saying the same about Kit."

Trystan grinned at Beth. "You know they're going to end up arguing all evening if we don't get down there and help them out."

"Off you go and have fun," Mirren said as she wandered back inside. "I'll keep an ear out for Ellie."

"Thank you," Beth called after her, then lowered her voice for Trystan. "I'm so embarrassed."

"Why?"

"Because your mum just caught me draped all over you."

"Do you honestly think she didn't already know there's something going on between us?"

"I assumed she knew. But there's a difference between knowing something and seeing something. I don't want to make her uncomfortable in her own home."

He told her not to worry about it and smiled as another message came through from Kit telling him to hurry up and get to the pub.

They arrived with impeccable timing just as the first question was read out. Beth whispered the answer to Kit, who was poised with a pen over the paper and a blank look on his face that matched Keira's beside him. For the next hour they huddled together, whispering possible answers to the questions.

The more wine she drank, the more Beth's smug smile intensified as she answered questions while teasing Kit and Keira for not pulling their weight.

"Have you two answered anything so far?" she asked, during the break at the halfway point of the quiz. Her cheeks were flushed from the wine, and Trystan struggled to keep his eyes off her. If he could think up a reasonable excuse he'd abandon the pub and take her back to his place immediately.

"We knew most of the answers," Kit said. "We're just not jumping to say them because they're so obvious."

Trystan grinned at Kit. "You tell yourself whatever helps you sleep at night."

"Fine," Kit huffed, slouching back in his seat. "We're not getting as many as you. But that's because the questions so far have been aimed at an older audience. You have a definite advantage since so many of the questions have been about history. You lived it – of course you know more!"

Beth shook her head as she laughed. "The questions have mostly been on pop culture."

"I'm fairly sure pop culture from the eighties and nineties counts as history, right?" Kit turned to Keira for confirmation.

"I'd have to agree," Keira said, deadpan.

"I think you're both being very rude," Beth said, trying but failing at a mock stern expression. Her eyes were too bright and happy.

"Maybe I didn't express myself clearly," Kit said, beaming. "I'm very grateful you're so knowledgeable about the olden days." He ducked away when Beth swatted at him. "This is why it's good to have a diverse quiz team. When the questions on contemporary culture come around we'll clean up."

Beth untangled her fingers from Trystan's and stood up.

"I didn't really offend you, did I?" Kit asked. "Please don't leave. We might have a chance of winning because of you."

She raised an eyebrow as she moved to pass him. "Because I'm so old?"

"No! You're not old … you look as though you're in your prime to me … and being a genius is nothing to do with age."

"You can stop with the flattery." She patted his shoulder. "I'm only going to the bathroom."

"Phew." Kit sighed dramatically. "Hurry up. We need you back here for the next round."

Trystan's eyes stayed on her as she moved across the room.

"How was your afternoon with Ellie on Friday?" Keira asked, breaking his trance.

"Exhausting, but fun." He clocked Kit's smirk and was fairly sure he didn't want to know what was going on in his brother's head but couldn't help but ask. "What's that look for?"

"I think it's interesting that you split up with Jenny because you didn't want kids and now you're completely smitten with your new girlfriend's kid."

"I'm not…" He trailed off, realising he wasn't sure which part of the sentence he could argue with. "Things just weren't right with Jenny."

Kit smiled. "I notice you didn't deny that you're smitten with Ellie, or that Beth is your girlfriend."

"Ellie is very cute." If he was honest, he was surprised by

how fond he was of her. "I'm not sure how I'd describe my relationship with Beth."

"I think she's lovely," Keira said. "What are you going to do when she leaves, though?"

"We haven't talked about it."

"It's only a couple of weeks away, isn't it?" Kit asked. "You go back to London at the end of the month, right?"

"I need to be back by the first week of September."

"Do you miss the city?" Keira asked.

He shook his head, locking eyes with Beth as she walked towards them. "Not at all," he muttered, a feeling of dread creeping into his stomach at the thought of going back to real life.

Beth hadn't taken much persuasion to go back to Trystan's place after the pub. She'd been on a bit of a high after they'd won the quiz and had a nice buzz from the wine. Time alone with Trystan finished the evening off perfectly. At least until her eyes started to close in the comfort of his bed. Her back was pressed against his firm chest while his arms circled around her in a tight cocoon.

"I can't fall asleep here," she said, knowing that she was already on the verge of sleep and needed to move before she was enveloped by it.

His words tickled her neck when he murmured beside her ear. "I'd like to fall asleep with you. And wake up with you."

"Me too. I can't though." Once or twice, Beth had contemplated setting an alarm and creeping back to the house at the crack of dawn but couldn't bring herself to do it. "I really need to go," she said, not moving a muscle.

"I'm not stopping you." He tightened his arms around her, snuggling his cheek in the space between her shoulder and jaw.

"You're definitely not making it easy to leave."

"No. I'm not going to do that." When she turned in his arms, his features were serious. "The summer is going so fast."

"I keep thinking the same. Two weeks from now, Ellie will have had her first day back at school."

"Have you already booked your flight home?"

"Yes." Her heart felt heavy. "A week on Wednesday."

"That's soon."

"I want to be back a few days before school starts to give us time to unpack and make sure we have everything ready for school."

He moved his head so his breath tickled her face when he spoke. "Do you think we'll stay in touch?"

"I … um … I think so … will we?"

He pressed his lips together. "If you want to?"

His hesitation made her heart race. "I can't imagine leaving and never speaking again …" She sat up, holding the bedding against her chest as she tried to read his features. Behind his tight smile she had no idea what was going on in his head. "What were you thinking would happen when we go back home?"

"I don't know. I just wondered what you were thinking…"

"Everyone knows long-distance relationships don't work. Right?"

He propped himself on an elbow. "I've heard that."

"And you've just come out of a serious relationship … so I wouldn't imagine you were looking for anything more than a holiday fling…"

His eyes brightened. "I can't say I was even looking for that."

"I'm like a rebound thing, no doubt!" She was fairly sure jokes were the only way she could make it through the conversation.

"Definitely." He trailed a finger over her back. "And you made it very clear that you think kissing is a good antidote to grief …"

"Absolutely. It's the only reason I've ever kissed you!" Her smile died on her lips. "Seriously. I've had an amazing summer with you. But we have such different lives. And it's not just us to think of. I don't want Ellie to be unsettled."

"Yeah."

"We still have more than a week here," she said, running a hand through Trystan's hair. "I don't even want to think about going home. I just want to enjoy the rest of our holiday."

"Me too." He sat and kissed her neck, then reached for his clothes when she began to dress.

"Are you cold?" she asked, giving him a sidelong glance.

"No. Thought I'd walk you home."

"You don't need to."

"I know. But all your talk of leaving has depressed me. I want to spend as much time with you as possible."

CHAPTER TWENTY-FOUR

The last week of Beth's holiday was as relaxed and easy as all the previous weeks. Every day felt wonderfully carefree as they explored the islands on foot and by boat. On the days when Trystan had to work, Beth felt as though she was wishing the day away until he joined them in the evening. She did her best to avoid thinking about the future, but it got more and more difficult as the days slipped away. It wasn't even just Trystan she was going to miss, but Mirren and Kit and the rest of the family too.

Trystan took the entire day off on the day before they were due to fly home. The weather was glorious and they spent a lazy morning in the garden, then moved down to the beach after lunch. After splashing around in the sea for a while, Trystan helped Ellie build a sandcastle, then left her to fetch water for the moat and joined Beth to lie on their towels in the sun.

"I really ought to go and start packing soon," Beth said, propping herself on her elbow to look over at Trystan, who'd closed his eyes.

"Later," he muttered.

"I'm not going to have much time later if everyone's coming over for dinner."

"Don't bother then," he said, his face looking perfectly peaceful. "Stay here instead."

A smile tugged at the corners of her lips. "Don't tempt me."

"We'd easily find jobs," he said wistfully. "A guy I went to school with has been trying to get me to work at his travel firm for ages, so that would be me sorted. We'd figure out a way for you to make a living from your photography here. There's a good school for Ellie. I already have a house. It'd be very easy."

"You've definitely made it sound very easy." She gazed at the contours of his face, happily losing herself in his little daydream for a moment.

"Are you quietly considering it?" he asked, eyes still closed.

"No." She smiled as she studied his face, committing every detail to memory. "Do you think you'll move back here?"

He opened an eye, then closed it again. "What?"

"You seem very at home here. And you're so close to your family. Do you plan on staying in London long term?"

His chest expanded as he inhaled deeply. "I have no idea."

"I could imagine you living here." Dragging her eyes away from him, she glanced up at the cottage, letting herself imagine it being home. She only realised she was frowning when Trystan nudged her leg.

"What are you looking so serious about?" he asked.

"I just thought …" She smiled at him. "Never mind."

"What were you thinking?"

"I was wondering how you can afford to own a house here and a flat in London …" Her brows drew together. "Are you rich?"

He laughed loudly. "What kind of question is that?"

"Well you don't seem to have any money worries … Your flat in London can't have been cheap."

He raised his arms, interlocking his fingers to a pillow behind his head. "It's only a one-bedroom place. We bought at a good time and both Jenny and I had decent incomes."

"But you also own the cottage here. How much does it pay to

be a relocation specialist? Even if you have a great salary, that doesn't seem to add up. Or do you have a huge mortgage or something?"

"The cottage was a good investment because the holiday rental market is thriving here." He shifted his weight then sat up. "I also inherited some money, which was how I could afford to buy the cottage."

Beth brushed sand from her calves. "Did you inherit money when your dad died?" she asked softly.

"No." Creases appeared in his forehead. "It was a couple of years before he died … I didn't really *inherit* the money …" Trystan glanced around as though worried he might be overheard. "It's kind of a weird story."

"You're being very mysterious," Beth teased. "Do I even want to know? It's starting to feel as though it's dangerous information…"

He laughed again and the tension left his features. "The money was a gift from Lowen," he said quietly.

"Your brother just gave you a load of money?"

He nodded. "A hundred and fifty thousand pounds."

It took a moment for Beth to digest the information. "Why? How did Lowen have so much money? He just gave it to you?"

"He gave the same to all his brothers. Kit used his money to buy the train. Noah and I each bought a cottage from our parents. No one's quite sure what Jago did with his, but I think a lot of it went to pay off debts."

"Where did Lowen get the money from?"

"He inherited it from his maternal grandparents. He spent a lot of time with them when he was growing up. Every school holiday he went on these fancy holidays with them. When they died within a year of each other, Lowen inherited a lot."

"How much?"

He shrugged. "He'd never say. Only that what he gave us was a drop in the ocean. He bought the pottery studio and his house on Bryher, but he's never been very extravagant with the money, at least not for himself. One time Seren was complaining about not being able to afford a car and Lowen bought her a brand-new Mini and had it shipped over."

"Wow." Beth smiled lightly. "I don't think I've ever cared about being an only child until now!"

Trystan dug a hand into the sand, then let it fall through his fingers. "When Lowen gave us the money, he insisted it was nothing to him and that we never need mention it again. He didn't want any of us to feel indebted to him because of it. So we don't really talk about it. There was a lot of speculation on the island about how we'd suddenly come into money, but most people don't know about Lowen's other family so we kept it quiet. Which likely just spurred more rumours."

"Was Lowen close to his grandparents?"

Trystan scratched at his jaw. "I'm not entirely sure."

"I thought you and Lowen used to be close."

"We were. And we talked about pretty much everything … just not his grandparents. It was kind of a sore subject. It caused some conflict between him and Jago when they were teenagers." He frowned as he gazed out to the horizon. "Jago was jealous of all the travelling Lowen did. Money was tight when we were growing up, but Lowen got to spend his holidays travelling in first class and being taken on fancy shopping sprees … it caused tension. I guess in the end he decided it was best not to talk about it."

"He must have had a tough time, losing his grandparents close together and then your dad …"

"He went a bit weird after his grandparents died. I think he felt guilty for not seeing much of them in the years before they died. He was caught up in work and life. I guess you always think you'll have more time." Pausing, he exhaled slowly. "I'd like to say the inheritance softened the blow, but I think the money caused him quite a lot of stress. When Dad died he completely lost the plot. He moved to Bryher and hid from the world."

"It's really sad. All that money and he's miserable."

Trystan stretched his neck. "Can we change the subject now?"

"Sure." Beth nestled her head on his shoulder. "But I'm afraid I'm going to have to change it back to the packing I should be doing."

"I can stay here with Ellie if you want to go and pack in peace," Trystan offered.

"That would be great. Thank you." She dropped a kiss on his shoulder, then called out to Ellie to tell her the plan.

Putting her bucket down, Ellie came over and plonked herself on the towel beside Trystan. "Can we go on the train today?"

"I think we probably can." Trystan checked his watch. "We'll have to hurry to make it in time."

"You can give me a shoulder ride," Ellie said. "Then we can go quicker."

He grinned at her. "You're full of good ideas, aren't you?"

Beth forced herself to ignore the knot of anxiety in her stomach at the thought of how much they were both going to miss him. After collecting up the beach things and waving Trystan and Ellie off, she headed to the house to face the packing. The task was about as depressing as she'd expected. She'd just managed to squeeze everything in the case when she checked the wardrobe once more and spotted her mum's ashes stashed on the top shelf.

During their week in Peswera Cottage, scattering the ashes had been on Beth's mind almost constantly. The fact that she'd hardly thought of them since meeting Trystan made her think that they'd both needed someone to prop them up. She'd kept his mind from his break-up and he'd been the perfect distraction from everything she'd wanted to avoid thinking about. Now she was going to have to figure out how to move forward with her life without his support.

After staring at the urn for a few minutes, she abandoned the packing and wandered out of the bedroom and down the stairs. Not bothering with shoes, she walked barefoot through the garden and onto the lane before dropping down onto the beach. She still had no clue which beach had been her mum's favourite, but she absolutely knew which hers was.

That would have to do.

CHAPTER TWENTY-FIVE

F or the briefest moment on the deserted beach, Beth felt completely at peace. She twisted the lid of the urn and was all set to let the ashes go when she happened to glance around. Her gaze lingered on Peswera Cottage, then swept over to Mirren's house, looming up on the headland. With a racing heart she returned the lid to the urn before sinking to sit on the sand.

She'd lost all track of time when Trystan called out to her.

"Don't worry," he said as he strode across the sand. "I didn't lose Ellie. She wanted to help Kit wash the train. He said he'd bring her back afterwards."

"Ellie will like that," she said.

His shoulder knocked against hers as he sat beside her. "Are you okay?" Following her gaze to the urn, he let out a sympathetic sigh. "Did you …?"

"No. I was about to, but …" She trailed off and shrugged.

"If you're not ready, you should wait. One day it'll feel right."

"It did feel right." She pushed her hair from her face as the wind pulled it around her. "I don't know which beach was Mum's favourite but I know this is mine and I thought that was good enough. I think Mum would approve."

"What stopped you then?"

"You," she said, her forehead crinkling to a frown. "I looked back at your cottage and realised that I don't know what's going to happen with us. Wherever I scatter Mum's ashes should be a place that I want to come back to time and again, but what if this place ends up being somewhere I'm not comfortable coming back to?"

The silence that hung between them felt loaded.

"I can't give you impartial advice about this."

"Tell me what you're thinking." Squeezing his hand, she pleaded with her eyes.

"I'm thinking that I'd like it if you always had a reason to come back here. But you need to do what feels right for you."

"I don't know what to do." Anger bubbled inside of her. "I feel as though I never know what to do any more. Every decision I make, I want to run it by my mum and I can't. I don't have anyone to help me figure things out and I hate it."

Trystan rubbed her back and she nestled into him, resting her head against his chest. "I think you're better at figuring things out for yourself than you think."

"Sorry," she sniffed. "It's my last day here and I'm wasting it."

"No, you're not."

"I feel as though I am. I'm sitting here being miserable when I should be enjoying the time with you."

"Well, that's a good point." He tilted his head as he leaned towards her and she felt the familiar flutter of butterflies dancing in her stomach as their lips met.

When she finally peeled herself away from him, Trystan's features were deadly serious.

"Can I see you again?" he asked. "Once we get back to real life. I don't know how it would work, but I hate the thought of not seeing you."

"I feel the same," she whispered, clutching his hand. "While I'm here with you it seems impossible that we won't see each other again. But I've no idea what's going to happen when we're back home. I need to get Ellie back into a routine and figure out what I'm going to do for work. And while we're busy falling back into our routines in Plymouth, you'll be doing the same in London. Once you're caught up in the grind of real life, who knows what you'll want."

He rested his head against hers. "I'm fairly certain I'll still want to be with you."

"You can't know that for definite until you're away from this lovely little bubble we've created. Everything is easy here because we're on holiday. It's not real life. After a few weeks at home, everything will feel different."

"I don't think I'll feel any different, but there doesn't seem to be much point arguing about it."

"Let's just wait and see what happens."

He kissed the side of her head. "Did you finish packing?"

"Almost." She checked her watch, realising she needed to hurry and make sure she had everything organised before dinner.

Standing, she hugged her mum's ashes to her chest and they set off back to the house in silence. As she squeezed the urn into the suitcase, Beth felt a pang of regret over not having the courage to scatter them.

By the time she'd finished with the packing, chatter drifted up to her through the bedroom window. Her heart felt heavy when she looked down at the Trenearys gathered on the patio. Ellie's face was gleeful as Noah held her upside down on the grass. Her gentle giggles morphed to a high-pitched squeal when Keira tickled her.

As though he could sense her watching, Trystan broke his conversation with Kit and Seren to look up at her. Opening the window, she told him she'd be down soon, then moved to sit on the bed. Going downstairs and pretending her heart wasn't breaking at the thought of leaving felt overwhelming, and being surrounded by so much love and laughter would only serve to highlight the lack of it when they returned to real life.

After a few minutes she shook herself out of her pity and set off down to enjoy their last evening. Music hit her ears halfway down the stairs and she found Trystan and Ellie dancing around the kitchen.

"I was about to come up and find you," Trystan said. "Are you all organised?"

"I think so."

Ellie's skirt fanned around her when she twirled on one foot. "I washed the train with Kit," she said proudly.

"I'll bet he was glad of the help," Beth said, then burst out laughing as Trystan took her in his arms and danced her around the room.

Ellie stared up at them. "Kit says we can have a water fight after dinner. He's got water guns. I'm going to choose the one I want." She ran out of the kitchen to join the others outside.

"We should go out too," Beth said half-heartedly.

Trystan continued to waltz her around the room. "After this song."

She touched her cheek to his, inhaling his scent and attempting to commit every detail of the moment to memory. When the song came to an end he kissed her softly, then led her outside and straight into a discussion between Seren and Kit about how long to cook steaks for.

Eating out on the patio as the sun went down felt magical, and Beth tried her best not to dwell on the fact that it was the last time she'd be with these wonderful people for a while. Ellie was in her element amid the bustle of the family meal, especially when Kit and Noah ran around the garden with her after dinner. It was hard to say who enjoyed the water fight the most.

When Kit and Noah ran out of energy and moved back to the table, Beth took Ellie upstairs to get her pyjamas on, promising her she could stay up a little longer once she was ready for bed.

As it was, she curled up on Beth's lap when they re-joined the others and her eyelids drooped to the hum of easy conversation.

"I think you need to go to bed," Beth said eventually.

Ellie opened her mouth wide to yawn. "I'm not tired."

"*I* am," Kit said, stretching his arms above his head, then giving Seren a gentle nudge. "We should get off."

"We'll go too," Keira said, smiling at Beth. "Let you get her settled."

Emotions bubbled in Beth's chest and she was amazed she made it through all the hugs without crying, especially when she got to Kit and quietly thanked him for all he'd done to make their summer so special. As she watched the four of them file off across the garden, she hoped it wouldn't be long before she'd see them again.

"Now, it's really time for bed." Beth took Ellie's hand but she didn't budge.

"Can Trystan read my bedtime story?"

He was out of his chair in an instant. "I'd love to."

"Can you carry me?" She raised her arms, then settled her head on his shoulder once he'd lifted her up.

Beth smiled as she watched them go inside, then took a seat again.

"You two are going to be missed around here," Mirren said.

"Don't make me cry." Beth put a hand over her heart and fought off tears. "I can't believe how fast the summer has gone. We've loved every minute of it thanks to you and your wonderful family."

"I've loved having you." Mirren looked a little choked up too. "You know you're welcome back anytime, don't you?"

"Thank you." She gazed out at the view, which had become so familiar. With the sun low on the horizon, everything was bathed in a warm orange glow. "I should settle the bill so I don't have to think about that in the morning. I'll grab my credit card now."

Mirren gave a discreet shake of the head. "Don't bother."

"Would you rather do it tomorrow?"

"No. I'd rather we forget all about it. I've enjoyed having you here far too much to take your money."

"Don't be silly," Beth said, the lump in her throat making it difficult to speak. "Of course I have to pay you."

"You and Ellie feel like family. How can I take your money?"

"You're running a business," Beth said. "We've been here for the entire summer. *And* you've done so much for us."

"The two of you have brightened up my days. I'd keep you for longer if I could. And I've loved seeing Trystan so relaxed. That's all your doing."

"I imagine Trystan's always pretty relaxed."

Mirren bobbed her head. "Yes and no. Since his dad died he's been coasting a bit. The issue with Lowen has been difficult for him – I'm sure he's talked to you about that – and his break up with Jenny wasn't easy. I'd expected him to spend the summer putting on a brave face, but he's been happier than I've seen him in a long time."

"He makes me happy too." Beth glanced up at the window, imagining him settling Ellie down for the night. "I just don't know where we'll go from here."

"You'll figure it out."

"I'm terrified of how much I'm going to miss him," she said, while Mirren filled up their wine glasses to polish off the bottle.

"I'm certain he'll be keen to keep in touch. London isn't so far from Devon."

Beth took a long swig of her wine, not commenting that the distance felt insurmountable. And not just in miles; they had different lives. Continuing their relationship felt utterly unrealistic. Sinking further into her seat, she focused on enjoying the stunning sunset for one final time.

"I wonder if Ellie's asleep," she finally said, breaking the comfortable silence. "Or Trystan, or both of them."

"I reckon both of them is a good bet."

"Ellie will have begged him to stay with her until she fell asleep."

"Go and nudge him awake. I'm happy to listen for Ellie if you two want to go out."

Beth thanked her and went inside. As she suspected, Trystan was fast asleep – with Ellie curled into his chest and sleeping soundly too. She tried to wake him, but when he stirred and went back to sleep, she gave up and changed into her pyjamas.

With her emotions all over the place it was hard to imagine she'd be able to sleep at all, but once she was snuggled beside Trystan she slipped easily into a peaceful slumber.

CHAPTER TWENTY-SIX

A s he drifted out of sleep, Trystan became aware of the pressure in the centre of his forehead. Instinctively, he moved his hand to the spot and heard a childish giggle at the same time.

A smile hit his lips as he opened his eyes to find Ellie beaming down at him. The sunlight streaming through the window caught her hair, giving her an ethereal glow.

"What are you up to?"

"Poking you." She moved her delicate finger to the side of his nose, making him laugh and swat her away.

"Why are you poking me?"

"To wake you up," she said as though it should be obvious. "You slept in our bed."

"It's a very comfy bed." He glanced at Beth, who was nestled beside him, her breath sweeping over the skin at his neck.

"Can we go to the beach today?" Ellie asked.

Trystan's heart felt as though it stopped dead and a dull ache filled his chest. "You're going home today, remember?"

"Are you staying here?"

"Just for a few days, then I'm going back to London."

"Will you come to our house to see us one day?"

"Maybe." He certainly hoped so, but he had no idea what was going to happen.

"I'm going to see if Mirren is awake," Ellie said, hopping off the bed and running out of the room.

Holding Beth closer, he stared at her while she snoozed on his chest.

"I'd like to wake up like this every day," he whispered, when her eyes flickered open.

She searched for his hand, pulling it to her face to kiss his palm. "Me too."

"I know I'm starting to sound very needy, but I don't want us to leave and not see each other again."

Her silence and the way her forehead wrinkled didn't do anything to allay his fears. Slowly, she tilted her face to look at him. "We'll keep in touch," she said. "I just don't want us to make promises we might not be able to keep."

"I wasn't thinking of breaking any promises." He pushed her hair from her face and traced his finger over her hairline.

"Let's give ourselves time to settle back into real life. Then we'll see how things look."

"That sounds like a brush-off."

"It's not. I'm trying to be realistic."

He wished she wouldn't, because he wanted them to declare their love for each other and promise that the distance wouldn't be an issue – that no matter what, they'd figure out a way to be together.

"I have to think of what's best for Ellie," Beth said.

He nodded, fighting the urge to plead his case. The thought of them parting was bad enough without them leaving on a sour note. All he could do was hope that if he gave her space, things would work out in the end.

She lifted his arm to check his watch, and the flash of sorrow in her eyes gave him hope that this was as hard for her as it was for him.

"I have to get moving." She propped herself on her elbow to kiss him. "Can we make this morning as painless as possible?"

Sitting up, he cocked an eyebrow. "As long as that doesn't mean me not coming to the airport with you."

"Considering I have luggage and a five-year-old to deal with, I'm definitely not going to refuse you coming to the airport."

"What did you mean then?"

"I was talking to myself really." She rubbed her hands over her face. "And I wish I knew what I meant. I don't know how to make this painless. Saying goodbye to you already hurts and I haven't done it yet."

He kissed the side of her head. "Let's get breakfast and take it from there."

The morning passed in a blur. Beth was acutely aware that she was rivalling her daughter with her ability to make inane conversation. Anything to avoid facing the reality of leaving. Their summer holiday had gone so fast, but those final couple of hours felt excruciatingly slow. Waiting to leave was unbearable, and she found herself wishing to be on the plane just so she could stop dreading the moment she had to say goodbye to Trystan.

Even saying goodbye to Mirren was heart-wrenching. Beth was too emotional to express her gratitude properly and only managed a quick but heartfelt thank you as they embraced. She promised she'd be in touch, then switched her focus to getting Ellie and their bags out of the door.

Trystan drove them around to the airport in the golf buggy, and Ellie excitedly pointed out the plane coming in to land as they pulled up.

"This is horrible," Beth said once their suitcase had been checked in. Her hand was shaking as she slipped it into Trystan's. She looked over at the door to the boarding area. "I think we have to go."

He walked over with them, then scooped Ellie into his arms. "Give me the biggest squeeze you can manage," he told her with a smile. "Harder than that," he said when she hugged him. They both laughed when he pretended to choke. Shifting her onto his right arm, he drew Beth into a hug.

Holding him tightly, she couldn't think of anything to say. The only thing which sprang to mind was to tell him that she loved him. The words were on the tip of her tongue, but she was terrified of saying them out loud. Declaring her love for him wasn't going to make getting back to real life any easier. How could she be in love with him anyway, when she'd known him for such a short time? It was like she'd told him; they were on holiday, which made everything easy and heightened their feelings. But it wasn't real.

"Let me know when you're home safely," Trystan said, releasing his grip on her and setting Ellie down.

"I will."

"Promise? Message me as soon as you're home."

"Promise." She let her lips linger against his when he kissed her goodbye, then she shepherded Ellie away and willed herself not to cry.

CHAPTER TWENTY-SEVEN

The first few days back at home were a bit of a haze. Between unpacking and washing and buying school supplies and visiting her dad, Beth managed to ignore the ache in her chest fairly effectively. At least during the daytime. Once Ellie was in bed in the evening and she sat down to the deafening silence of the house, she missed Trystan with an intensity that was hard to block out. That was when she was most tempted to call him.

They hadn't had any contact since she'd left. Guilt niggled at her that she hadn't messaged him to let him know they'd arrived home safely as she'd promised. Instead, she'd messaged Mirren to let her know they were home and thanked her again for a wonderful summer.

Adjusting to it just being the two of them was hard, and made more difficult by Ellie's frequent questions about when they'd see Trystan again – and Mirren and Kit.

Ellie's first day back at school gave Beth a break from the questions, but it wasn't long before having so much time to herself bothered her far more than Ellie's questions ever did. It also reminded her that she needed to figure out what she was going to do for a job.

The first day back at school left Ellie worn out and irritable. From the moment Beth collected her, everything was wrong. After making the wrong dinner and serving it on the wrong plate, Beth sent Ellie up to play in her room, hoping it would give them both some respite.

She was emotionally drained when her phone rang, but the sight of Mirren's smiling face when she answered the video call perked her right up.

"You don't mind me calling, do you?" Mirren asked, once they'd got the greetings out of the way. "I kept thinking of Ellie going back to school today and wondered how she'd got on."

"Of course I don't mind you calling." Beth was touched that Mirren was thinking of them. "I think school was fine, but Ellie's in a terrible mood. It was tiring for her."

"It'll take her a while to settle back into the routine. Can I say hello to her?"

"Yes. She'd love that. Hang on a second." Upstairs she found Ellie sitting on her bedroom floor with her dolls spread around her. She scowled at Beth when she glanced up but brightened when she realised Mirren was on the phone.

"How was school?" Mirren asked her.

Ellie held the phone in her lap and stared down at it. "Okay. But Sophie had pink nails with pictures of butterflies on them. I want some too but Mummy took me to the shop after school and they didn't have them."

"Oh!" Mirren sounded taken aback and mildly amused.

"Daisy said she has nail stickers at home too and she's going to wear them tomorrow. It's not fair that I don't have any."

"I said you could have the ones in the shop," Beth put in.

Ellie glanced up at her. "They weren't the right ones, Mummy!"

"Was everything okay apart from the nail situation?" Mirren asked lightly. "I'll bet your teacher was glad to see you again."

"My teacher is very nice," Ellie said, then wittered away for a few more minutes until Beth took the phone back from her.

"Kids are funny," Mirren remarked as Beth wandered across the landing and into her bedroom to perch on the edge of the bed. "What was all that about the nails?"

"Apparently nail art is a hot new trend with five-year-olds. Evidently I'm not cool enough to figure this out before the first day of term. I looked online but whatever I suggest is wrong. Everything was wrong this afternoon."

"She'll be fine in a few days."

"I know. We're both missing our lazy beach days. We had it too good over the summer, that's our problem."

"Have you and Trystan been in touch?" she asked tentatively.

"No." Beth tried to sound nonchalant but suspected she missed the mark somewhat. "We agreed we'd need time to settle back into normal life." She smoothed the duvet beside her. "He flew back to London today, didn't he? I bet you'll miss having him around."

"He ended up going back on Friday."

"Really? I thought his flight was today …"

Mirren looked suddenly unsure of herself. "He had to change his plans. He took the ferry back on Friday."

"Oh." Beth fought the urge to ask questions. It hit her hard that she no longer knew what was going on with him. It was her own fault though. She could get in touch with him if she wanted. "I guess it makes it a long trip. Getting from Penzance to London must be a bit of a trek."

"Yes." Mirren cleared her throat. "Anyway, he's made it back to London. I'll give him a call later and see how he got on being back in the office today. Speaking of which, have you given any more thought to what you're going to do jobwise?"

"Not really. I still have two weddings lined up, so I'm putting off doing anything about it until after that. I suppose I should really think about it and make some decisions."

"Don't rush into anything. If you can afford to take your time, it makes sense to do that."

"I suppose it's a bit lazy of me to not be working now that Ellie's back in school."

Mirren's features drew serious. "You've had a difficult year. You're not being lazy. Give yourself time."

"Thank you." Beth smiled into the phone. "And thank you for calling. It's so lovely to talk to you."

"My house seems incredibly quiet since you two left. And not in a good way! Though Kit and Seren came over for dinner last night, so that was nice."

They chatted away for another ten minutes. Beth loved hearing about the rest of the family, and felt a knot in her stomach when she heard about the guests who had arrived that day to stay in Peswera Cottage.

"I should let you get back to Ellie," Mirren finally said. "She'll probably need an early night after the excitement of the first day of school."

"I think I need an early night too," Beth said. That probably wouldn't happen though, since Dee was coming over later to catch up and celebrate the kids being back at school.

By the time Beth had battled to get Ellie settled, she was happy to have Dee to drink wine with and vent about how difficult Ellie had been.

"All kids are the same after the summer holidays," Dee said, reclining back on the couch. "She just needs time to adjust. Ferne's been the same this afternoon. Everything I did or said was wrong. She was still wide awake when I left. Hugh's going to have a frustrating evening with her no doubt."

"How are things with Hugh now?" Beth took a long sip of wine and set her glass on the coffee table.

"Okay. He's been coming over more." She shook her head. "He's not moving back in, that's for sure, but it's kind of nice having him around."

"That's good."

"Have you spoken to Trystan since you got back?"

"No."

Dee scrunched her nose up. "Why not?"

"Because I think it's probably better if we leave what we had as a nice holiday thing and not try and drag it out to something more than that."

"So you haven't had so much as a message from him?"

"No." Beth stared into her wine. "But…"

"But what?"

She shrugged. "I promised I'd message him to let him know we got home okay … but I messaged his mum instead."

"Why?"

"Because I knew that if I messaged him, messaging him would become a thing. Then messaging would turn into phone calls and phone calls would lead to him coming to visit us."

"I take it he was keen to keep seeing you then?"

"Yes."

"You're an idiot. You realise that right?"

"I have Ellie to think about. Having Trystan show up every now and again will confuse her."

"No, it won't." Dee rolled her eyes. "If you explain that Trystan lives in London and can't be here all the time, Ellie will absolutely understand that."

"It's completely unrealistic to think we can maintain a long-distance relationship." Beth rested her elbow on the arm of the chair. "Especially since my life is exactly what he didn't want with his ex. He doesn't want to settle down and have a family. Which is what he'd be getting with me. I miss him like crazy, but that will fade."

"Or maybe it won't." Dee flashed her a smug smile. "You might miss him forever and spend the rest of your life wondering what might have been."

"He hasn't even messaged me anyway. He's probably forgotten all about me already." She reached out to give Dee's leg a playful slap. "Stop rolling your eyes at me."

"Stop saying stupid things then!"

"Let's not talk about Trystan. I need to stop thinking about him and settle back to real life." She curled her lip. "Figuring out what I'm going to do for work would be a more productive use of my mental energy."

"I thought you could afford to take some time off. You said you could easily take the rest of the year off …"

"I can, but watching my savings dwindle isn't exactly fun. Besides, I need something to occupy my mind."

"So set up a website with your new services and start advertising."

"What are my services going to be though?"

"School photography, professional head shots … workplace photography … anything that you can do during school hours."

"It seems like such a step down from wedding photography."

"It's a sidestep, that's all. And it's only temporary. Ellie won't be this little for long. In ten years she'll be self-sufficient and you can do whatever you want."

Beth rested her head on her hand on the arm of the couch. "Don't say that. I don't want her to grow up."

"I'm afraid that's one thing you really have no control over." Dee smiled mischievously. "But you do have control over whether you see Trystan again. Send him some flirty messages to make up for you blanking him since you got home."

"You were supposed to distract me from my urge to get in touch with him, not encourage it."

"Just do it," Dee pleaded.

"I need to think about it," Beth said. "It's probably a bad idea."

"Thinking causes all sorts of problems. If I were you I'd give it up."

Beth wished it was that easy. All she seemed to be able to think about was Trystan, and no matter how much she pondered what to do she couldn't reach a definite conclusion. The rational part of her brain told her she was living in a dreamland if she thought it could be anything more than a holiday fling, but that was overshadowed by the fact that she missed him so much.

It seemed impossible to Trystan that he'd ever enjoyed wearing a suit. Arriving home on Tuesday evening, he began to undress the moment he walked through the door. Once he'd changed into a pair of shorts and T-shirt he felt he could breathe again. Sitting at the kitchen island, he read the messages from his brothers that he'd avoided looking at all day. As he'd suspected, his group chat with Kit and Noah consisted mainly of photos intended to taunt him. Pictures of Porthcressa Beach and Old Town Bay with comments about how they hoped Trystan's view was just as good.

He smiled at the most recent messages sent an hour ago. Kit had sent a photo of his beer on the bar in the Mermaid Inn, then Noah had sent a similar one with a glass of water and slice of lemon along with a message about it being more to Trystan's taste.

Hate you both, he replied, wondering how long they'd keep up with their campaign to get him to move back there permanently.

At least *someone* missed him.

With his phone still in his hand, he flicked into his messaging chat with Beth, scrolling to read their last messages before switching to his camera roll to torture himself with photos of her and Ellie. Finally, he tossed the phone aside and contemplated going for a run. He hadn't been to the gym that morning so he probably ought to. Jogging in the city wasn't appealing though, and he flopped onto the couch instead, only moving when his phone rang an hour later. He was tempted to ignore it, but on the off-chance it was Beth he forced himself to the kitchen for his phone, then didn't have the heart to ignore his mum's call.

"I meant to call last night," she said as he took himself back to the couch. "But Keira called in for a drink and a natter. It was too late by the time she left."

He made a noise of acknowledgement.

"How is it being back in the office?"

"Okay," he mumbled, massaging his temples.

"You don't sound too thrilled."

"It's fine. Same as ever."

"Have you spoken to Beth since you got back?"

His jaw clenched. "No."

"Why not?"

"Because she didn't seem keen to have a long-distance relationship. And if she wasn't clear enough on the fact that she wanted to get on with her life and forget about me, she didn't even bother to message me when they got home like she said she would."

"Maybe you should have messaged her to check they'd got home safely …"

"No," he said through gritted teeth. "Because she messaged you deliberately so I'd know they got home. She just didn't want to be in touch with me."

"Just message her," Mirren said with an air of exasperation. "You obviously miss her and I'm sure she misses you too."

"How did you reach that conclusion? Clairvoyant now, are you?"

"No!" She sighed heavily. "I was chatting to her last night …"

Trystan squeezed his eyes shut as he shook his head. "What … Why?"

"I wanted to see how they were doing and find out how Ellie got on at school."

"So you just called Beth?"

"Yes. You press a few buttons on the phone, wait for her to answer, then talk. You should try it!"

"Did she say she missed me?"

"Not in so many words."

"What *did* she say?"

"Just asking if you were back in London yet. I almost put my foot in it there. I mentioned that you'd got the ferry back. She seemed curious as to why, but I changed the subject quick. I didn't want to start talking about Jenny with her."

Trystan's gaze automatically roamed to the cardboard box at the side of the room that contained the dinner set Lowen had made for Jenny. When she'd called and asked him to transport it back for her, he'd agreed without much thought. He'd known as soon as he'd picked it up from Lowen there was no way he could take it on the plane given the weight of it. At Jenny's pleading he'd taken it on the ferry instead. He'd then stupidly declined her offer to pick him up from Penzance, saying he could get the train.

"That bloody dinner set weighs a ton. I've got blisters on my hands from where the box cut into my fingers. Carrying that and my luggage was a nightmare."

"I'm sure Jenny appreciates it."

"I hope so. She hasn't picked it up yet." He leaned back on the couch, propping his feet on the coffee table. "What else did Beth say?"

"I can't remember. Why don't you call her if you want to know what's going on with her?"

He let out a low growl. "Is Ellie okay? Was she happy to go back to school?"

"Yes, I think so." She chuckled. "She's so funny. The things she comes out with make her sound like a teenager sometimes."

"Why, what did she say?"

"Telling me about a girl at school who had nail stickers. Ellie wanted some the same, but Beth took her shopping and they couldn't find the right ones. Beth said she had a tantrum in the shop."

"Nail stickers?" He chewed on his bottom lip. "What is that? Instead of nail varnish?"

"You put the sticker on after nail varnish. Nail art."

"What was it that Ellie wanted that they couldn't find?"

"Butterflies, I think she said."

"I can probably find some. There'll be more choice in the shops here."

Mirren laughed. "Or you could just call them for a chat if you're so keen to be in touch with them."

"Can you give me Beth's address? I'll go shopping after work tomorrow and put something in the post for her."

"I'm not sure if I should really share confidential guest information with you."

"Mum! Don't be annoying."

"Message Beth and ask for the address."

He squeezed the bridge of his nose. "You know Beth won't mind. Can you please just give it to me?"

"Fine. I'll find it and message it to you."

"Thank you."

When he hung up, it was with a small smile on his face as he imagined how excited Ellie would be to receive post.

He couldn't be certain that Beth would get in touch to thank him. But he suspected she probably would.

CHAPTER TWENTY-EIGHT

A fter managing to get through the week without contacting Trystan, Beth felt her resolve wane on Friday morning. She was slightly stung that he hadn't been in touch with her, which was ridiculous given that he was only doing exactly what she was. And she was the one who'd promised to message and hadn't.

As she walked home from taking Ellie to school, she contemplated having a glass of wine that evening and calling him. She probably shouldn't though. There was a definite chance he'd settled back into his life in London without giving her a second thought. It crossed her mind to call Mirren instead and try to find out if Trystan had said anything about her. Squeezing his mum for information was pathetic though.

"Hello!"

The deep voice dragged her from her thoughts and she smiled at the postman standing outside the house. She thanked him as he handed over a couple of envelopes and a small parcel. With her key in the door, she caught the return address on the parcel and almost dropped everything.

Muttering to herself, she pushed the door open and deposited her keys and the rest of the post onto the hall table. The parcel was addressed to Ellie with Trystan's name and address written clearly as the sender.

"What have you sent?" she mumbled, giving it a gentle shake as she took it to the kitchen. The desire to open it was overwhelming, and she had to stop herself a few times. She even contemplated opening it and then closing it up again, but decided she'd just have to wait until Ellie got home.

The day stretched out before her and the few household jobs she had to do didn't distract her nearly enough. She caught herself smiling to herself throughout the day and felt a spark of hope. Trystan hadn't forgotten about them after all.

By the time she collected Ellie from school, Beth was almost beside herself. Thankfully, Ellie walked slightly faster than usual once she heard there was something exciting for her at home.

"What is it?" Ellie asked, climbing up to the kitchen table to peer at the package.

"I don't know." Beth fetched the scissors. "Trystan sent it. We have to open it to find out."

They opened it together and Ellie's eyes lit up at the set of nail varnishes and multiple packets of nail art stickers.

"These are the ones I wanted, Mummy!" Ellie waved the butterfly stickers in Beth's face.

"He sent a letter too," Beth said, plucking the envelope from the box. "Do you want to open it?"

"No." Ellie spread out the packets of stickers. "I want to look at these. Can I put some on now?"

"Yes. But you should open this and see what Trystan said." She checked the package in case she'd missed something for her, but apparently he'd only sent stuff for Ellie.

"You read it," Ellie said without looking up.

Hastily, Beth opened the envelope and unfolded the single sheet of paper. Her heart felt as though it was taking up more space in her chest as she read his writing.

"Dear Ellie. I thought you might like these nail stickers. Make sure you make Mummy's nails look pretty too." She smiled widely, knowing that she was going to end up with tiny animals on her nails and imagining the mischievous twinkle in Trystan's eye when he wrote it. "I hope school is going well. Lots of love, Trystan." The three kisses after his name made tears well in Beth's eyes and she clutched the letter to her chest.

"When is Trystan coming to our house?" Ellie asked, still scouring through her treasures.

"I don't know if he is."

"He said he would."

"When did he say that?"

"At Mirren's house. I asked him and he said he'd come." Her gaze shifted to Beth. "He said maybe. But that means yes, I think."

"It doesn't really mean yes or no."

"I think he meant yes. Can you call him and ask him?"

"He's probably at work. Let's do our nails and call him later so you can say thank you."

"I'll ask him when he's coming to our house, too."

"I suppose you could if you want." Beth pulled the chair out and sat down with Ellie.

"How did he know about the butterflies?" Ellie asked, showing them to Beth again.

"I think Mirren probably told him."

"Can we call Mirren today too?"

"Yes."

"Can I call Kit as well?"

She smiled lightly. "I suppose so. Just a quick call though. He might be busy."

"He'll like to talk to me, Mummy. He thinks I'm very important, remember?"

"Yes. I remember." Beth picked up the pack of nail polish bottles, deciding which colour she wanted.

They spent a good half hour giving each other manicures, then called Mirren to show her the results. She didn't seem at all surprised by Trystan's gift for Ellie, and it only then twigged with Beth that he would have had to ask her for the address.

"Can we call Trystan now?" Ellie asked when they got off the phone to Mirren.

Beth checked the clock on the microwave. "I think he'll probably still be at work." While she wasn't overly concerned about disturbing him, it would be annoying to call when he didn't have time to chat.

"Kit then. Or will he be driving the train?"

"No. I think he'll be finished for the day." He'd sent Beth photos from the kids' club so she had his number saved. She just hoped he didn't find it too strange for them to call him. Of course, she was worrying about nothing and he seemed genuinely excited to hear from her.

When she passed the phone over to Ellie and she told him about her new nail stickers, he insisted they switch to video so he could see. He and Ellie chatted away for ten minutes, and Beth smiled at the ease of the interaction.

"Do you want to come to our house one day?" Ellie asked eventually, making Beth wince.

"I'd love to," Kit said breezily. "I can't leave the train at the moment though."

"Keira could drive the train," Ellie said. "She won't mind."

"Kit can't leave Seren," Beth said, leaning into the frame to help Kit out with the conversation.

"She can come too," Ellie said confidently, much to Kit's amusement.

Beth rolled her eyes. "How about we say goodbye to Kit and let him get on with his evening."

"What are you having for dinner?" Ellie asked him.

"I don't know. I'm going over to Seren's place. I think she's cooking."

"See," Beth said. "We really have to let Kit go. Poor Seren's waiting for him."

"Yep," he agreed. "If I keep her waiting too long I'll be in trouble!"

For a moment, Beth had the feeling that he was making a reference to her not being in touch with Trystan, but when his smile fell away it was clear from the slight panic in his eyes that he hadn't intended that at all.

"You definitely shouldn't keep her waiting." Beth tried to smile despite the awkward subtext.

"It was really good to talk to you both," Kit said, his natural smile returning.

"You too."

There was a lot of waving and grinning at the screen before they finally got off the phone.

"Now can we call Trystan?" Ellie pleaded.

Glancing at the clock again, Beth realised she wasn't only worried about him being at work, but that he'd been annoyed with her for not getting in touch sooner.

"Let's get some dinner first," Beth said. "Then we'll call him."

Trystan had two missed calls from Kit. He called him back as soon as he got home from work on Friday, putting the phone on speaker and dropping it on the bed so he could get changed while he waited for the call to connect.

"What's up?" he said when Kit answered.

"I spoke to Beth."

Trystan pulled on a pair of shorts, wondering if he'd heard right. "You did what?"

"She called me earlier."

"Beth called *you?*" Roughly, he pulled a T-shirt over his

head, shoving his arms into it before snatching up the phone. "Are you kidding me?"

"No. I think it was Ellie's idea. She wanted to show me her new nail stickers."

"I sent the nail things," he growled, walking back to the living room.

"Yeah. She told me that."

"Why the heck did she call you and not me?"

"I'm not sure."

"Did Beth say anything about me?" He ran a hand through his hair as he sat on the couch.

"Not really. But I said something stupid and it got a bit awkward …"

"About me?"

"Not really." He sounded as though he was speaking through gritted teeth. "I was talking about Seren, but I said something about how she'd be annoyed if I kept her waiting too long … it totally sounded as though I was making a comment about you."

"What did she say?"

"Nothing really. I don't understand why she hasn't been in touch with you. Why don't you just call her?"

"I don't know." He flopped back on the couch. He'd really expected that she'd get in touch when they received his parcel, but maybe she really was set on not seeing him again. The thought made his chest tighten. "I can't believe she called you and Mum, but not me."

"Sorry," Kit said. "Your phone's doing something weird. I keep hearing beeps like there's another call coming through. If it's a work call ignore it. Also if it's Noah, ignore it. Or Mum. Don't hang up on me for any other family members."

Trystan sat up straight and stared at the phone.

"Are you still there?" Kit asked.

"It's Beth."

There was a momentary pause. "You can hang up on me for Beth," Kit said. "Call me back later, okay?"

"Okay." He swallowed hard as he pressed the button to switch the call. The hairs on the back of his neck stood on end at the sound of her voice quietly saying hello. "Hi," he replied, then smiled at the sound of Ellie in the background asking for Beth to show her the phone.

"It's not a video," Beth told her.

"Do a video, Mummy, then I can see Trystan."

"Sorry," Beth said into the phone. "Do you mind if we switch to video?"

"No. It's fine." There was a momentary pause before Ellie's smiling face appeared on his screen. "Hi!" he said, grinning back at her. "How are you?"

"I've got butterflies on my nails." She twirled around, making her image blur.

"Show me …"

The screen blurred again as she waved a hand in front of the screen. "I can't see them. Stay still!" Beth's hand appeared, directing Ellie's hand so he could finally make out her nails. "I love them," he said.

"Say thank you," Beth whispered.

"Thank you!" Ellie shouted, then laughed.

"How was your first week back at school?"

"Good."

"What did you learn about?"

"I don't know. But we had chips for dinner today."

"That's weird. I thought you always eat healthily when you're not on holiday."

Beth's gentle laughter in the background made every muscle in his body relax. He sank happily into the couch.

"There's nothing wrong with a Friday treat," Beth said from somewhere over Ellie's shoulder.

"Do you want to come to our house one day?" Ellie asked.

He smiled into the phone, unsure how to answer. He'd get in the car immediately if Beth gave him the green light.

"Give me the phone for a second," Beth said, before her face filled the screen. "Hi."

"Hi."

"Thank you for Ellie's nail things. She loves it."

"She's very welcome."

Beth glanced away before looking back at him. "I should have got in touch sooner." She bit down on her lip. "I wanted to … but …"

"It's okay," he said, letting her off the hook. "It's just nice to hear from you."

"It's really nice to see you." The corners of her mouth pulled to a smile.

"Mummy!" Ellie shouted. "Can I talk to Trystan again?"

"Okay." She smiled at Trystan. "Have you got time to chat?"

"Yes."

He had all the time in the world, and for the next hour Ellie kept up a running commentary while proudly giving him a tour of the house and her toys. Beth and he managed a disjointed conversation in between Ellie's chatter.

"You look tired," he told Ellie when she yawned for the second time in five minutes.

She rubbed at her eye. "I'm not."

"You always say that. Then you fall asleep in about two minutes flat."

Beth appeared beside Ellie. "I should get her into bed." From her tight smile he suspected she was as reluctant as he was to get off the phone. Or maybe he was just seeing what he wanted to see.

"I have no plans for the evening," he said, nerves twisting his gut. "If you feel like calling me back later."

"I'd like that," she said.

"Great." His relief felt almost palpable. "I'll talk to you later then. And I'll talk to you another day, Ellie."

"Okay."

He blew her a kiss and the screen turned to a blur of pink as she kissed it in reply.

"Talk to you later," Beth said, her smile lingering in his mind even after she hung up.

All the stress of the last week vanished and he lay back on the couch with the feeling that the world made sense again.

CHAPTER TWENTY-NINE

As soon as Ellie was tucked up in bed on Friday evening, Beth called Trystan back and they spent the entire evening on a video call. There was no mention of the time since they'd left Scilly. No questions about why she hadn't been in touch like she'd promised. Talking to him was as easy as it always had been.

She then spent the weekend thinking of him more than ever and wanting to message him about every part of her day. With effort she held out until Sunday, when they exchanged a flurry of messages which spilled over into the beginning of the week. When they spoke on Wednesday evening, Trystan's question about her plans for the weekend felt loaded.

If it weren't for the wedding job in Falmouth on Saturday, she was sure she'd have invited him to visit them. Seeing him through the phone screen wasn't nearly enough.

Beth's nerves about the wedding steadily increased over the week. She spoke with the couple again to confirm everything, which should have put her mind at ease since they both seemed very relaxed. Nevertheless, having such a long break had shaken her confidence.

On Friday afternoon, Beth fired off a message to Dee

reminding her that she'd be on her doorstep at six o'clock in the morning to drop Ellie off. She half expected a reply telling her that Ellie should come for a sleepover to save them all the early morning, but there was no reply at all. It didn't even seem as though Dee had received the message. Beth waited half an hour before calling Dee's mobile, and then the house phone. There was no answer on either, and Beth slowly began to panic. It wasn't like Dee not to pay attention to her phone.

Once Ellie was ready for bed, Beth tried Dee's mobile again, but it seemed to be switched off. She was probably out somewhere and the battery had died. No doubt she'd call as soon as she got home. The niggling feeling that something was wrong stayed with Beth as she read Ellie's bedtime story and settled her down for the night.

She was pacing the kitchen when her phone finally rang and she scrabbled to accept the call.

"I'm so sorry," Dee said in a rush. "I had the afternoon from hell and I only just saw your calls."

Beth sank onto a chair. "What happened? Where are you? You sound strange."

"I'm in the children's hospital with Ferne. We were at the swimming pool this afternoon and she slipped and cracked her head open."

"Is she okay?"

"She needed a few stitches and they're keeping her overnight for a suspected concussion."

"Are *you* okay?" Beth asked, trying to focus on Dee while in the back of her mind she was wondering how she'd be able to look after Ellie tomorrow.

"I've acquired a few more grey hairs but I'll survive."

"Are you staying in the hospital with Ferne tonight?" Beth's heart was beating faster, knowing there was no way Dee would be able to have Ellie for the day.

"Yes. Hopefully, she'll be able to go home tomorrow."

"I hope so," Beth said, trying to sound sympathetic. "The poor thing."

"Is there someone else you could ask to look after Ellie tomorrow?"

"Um …" Beth wasn't sure there was but couldn't exactly say that. "I can ring around her school friends.

"I'm sorry. Maybe I can ask Hugh to have her if you're stuck …"

"No. He'll want to be with you. Don't worry about it. Just focus on Ferne. I'll figure something out."

Dee apologised again before they ended the call. There were only two of Ellie's school friends whose mums Beth knew well enough to ask them to look after Ellie for the day. The first had a family day out planned and the second had dance lessons and a visit with grandparents.

As she sat on the couch, Beth leaned onto her knees and pondered what on earth she was going to do. She tried not to dwell on the fact that her mum should be there to take care of Ellie, but it was hard not to go there.

She smiled sadly when a message came from Trystan asking how the rest of her week had been. Slowly, she tapped out a reply saying it had been fine until that afternoon when it had gone downhill quickly.

The phone rang immediately and she felt overwhelmingly emotional as she answered the video call.

"What's wrong?" Trystan asked, the skin around his eyes crinkled in concern.

She swallowed the lump in her throat and inhaled deeply in an attempt to keep her tears at bay. "Dee can't look after Ellie tomorrow. I've called around a couple of her school friends to see if anyone can look after her, but they're all doing family stuff. Plus, I guess no one really wants to look after someone else's child from six o'clock on a Saturday morning." She'd expected him to be sympathetic but he went silent. "I'll have to take her with me."

"You're going to take her with you?" His brow creased. "To the wedding?"

"I suppose there's finally something positive about me getting out of the wedding business – I don't need to be concerned about developing a bad reputation."

Trystan shook his head. "You can't take Ellie with you while you photograph a wedding."

She caught a tear at the corner of her eye. "I'll tell her she's my assistant and make a game of it. It'll be fine. It's just made me miss Mum."

The sympathy in his eyes did nothing to calm her emotions. "I could look after Ellie," he said.

The offer wasn't a complete surprise, but it also wasn't a practical solution. "The wedding is tomorrow," she told him. "And you live in London."

"I realise that. I can set off now."

"You wouldn't get here until midnight, or later."

"So?"

"I can't ask you to do that."

"You're not asking – I'm offering."

The thought of seeing him in a matter of hours made her heart leap, but it would also complicate everything. If she was going to see him it would have been better if she'd come to that conclusion without the childcare dilemma. "I don't know," she whispered. "It's a really long drive for you … and then you'd have the entire day with Ellie. It's sweet of you to offer but—"

He cut her off. "Let's not pretend I'm being completely self-less here. I'm using the situation to my advantage so I get to see you both. If you don't want me to come you're going to have to stop with your flimsy excuses and tell me you don't want to see me."

"I can't do that," she said as a tear ran down her cheek.

"Good. I'll throw a few things in a bag and be there as soon as I can." His reassuring smile only induced more tears. The mixture of relief at not having to take Ellie to work with her and excitement at the thought of being with Trystan was a lot to deal with. "Go to bed," he said gently. "Just make sure your phone isn't on silent; I'll call when I arrive."

"Thank you," she spluttered while swiping tears from her cheeks.

Even though she was sure there was no chance of sleeping before he arrived, Beth got changed into her pyjamas and curled up on the couch to wait for him. Sometime after midnight, she drifted out of a light sleep to check once again that the ringer was turned up on the phone. At the same time, the room was illuminated by headlights on the road and she stumbled off the couch and to the front door.

"Hi," she whispered loudly at the sight of Trystan getting his phone out as he stepped from the car.

The noise of the car door closing and the subsequent click of the lock sounded incredibly loud on the quiet street. But it was nothing compared to the thudding of Beth's heart as Trystan walked towards her with his sports bag slung over his shoulder.

He picked up his pace on the front path and held her gaze with quiet intensity until he crashed right into her, lifting her off her feet as he kissed her eagerly. With her body moulded to his, the scent of him filling her nostrils and the taste of him on her lips, she couldn't think of a single reason why she'd tried to keep him away.

"You'll freeze," he muttered, his lips pulling to a radiant smile as he walked her backwards into the house and closed the door behind them.

She kept her arms hooked around his neck and her body pressed against his. "I missed you."

"Really?" He dropped his bag to the floor before pushing her back against the wall to continue kissing her.

"Why do you sound as though you don't believe me?" she asked breathlessly between kisses.

His lips barely left hers as he spoke, the feel of his breath on her lips making her head spin. "It took you a long time to call. And you only called then because I sent that stuff for Ellie."

Their lips met again before she broke away to speak. "That was pretty manipulative of you – sending Ellie stuff to get me to call."

"That's not why I sent it."

"Liar," she murmured, while his mouth moved to her neck, bringing a fresh rush of desire. "You knew I'd have to call to say thank you."

"Not true. I added the return address so Ellie could have written a thank-you note. There was no obligation to call."

"So you didn't just send it hoping I'd call."

"No," he said breathlessly. "I sent it because my mum told me Ellie wanted nail stickers, and I knew she'd enjoy getting post." He drew back slightly, quirking an eyebrow. "Nice that you called my mum, by the way. I heard you spoke to Kit too. I was last on the list."

When his lips sought hers again, she drew back. His small smile hadn't hidden the hint of bitterness in his tone. "I wasn't trying to hurt you."

Inhaling deeply, he pushed the hair from her face. "I'm not really annoyed. It's fine. I just missed you."

"I missed you too." She touched her forehead to his as her breathing slowed. "If it was only about me I'd have had no hesitations, but I'm worried about how it will affect Ellie to have you around. I don't want to confuse her."

"Were you really annoyed with me for sending her the nail stuff?"

"No. It was sweet."

He scrunched his nose up. "I was *hoping* you'd call to thank me. But it's not as though that was the *only* reason I sent it."

"I know." Smiling, she kissed him again, slowly this time, savouring the scent and smell and feel of him. Eventually, she suggested they take their reunion upstairs where she savoured him even more.

It took Beth a while to figure out it was her alarm that was interrupting her sleep. And then another moment to remember she had to get to Falmouth to photograph a wedding. The thought of it brought a rush of adrenaline that jolted her upright. Trystan released a low groan when she switched the lamp on, then went back to sleep while she showered and got herself ready. Her equipment was waiting in the hallway, and she checked through it again while she waited for the coffee machine to produce a coffee for her takeaway mug.

When she was sure she had everything ready and had loaded up the car, she sneaked back upstairs, lingering on the landing as she pondered whether to wake Ellie. With her brain whirring, she went back to her bedroom and perched beside Trystan to gently nudge him awake. The sight of his bare chest made her smile.

"You're going to need to put some clothes on," she told him. "Ellie will be surprised enough to see you without finding you naked."

Chuckling, he roused himself and got dressed. "I might need to invest in pyjamas," he said, flopping back onto the bed in a pair of jeans and a T-shirt.

Beth couldn't help but smile at the idea that waking up with Trystan in her bed might become a regular occurrence.

"I don't know what to do about Ellie," she told him, grimacing as she checked the time. "Shall I wake her now or leave her to sleep?"

He shifted onto his side and propped himself on his elbow. "Will she freak out when she wakes up to find me here and not you?"

"I don't think so. I imagine she'll be over the moon to see you, and I'm sure she'll be very happy to have you to herself for the day." She chewed her lip. "She usually doesn't wake up until between eight and nine. If I wake her now, she might end up being grumpy for you all day."

"Whatever you think," he said.

"I also need to leave really soon to make sure I'm not late." She blew out a breath. "I think I'll just go. I'm sure she'll be fine. That way you both get to sleep longer."

"What happened with Dee, by the way?"

"Ferne fell at the swimming pool and ended up in hospital." Beth made a mental note to message Dee later to see how everything was.

"Ouch. Is she okay?"

"Yeah. Just needed to stay overnight to be on the safe side." She leaned down and kissed him. "Thank you so much for this. You're a lifesaver."

"Have a good day." He smiled and gave her another quick kiss. "I'll see you tonight."

CHAPTER THIRTY

Trystan's fog of sleep lifted quickly when he rolled over in bed to find Ellie staring at him.

"Hi," he said gently.

"Where's my mummy?" she asked with a trembling lip.

He sat up in a rush and reached out to her, but she shrank back until she collided with the wall.

"It's okay," he said. "Mummy had to go to work, so I'm going to look after you today."

Ellie shook her head and scowled. "I'm going to Ferne's house when Mummy goes to work."

"Yes. That was the plan, but Ferne fell over and had to go to the hospital, so I said I could look after you instead."

Tears pooled on Ellie's lower lids before spilling down her cheeks. She turned and fled before he could say any more, and he followed her to her bedroom, where she curled up on her bed.

"It's okay," he said, lingering in the doorway.

"Ferne's hurt and Mummy's gone," she sniffed, hugging a teddy to her chest.

"Ferne's fine." He silently cursed himself. Why had he told her that her friend was in hospital? "And Mummy will be back later. I'll be here with you until she gets home. We can play and do whatever you want …"

"I want Mummy."

"Okay." He glanced behind him in a panic. "How about we call Mummy? That's a good idea, isn't it? She can explain that everything is fine." At the slight drop of her shoulders he backed out of the room. "I'll get my phone …"

When Beth didn't answer, he left her a message asking her to call back.

"We just have to wait a little bit," he told Ellie nervously. "Mummy might still be driving or busy with work, but she'll call back really soon and you can talk to her." He wanted to comfort her but was nervous of making the situation worse. After pacing the landing a few times, his phone rang and he swiped a finger over the screen before pressing it to his ear. "I'm sorry. There's a bit of a problem."

"I take it that means you can't meet me this morning after all?" The prickly voice didn't belong to Beth.

He grimaced as he remembered he'd told Jenny she could come over to his place that morning to pick up her dish set.

"I was about to set off," she said accusingly. "Would you even have let me know if I hadn't called?"

"Sorry. I'm kind of in the middle of something."

"What's going on? You sound weird?"

"It's a long story." He shook his head, wondering the best way to get her off the phone. "You can still pick up your stuff. You have your key. Help yourself and leave the key when you go …"

"Trystan," she growled. "What's going on with you?"

"Nothing. I just can't talk now." He set off pacing again at the sound of Ellie crying softly. "You'll probably need someone to help you carry the box," he said to Jenny. "It's heavy. I struggled with it."

"I'll come another time instead," she said wearily. "I also wanted to talk to you."

"Just call me sometime."

"I want to speak to you in person. There's something I need to tell you. It's important."

His phone beeped with a video call from Beth. "Come another day then. Whatever you want. I need to go though. Sorry." He hung up on Jenny and connected with Beth.

"Is everything okay?" she asked.

"Yes." He shook his head. "No. Ellie freaked out about you not being here, then I stupidly mentioned that Ferne is in hospital. She's really upset. I don't know what to do."

Beth sighed gently. "I should have woken her up before I left. Just let me speak to her. I'm sure she'll be fine."

He held the phone out to Ellie, who took it from him and scooted back along the bed.

"Hey, sweetheart," Beth said soothingly. "I had to go to work when you were still asleep. But Trystan's going to look after you today. That's nice, isn't it?"

Ellie glanced up at Trystan, apparently unconvinced. "Ferne's in the hospital," she said, sniffing loudly.

"She's fine though. The doctors made her all better. We can visit her tomorrow and you'll see she's okay. Just a bumped head."

"When are you coming home?" Ellie asked.

"Today. It might be after dinner time. I can call you again later if you want. But you'll probably be having too much fun with Trystan, won't you?"

She shrugged and eyed him warily.

"Give the phone back to Trystan," Beth prompted. "I have to go to work, but I promise you'll be fine and I'll be back later. Trystan will look after you." She looked at him apologetically when he took the phone back. "I'm sorry, I have to go. I think she'll be fine though. I'll call again when I get a minute."

"Thanks," he said, slipping the phone into his pocket when she disappeared from the screen. He took a step into Ellie's room and smiled at her. "Are you okay?"

Her chest hitched as she started to cry again. "Who's going to make my breakfast?"

"I will," he said, crouching by the bed. "Toast with loads of jam, right?"

She nodded solemnly and wiped tears from her eyes.

"Can you help me find the bread and the plates?"

She nodded again. "You'll need a knife and the butter too."

"Shall we go down and make it now?"

"Okay," she whispered, sliding off the bed and giving him another uncertain look before leading the way downstairs.

It took the entire morning and another phone call from Beth for Ellie to warm up to Trystan again. In the afternoon she was back to her usual self and bossing him around the place, insisting on one game after another. Since the weather was so nice, they ended up in the garden, playing a game of chase before Trystan insisted he needed a rest and flopped into one of the patio chairs.

"What are we going to eat for dinner?" he asked when Ellie climbed onto his lap. He'd made sandwiches for lunch but noticed the fridge was pretty bare.

"I don't know," Ellie said.

He checked his watch. "We could go out to eat …"

She nodded. "I like chicken nuggets at McDonalds."

"Let's see how far it is." He checked on his phone. "It's too far to walk and I don't think I can take you in my car without a child seat."

"You can't," she agreed while he continued searching the nearby area on his phone.

"There's an Italian place not far away. How does pizza and pasta sound?"

"Good. But can I ride on your shoulders so I don't have to walk?"

"Go on then." He shuffled her off his knee and picked up the spare key before they set off out the door.

The food in the restaurant was decidedly average but the

staff were friendly and Ellie enjoyed her spaghetti bolognese and ate a slice of Trystan's pizza too.

Her stream of chatter, which had been constant that afternoon, began to fade, which he took as a sign that she was getting tired. While Trystan paid the bill, she wriggled down from her chair and leaned her head on his arm.

The young waitress smiled down at her while she handed over the receipt. "Someone loves their daddy, don't they?" She gave a breezy smile before waltzing away.

"I think we ought to get home," Trystan said, smiling tightly as he tapped Ellie's nose. "It'll be bedtime soon."

She kept quiet until they were outside, where she asked if he'd carry her. There was something unnerving about the way she stared at him as he walked with her on his arm, and he wondered if he ought to have said something about the waitress's remark. Not that he had any clue what he'd say. Maybe Ellie hadn't even heard. She was probably miles away in a daydream.

They were halfway home and she'd tangled her fingers into his hair when she finally spoke.

"Are you my daddy?"

He shifted her onto the other arm and felt a tug at his hair roots before her fingers broke free. "No. I'm not."

"The lady in the restaurant said you are."

"She just guessed because we were together … people like to guess things about other people."

"You didn't tell her you aren't my daddy."

"No." He puffed his cheeks out. "She'd already walked away. And I'm not sure what I would have said anyway," he muttered under his breath.

"Why not?" Ellie asked. "You could tell her you're just Trystan and not my daddy."

"She would have thought that was strange. I'd have had to say 'I'm your mum's boyfriend'."

"Why didn't you say that?"

"I don't even know if it's true." He shook his head. "I'm friends with your mum … but I don't know if … I just don't know."

She stroked his hair affectionately. "You don't know very much, do you?"

"It certainly feels that way at the moment."

"That's okay." Resting her head against his, she continued to stroke his hair. Briefly, Trystan thought the conversation was over. Until she drew back to aim a piercing stare at him.

"I don't think I have a daddy," she said.

"No," he replied softly. "You don't." He decided that getting into technicalities probably wasn't appropriate.

"Why don't I?"

"Not everyone has a mummy and daddy."

"Do you have a daddy?"

"Yes, but he died."

"Did my daddy die?"

Trystan winced and picked up his pace, hoping that arriving home would put an end to the conversation. "No, he didn't." He had no idea what else to say on the matter and was fairly sure this entire conversation was what Beth was talking about when she mentioned not wanting Ellie to be confused.

"I just don't have one?" Ellie asked.

"That's right. All families are different."

"A boy in my class has two mummies."

"See! Some people might have two daddies. Or just live with their daddy. Some kids might live with grandparents." He was about to mention step families and half siblings before deciding that would probably inspire more questions. "Some people have brothers and sisters," he said instead. "And some people don't."

"You have lots of brothers," she stated.

"I have four brothers."

"I'd like a brother."

He raised an eyebrow. "Would you?"

"Yes. Kit."

A burst of laughter bubbled out of him. "What?"

"I'd like Kit to be my brother. He'd be the best brother in the world. You're very lucky."

"He's a very good brother," he agreed, then set her down as they reached the house.

As he drew the key from his pocket, Ellie tipped her head back to look up at him.

"You're a boy," she stated, matter-of-factly.

"Yep." He smiled down at her as the key clicked in the lock.

"You must be Mummy's boyfriend. If you're a boy and her friend."

"I suppose so … maybe …"

She stepped inside, ahead of him. "Does that mean Kit's my boyfriend?"

"No. He's just your friend."

"That doesn't make sense," she mused.

He shook his head, completely lost as to how to explain the world to a five-year-old. "Would you like to watch TV for a while?"

"Yes, please." She beamed at him and he breathed a sigh of relief that he'd brought the conversation to an end.

CHAPTER THIRTY-ONE

A fter feeling increasingly nervous about the wedding, the panicked phone call from Trystan at the start of the day should probably have unsettled Beth even more. As it was, she put it out of her mind, assuming that Ellie and Trystan would be okay and that worrying otherwise wasn't going to help anyone.

She slipped automatically into professional mode as soon as she greeted the bride, and everything went smoothly from there. When she found a moment to check up on Trystan and Ellie later, they were fine, as she'd suspected.

The day went by in a blur of dresses, confetti, speeches and dancing. Once she'd taken the formal photos, directly after the ceremony, she relaxed even more. The afternoon photos were informal ones of the speeches and a few of the dancing. The excitement of the day stayed with Beth as she left the venue, where the guests were really getting into the swing of the party.

Before setting off for home she quickly checked in with Trystan. She also called Dee and was relieved to hear that Ferne was back at home and on the mend.

The house was quiet when she arrived home. In the kitchen, Trystan was bent over his laptop but leaned back in the chair, leaving room for her to perch on his lap and drape her arms around his neck.

"It's very nice to come home to you," she told him happily. "I presume Ellie's already in bed?"

"Yes. She went out like a light."

"That's good. How was your day?"

"Fine." His smile didn't cover the flash of nervousness in his eyes.

"What was that look for?" she teased. "Were you subjected to one of Ellie's tantrums?"

"No." His smile widened but still didn't reach his eyes. "She was really good."

"I'm not sure I believe you. If you had a stressful day you can say so …"

"You already know the small matter of Ellie waking up to find you not here and me dealing with that by giving her the news that her friend is in hospital…" He raised an eyebrow. "Once she recovered from that, we were pretty much all good."

She decided not to dwell on the fact that he'd only said *pretty much* all good. "Sorry. I really should have woken her before I left. I don't know what I was thinking."

"It was fine in the end," he said dismissively.

"Did you find something to eat here?" she asked, glancing around the kitchen and realising she'd given no thought to food since she'd expected Ellie to be at Dee's place.

"We went out for dinner. Found an Italian restaurant not far away."

"You took Ellie in a restaurant that wasn't a fast-food place?" Beth asked, amused at the thought of the two of them out for dinner.

"Yep."

"I presume she was well behaved for you?" Beth was unnerved by his slight hesitation. "Oh god. Was she a nightmare?"

"No. Of course not. She was fine." He tightened his arms around her waist. "How was your day?"

She had an inkling there was something he wasn't telling her but decided not to push him on it. If it was important he'd say. "Really good." She wrinkled her nose, thinking about how beautiful the wedding had been. "It made me a bit sad that I can't do that any more."

She brightened immediately, determined not to dwell on it and remembering what Dee had said about it not being forever. "A change might be good. Maybe I can find something I like just as much as wedding photography. If not, I can come back to it when Ellie's older."

Trystan looked thoughtful. "You still have one more wedding lined up, right?"

"Yes, in two weeks. The editing and post-production stuff takes me a couple of weeks too so that means I can put off looking for more work for a while longer."

"Will Dee look after Ellie next time?"

"Yes." She paused, wondering if he'd offer, then felt slightly disappointed when he didn't. Maybe Ellie really had been hard work and it had put him off looking after her in future. She told herself she was being paranoid and cast a quick glance at his laptop. "Were you working?"

"Yes. But it's nothing important." He closed the lid decisively.

Beth trailed her fingers across his brow. "You look tired."

"I'm very tired." The light came back to his eyes as his lips pulled to a flirty smile. "I probably need an early night."

"I've had a very long day. I might need an early night too …"

His hand moved to the back of her neck and he drew her close. "I was hoping you might," he murmured, right before their lips met.

~

The following morning, Beth woke with a smile on her face that vanished when she realised she was alone in the bed. Thinking Ellie must have got Trystan up, she headed downstairs in search of them, only to find Trystan staring at his laptop at the kitchen table with a look of concentration on his face.

"Are you working on a Sunday morning?"

He startled at her voice.

"Sorry. I didn't mean to make you jump." She bent to kiss his cheek. "I assumed Ellie had woken you. Is she up?"

"She's still asleep."

"Why did you get up then?" She felt a pang of rejection that he'd passed up an opportunity to snuggle in bed. "Do you have that much work on?"

"Not really. I just woke up early." He closed his laptop and turned in his seat when she moved to set the coffee machine running. "And then I wasn't sure if it would be weird for Ellie to find us in bed together."

Beth frowned. "I don't think it would be an issue."

"Maybe I was overthinking it …" He tapped on the tabletop, his gaze intense for a moment before his features softened. "Are you making coffee?"

She'd stopped with the grounds in her hand but moved again at his prompting. As she filled the water tank for the machine, she looked out of the kitchen window, where an airplane divided the pale blue sky with its vapour trail.

"How come you didn't fly back from Scilly?" she asked, remembering her conversation with Mirren. When he didn't reply, she couldn't figure out if he hadn't heard or if he was deciding how to answer. "Your mum mentioned that you got the ferry. Doesn't that make it a long trip for you?"

"Yes … But I had a lot of stuff to bring back. The weight limit on the plane is restricting."

She set the coffee machine running, then turned to face him, leaning back against the sideboard. "What did you have that was so heavy?"

"A bunch of Lowen's pottery," he said with a nervous smile.

Beth's eyebrows darted upwards. "The set for your ex?"

"Yeah."

"I didn't realise you were bringing it back for her."

"Neither did I until the last minute."

The thought that they'd been in touch bothered Beth. As did the fact that they were obviously still on good terms if Trystan had changed his plans to accommodate her. "Did she like the plates?"

"She hasn't picked them up yet. I think she'll come to collect them next weekend."

Beth busied herself getting mugs out of the cupboard. "Did you also leave St Mary's earlier than planned?"

"Yeah." He sneaked up behind her, making her smile when he slipped his arms around her waist. "It was no fun being there after you left."

Setting the mugs aside, she turned in his arms and softly kissed him. "It's so lovely having you here," she told him.

"I like being here," he said, giving Beth the perfect opportunity to ask if it would happen more regularly.

Before she could get a word out, she was interrupted by footsteps on the stairs, then Ellie running in and launching herself into Beth's arms.

"I missed you," Beth said, squeezing her daughter and inhaling the scent of her hair.

"I missed you too, Mummy."

"Were you very good for Trystan?"

"Yes. I think so." She looked to Trystan for confirmation.

He'd taken over with the coffee but paused and smiled at her. "You were."

Ellie beamed proudly at Beth.

"You're getting far too heavy for me," Beth said as she set Ellie down and took her drink from Trystan.

Ellie stared up at him. "Are you going to live here now?"

"Um …" He opened his mouth a few times, then glanced nervously at Beth.

"Trystan just had a sleepover with us. Like you and Ferne have sleepovers sometimes."

Seemingly satisfied by the answer, Ellie moved to the table and clambered onto a chair. "What's for breakfast?

"Toast or cereal," Beth said, distracted by Trystan, who was staring into his coffee. "Or I could make eggs if you want?"

His head pulled up slowly as he registered she was talking to him. "What?"

"For breakfast … eggs?"

Ellie stared up at Trystan. "I like dippy eggs. Mummy makes good dippy eggs."

"I'm a talented chef," Beth joked.

"I can make pancakes if you want," Trystan said.

"Yes!" Ellie hopped off the chair to stand beside him. "Can I help?"

"Okay."

"What are we going to do after breakfast?" she asked him, while Beth pulled flour from the cupboard.

"I can't stay too long," he said, surprising Beth, who'd assumed he'd stay for the day. "I've got a meeting tomorrow that I need to prepare for."

Beth ignored the knot in her stomach. The fact that he wasn't his usual cheerful self wasn't necessarily anything to do with her and Ellie. Maybe this was just how he was when he was tired. He can't have slept well the last two nights, so it could just be that.

As the morning went on, she couldn't shake the feeling it was more than tiredness. She was keen to talk about their future but there was no opportunity with Ellie around. Her previous reluctance to embark on a long-distance relationship had been entirely erased and she hoped spending weekends together would become a regular thing.

After lunch in a local cafe, Trystan packed up his things and they wandered outside with him to say their goodbyes.

"Will you come and visit us again?" Ellie asked and Beth smiled gently as she waited for his reply.

He slung his bag into the boot and seemed to be contemplating how to answer. "I hope so," he finally said as he bent to hug Ellie.

"You're always welcome," Beth told him.

His lips curved to the same tight smile that he'd been sporting for most of the morning. "Thanks." He hugged her hard enough that she should have been reassured of his feelings for her, but she couldn't help but wonder if it was more of a "goodbye forever" hug than a "see you soon" kind of hug.

"Thank you so much for coming," Beth said, trying not to let her emotions overwhelm her as she gave him a lingering kiss.

"Talk to you soon," he said as he got into the car.

As Beth watched him leave the knot in her stomach twisted even tighter. Beside her, Ellie tugged on her arm as she bounced on the pavement.

"Mummy," she said, drawing Beth's attention. "Did you know that Trystan isn't my daddy?"

She closed her eyes as she sighed, suspecting she might have an idea why Trystan had been in such a strange mood. "Yes. I did know that. Did you ask him by any chance?"

"Yes. I did. He said he's not my daddy, but I think he might be wrong … there are a lot of things he doesn't know … he doesn't know if he's your boyfriend."

"Did he say that?"

"Yes. He thinks he's probably not your boyfriend."

"Right …" Beth led Ellie back towards the front door. "Trystan definitely isn't your daddy. It sounds as though you had some very interesting conversations with him."

"Yes." Ellie skipped ahead, then turned back inside the doorway. "I'd really like to have a brother."

"Okay. That's good to know." Her mind was spinning,

wondering what on earth Trystan was thinking after being subjected to Ellie's probing questions.

"Can I have a brother, Mummy?"

"I don't know. Probably not." She wondered if she'd talked to Trystan about that one too. Sighing again, she closed the door behind her. "How about we go over to see Ferne later and bring her some sweets to make her feel better?"

It would be good to see how Ferne was doing, and it would give Beth a chance to chat everything through with Dee.

CHAPTER THIRTY-TWO

With the editing work for the wedding photos, Beth had a busy week. It was absorbing enough that it took her mind off Trystan for a few hours a day. Sadly, there were a lot more hours in the day, and worrying about Trystan filled most of them. By Friday she felt as though she was going out of her mind and took Ellie over to play with Ferne again after school so she could vent to Dee.

"Something is definitely wrong," she said, while Dee made them tea.

"I don't understand why you don't just ask him straight out what's going on."

"I know what's going on … Ellie freaked him out with her questions and he realised that a holiday romance was one thing and real life is something entirely different. And the reality is not something he wants."

"You don't know that though. That's just the story you've created in your head. You need to ask him."

Beth dropped her head to her hands. "It was a little difficult to ask him anything since the couple of times I've spoken to him this week, he's conveniently had a lot of work to do and hasn't been able to chat for long."

"So just call him and ask him directly what's going on."

"I'm not sure I want to know what's going on. The fact that he's been avoiding speaking to me all week is a pretty big clue that he doesn't want to be with me." She pouted as a wave of sadness washed over her. "I miss him." What with him and her mum, she felt as though she spent all her time missing people. She was sick of it.

"Tell him that." Dee joined Beth at the table. "Why not go for a spontaneous weekend in London? You can leave Ellie with me if you want …"

"Thanks, but I can't."

"Why not?"

"Because I need him to decide what he wants without any pressure from me. I'm the one with all the baggage – if he can't deal with that, it's better for all of us if he figures that out now."

"From what I've heard about him, it doesn't sound as though a few questions from Ellie would put him off."

"He was definitely keen until he spent the day with her. That's when everything got weird."

"Men are so annoying. Why can't they just communicate properly?"

Beth tapped the side of her mug, suddenly tempted to drive to London and demand to know where she stood. Her mood dropped further when she remembered another reason she couldn't do that. "I can't go this weekend anyway," she said. "He's meeting up with his ex."

"He told you that?"

"Yeah. When I spoke to him yesterday, I asked him if he had weekend plans. To be honest I was hoping he might suggest coming to visit again. He said his car's being serviced, which I kind of took to mean that he might have come otherwise … but then he casually mentioned that his ex would come over at some point to pick up some stuff."

"They were together a long time, right? I don't think you

need to read too much into that. And the fact that he told you is a good thing. He's not hiding it."

Beth almost wished he *had* hidden it. She wasn't sure she'd managed to hide her jealousy on the phone. Plus, she was probably going to spend the entire weekend thinking about him with his ex.

"Do you really think I should go over there?" She ran her hands down her face. "I think we need to speak in person and I don't think I can wait another week to do that."

"Go then."

"I don't know … he's been so distant on the phone this week. I suspect he'd tell me not to come, then I'll feel even worse than I do now."

"Don't ask him then," Dee suggested. "You have his address, right? Turn up and surprise him. It'll be super romantic."

Beth leaned back in her chair, glancing at the ceiling. "That's surprisingly tempting."

"Wow. I expected you to laugh at the idea. I like it when you're spontaneous."

"I can't go right now though." She glanced at the kitchen clock. "I'd be driving in the dark and I'll probably end up lost in London. I'm going to ponder the idea, but I might go first thing in the morning. Are you sure you'd be okay to have Ellie?"

"I strongly suspect you're going to change your mind between now and tomorrow morning, but I'm very happy to have her."

Not bothering with the gym on Saturday morning, Trystan made a quick trip to the local bakery to pick up pastries in preparation for Jenny coming over. Her message earlier in the week insisting she needed to speak to him had left him intrigued. Usually, she wasn't the type to be unnecessarily mysterious, but it certainly didn't sound as though she wanted a general catch-up.

The doorbell sounded at eleven o'clock on the dot and he was on his way to answer it when the lock clicked. Jenny stepped inside, an intensity to her gaze as she stared at the key in her hand.

Finally, she looked up at Trystan. "I suppose that's the last time I'll do that. It feels weird."

"I'll bet," Trystan said, though it hit him that he wasn't particularly attached to the place. It felt like a part of his past. Which didn't make a lot of sense, considering it was his current home.

"How are you?" he asked as they moved through the living room.

"Fine, thanks."

"There's your crockery." He pointed to the box at the side of the room. "It weighs a ton. I spent most of the way from Bryher to here cursing you."

"Sorry. I shouldn't have asked you to bring it."

"It's fine. I managed. Do you want a coffee?" He continued to the kitchen. "I bought you a chocolate eclair from the bakery on the corner."

"You shouldn't have." She remained in the living room, looking slightly pained as she swept a hand through her blonde hair, changing the line of her parting.

"I thought you wanted to talk, but if you haven't got time don't worry about it."

"You're going to be really angry with me," she said quietly. "But I need you to know that I'd never hurt you intentionally."

"What are you talking about?" Leaning on the counter, he felt a jolt of nerves deep in his stomach.

She walked quickly to the other side of the island, a look of desperation in her features. "Please don't think I've done this to spite you or anything."

"What have you done?"

Slowly, she raised her left hand, the sunlight flashing on a large diamond.

Blinking a few times, Trystan managed to suppress a laugh. "You got engaged?"

"Yes. It all happened quickly and I know people will think it's crazy, but it feels right. I've been dreading telling you." She glanced at the box of stuff from Lowen. "I probably should have told you before you carted all that stuff back for me."

He stared at her. "Did you purposely not tell me because you thought I wouldn't bring it back for you?"

"No." She grimaced. "I was nervous of telling you. And I wanted to do it in person."

"Who are you marrying?" he asked as he moved to the coffee machine.

"Nathan Wadsworth." She grimaced again.

"Nathan who you work with?"

"Yes. I know this will all sound terrible. I swear to you that nothing ever happened before you and I broke up, but I did have feelings for him, which was part of the reason I knew I had to end things with you."

"Okay," Trystan murmured.

"I'm sure lots of people will think I'm being spiteful, that you wouldn't marry me so I found someone who would, but it's not like that." She spoke fast enough that Trystan didn't even try to get a word in. "I think you were right about marriage not being the right thing for us. Our relationship was so easy and comfortable, but there was always something missing. The thing that makes you want to dive in and take chances and never let go of each other no matter what." She took a breath. "I'm waffling, but the point is that with Nathan everything feels different. It feels one hundred percent right. I have no doubts."

Trystan put a coffee in front of her then moved to sit beside her when she shifted onto a stool. "I understand," he said flatly.

"You understand?" She eyed him incredulously.

"Yeah."

"I thought you'd be furious." Her shoulders sank as she

sighed. "I've been panicking about telling you because I thought you'd be upset."

"Would you rather I was upset?"

"No." She gave his arm a gentle shove. "I'm surprised you're so calm. I don't know why – you always take everything in your stride."

He tapped the countertop. "I met someone this summer, while I was on St Mary's. A woman was staying at Mum's place with her daughter and we got close."

"You got close to the daughter?"

"No. Sorry, that was a bad explanation. The daughter's five years old. I got close to her mum, Beth. We had a thing …" He trailed off, not entirely sure how to describe it.

"A fling?"

"Yes, but also more than that. I love her."

"You do realise the irony of you telling me you don't want kids and then falling for a woman with a kid?"

"It's been pointed out to me."

She tilted her head. "It was never that you didn't want kids, was it? You just didn't want kids *with me*."

"Yeah," he replied, an apologetic smile pulling at his lips. "I didn't really know what I wanted before. But with Beth … it's the same way as you feel about Nathan. I have no doubts."

"I think I always suspected it was children with *me* that was the issue, not children in general."

"I'm sorry," he said quietly.

"It's okay. We weren't right for each other. Maybe we should have admitted that sooner. I'm glad we both found the right person in the end."

"It's not that simple for me," Trystan said. "Beth and Ellie live in Plymouth. I thought we could have a long-distance relationship for a while and see how things go … but Beth was worried about it being unsettling for Ellie. I thought it was an excuse but now I think maybe she has a point."

"How come?"

He ran his hands over his face. "I went over last weekend and looked after Ellie while Beth was working. In the space of a day, I think I traumatised the poor child and possibly caused her lasting psychological damage …" He took a deep breath before recalling the events of the day, including how badly he'd handled her being upset in the morning and the many awkward conversations.

"It doesn't sound so bad," Jenny said when he came to the end of the story. "She sounds like an inquisitive kid. All kids ask questions."

"But I answered them all wrong! Ellie asking so many questions about her father is probably exactly the confusion Beth wanted to avoid."

"I doubt it. She was bound to ask eventually."

"But I didn't give her very informative answers to her questions, did I? Plus, she's probably going into school telling her teachers she's got a twenty-two-year-old boyfriend called Kit! Social services will be knocking on the door before we know it."

"You're being ridiculous." Jenny rolled her eyes in amusement. "What did Beth say about it?"

He closed his eyes, then peeked out of one. "I should have told her, shouldn't I?"

"Trystan!" She gave his shoulder a shove. "Of course you should have told her. Why didn't you?"

"I kept thinking about saying something, but I feel as though it will cause issues. She'd already told me she was worried about us being together because of how it would affect Ellie. I wasn't overly keen to admit she was right."

"Idiot," Jenny said lightly. "You need to talk to her about it. If nothing else, she should know that Ellie was asking questions about her father."

He leaned his elbows on the counter, letting the weight of his head stretch his neck. "When we were on holiday everything was easy. I looked after Ellie on St Mary's and it was fine, but Beth was right that it wasn't real life. In the real-world Ellie asks me questions that I've no idea how to answer and ..." He trailed off.

"And what?"

He let out a long breath. "If Beth and I are together I'm going to be a huge part of Ellie's life … What if I continue to have no idea how to answer her questions, or I answer them wrong? What if I get *everything* wrong?"

"I think the fact that you're worried about getting things wrong is a sign that you'll be fine. I have no doubt that you're great with her. And Beth must think so too or she wouldn't let you look after her."

"I guess so." He frowned. "I really need to talk to her properly. I've been avoiding the conversation all week, but she clearly knows something's going on."

"Well, pass me that chocolate eclair. Once I've polished that off and finished my coffee, I'll head off and leave you to call her."

"There's no rush," he said, as he went to get plates and the paper bag with pastries.

She was looking at him intently when he turned back to her. "I was expecting this morning to be stressful and awful. This is nice."

"It is."

"Have you got a photo of Beth?" A hint of a smile flickered at her lips. "Obviously, if she's younger and prettier than me I don't want to see."

"She's older than you," Trystan said, unlocking his phone and gazing at the screensaver photo of Beth and Ellie. "And beautiful." Switching to the camera roll, he handed the phone over.

"Oh, they're cute." While she swiped through the photos, Trystan peered over her shoulder to give a running commentary.

He was proudly regaling Jenny with his sandcastle-building skills when the phone vibrated in her hand and the photo of Beth and Ellie on the beach was replaced with a call from Beth.

"I'll tell her I'll call her back," he said as he took the phone.

Jenny was murmuring about leaving when he put the phone to his ear, but she was soon drowned out. It was hard to hear Beth given the bustle in the background, but he knew instantly that something was wrong.

"Are you all right?" He moved away from Jenny. "What's going on?"

"I'm in London." Beth's voice was garbled and he struggled to make out what she was saying. "I'm in such a mess. Can you help me?"

His heart went into overdrive as he told her to calm down and explain what was going on.

CHAPTER THIRTY-THREE

After not hearing from Trystan on Friday evening, Beth had a disturbed night's sleep and woke up even more determined to sort things out with him. She couldn't take a weekend of wondering where she stood.

When she got bored of waiting for Ellie to wake up, she went into her bedroom to pack an overnight bag for her.

"What are you doing?" Ellie asked when she stirred.

"You're going to play with Ferne today," she said. "And have a sleepover with her tonight. That's exciting, isn't it?"

"I don't want to play with Ferne." She sat up in bed. "I want to play at home."

"I'm afraid you can't. I need to go to London, so I need you to be really good and stay at Ferne's house. Okay?"

"Okay, Mummy." She sounded weary enough that Beth had a pang of guilt over having woken her.

"I just need to pack a few things, then we'll have breakfast and I'll take you to Ferne's house." When she went to her own room, Ellie followed, curling up on the bed to watch her throw a change of clothes into her bag. She felt slightly giddy at the thought of seeing Trystan and called Dee while she pondered what else to pack.

"I'm going to do it," Beth said excitedly when Dee answered the phone. "I'm packing a bag and going to see Trystan. Is it still okay for me to bring Ellie to you?"

"Um ..." The hesitation wasn't a good sign. "You *can* bring her here ..."

"I'm sensing a but ..."

"I'm so sorry," Dee said. "I feel as though it's just one thing after another at the moment. Ferne spent most of the night vomiting. She seems to have finally stopped and she's sleeping now. I guess she'll sleep for most of the day. So Ellie can come over, but it'll probably be a TV day."

Beth's heart sank. "Poor Ferne. You must be exhausted too. Of course you can't have Ellie. Is Hugh going to come over to help you today?"

"Apparently he has the same bug so he's out of action too."

"Do you need me to help with anything?"

"No. We're fine. I just feel terrible for messing things up for you."

"Maybe it's a sign that I shouldn't go."

"Don't be daft. You could always take Ellie with you."

"It's like a five-hour drive. That long in the car wouldn't be fun for either of us."

"Take the train. You can get directly into London and it's pretty quick."

"I might look into it. If the train schedule works out I'll take it as a sign to go. If not, we'll stay put."

"Let me know what you decide. But I really think you should go if you can. A little weekend adventure will be fun."

After ending the call, Beth sank to the edge of the bed and opened a browser on her phone to check the train timetable. There was a train leaving in an hour. It took three and a half hours to get to Paddington Station, which was a lot faster than driving.

With a jolt of determination, Beth turned to Ellie. "Would you like to visit Trystan today?"

"Not really, Mummy."

"You're still half asleep, aren't you?" Beth smiled gently. "By the time you wake up properly, you'll think it's a good idea. We can go on the train, and we'll get to see where Trystan lives. There are lots of fun things to do in London."

"Can we go to the shop where Trystan bought my nail stickers?"

"I think there are probably more fun things we can do, but we could also ask Trystan about that."

"Can I take my nail stickers so I can do Trystan's nails?"

"Yes. And you should take toys and books for the train. Grab a few things for your backpack. We'll need to leave soon."

Ellie moved annoyingly slowly while Beth encouraged her to get ready and eat some breakfast. They should have had plenty of time but ended up dashing onto the train just in the nick of time. It was a relief to find that it wasn't busy and they got four seats and a table to themselves. With her colouring book and crayons, Ellie was kept quietly entertained for the first hour, then they killed a little more time going to the buffet car.

"Aren't you hungry?" Beth asked when Ellie lacked enthusiasm for the snacks they'd picked out.

"Only a bit," she said, taking another bite of the muffin before picking up her carton of orange juice.

Beth sipped her coffee. "Do you want to do more colouring?"

"No. Are we nearly at Trystan's house?"

"It's still a bit further. We'll have to get a taxi from the train station when we arrive in London." It struck her that the surprise approach might be utterly foolish. She told herself that if things went wrong, they could find a hotel for the night and do some sightseeing, then shook the thought from her head. There was no way Trystan would turn them away. He'd be delighted to see them. Beth imagined his face lighting up at the sight of them on the doorstep.

"It's a very long way," Ellie said, breaking Beth's thoughts.

"Not really. And it's nice being on the train, isn't it?"

"I don't know," Ellie said, unconvinced.

"Shall I read you a story?"

"Yes, please." Ellie slouched in her seat as Beth read to her. Then she switched to quietly looking out of the window while Beth finished her coffee and polished off the snacks.

The closer they got to London, the more she grappled with doubts. What if Trystan really wasn't pleased to see them? She'd be left heartbroken and stranded in London. In an attempt to quieten the noise in her head, she messaged Dee. They had a short exchange before Beth got frustrated and called her instead.

"Tell me this isn't the most stupid thing I've ever done," she said in a panic. "Because it's really starting to feel like it. What if he's not happy to see us? He was distant with me all last week … maybe I should have taken that as a hint to back off, not force myself on him."

"Being a bit distant can mean anything. From what you've told me it's more likely he was just tired and stressed. You said he was having a busy week with work."

"Yeah." Beth let out a long breath. "That could have been it."

"And last weekend he was definitely happy to see you again?"

"Yes." She thought of how eager he'd been to visit and how enthusiastic he'd been at seeing her again. "Okay. This is good. I feel calmer. But do you think I should call him and give him a heads up?"

"How far away are you?"

"Another half an hour or so I think … then I think it's about twenty minutes in a taxi from the station."

"I like the idea of surprising him."

"Me too … I just wish I could know for definite he'll be happy about it." She frowned and tapped the tabletop. "What if we arrive and his ex is there?"

"She's only picking some of her stuff up, right? What are the chances of her being there exactly when you arrive?"

"I've no idea." She pushed her palm into her forehead. "Why am I putting myself through this?"

"Because you love him, that's why."

"Yes. I do." She glanced at Ellie who was watching the fields and trees go by. "I really do. I need this to go well."

"It will. How's the train trip been?"

"Surprisingly easy. Ellie's been as good as gold and hasn't complained of being bored once. How's Ferne, by the way?"

"Tired and quiet, but she's managed to eat something, so I guess we're over the worst."

"That's good."

"I better go and check on her, but keep me updated with how you get on."

She promised she would, then switched her attention to Ellie as she put her phone away. "We'll be there soon," she told her. "Are you excited to see Trystan?"

"Not really."

Beth's eyebrows knitted together. "Why not? I bet he's going to love seeing you?" She hoped so anyway.

"My tummy feels funny."

Automatically, Beth put her hand to Ellie's forehead while wondering how long her cheeks had been so flushed. "You feel quite warm," she remarked at the exact moment that Ellie lurched forwards and vomited all over the table.

For a moment, Beth froze. Until Ellie's crying jolted her into action and she attempted to comfort her while making a poor attempt at clearing up sick with a few napkins and a travel pack of baby wipes. As the stench of vomit permeated the stuffy air, most of the passengers around them made a quick getaway to other carriages. A woman with a small child passed her another packet of baby wipes before telling her she'd find the conductor.

By the time the conductor arrived, Ellie had also vomited over the gangway and a chair. Apologising profusely, Beth ushered Ellie into the tiny toilet cubicle where she peeled her soiled clothes from her and put fresh ones on, all the while reassuring her she was fine and she'd feel better soon. Beth washed her hands in the trickle of water from the tap, then turned back to Ellie who threw up again, managing to cover them both.

After getting clean clothes on them both and turning the sick-covered ones inside out to put them in the bag, Beth insisted Ellie stay by the toilet until they arrived. She'd only packed for one night so they were now out of clothes. Ellie had a pair of pyjamas but Beth hadn't even remembered to pack any for herself.

She poked her head out of the toilet to apologise again to the conductor and hand him a twenty-pound note which didn't even come close to compensating him for his task.

The only good thing about the stink of vomit around them was that people moved out of the way for them on the platform while Beth struggled to carry Ellie and their bags outside to the taxi rank. Almost as soon as she opened the door of the black cab, the driver turned his nose up at the smell which was mostly coming from their bag of vomit-covered clothes. They probably didn't have much hope of him letting them in the car, but any chance they had of convincing him was dashed when Ellie threw up on the pavement.

"My tummy hurts," Ellie whimpered as the taxi drove away with another passenger.

"I know." Beth set their bags down and lifted Ellie into her arms, then pulled her phone from her pocket and hit dial on Trystan's number. She only had a moment to ponder what she'd do if he didn't answer. His voice made emotions creep up from her chest, bringing tears to her eyes and making her throat so tight she could barely speak.

"Can you pick us up?" she asked, after giving him a garbled rundown of the situation. "I don't think any taxi is going to take us … you won't have a car seat for Ellie but it's not too far, is it?"

"No … it's not far, but the car seat isn't as much of an issue as the fact that I don't have my car … it's being serviced."

"Oh my god." Beth's arm ached from holding Ellie. "I'll have to put you down for a minute, sweetie. You're too heavy." She'd just bent to set her down when Ellie puked all down Beth's front. It dripped into her cleavage via her V-neck top. "Trystan?" she whispered into the phone.

"Yeah, I heard. Send me your location and I'll be there as soon as I can."

She didn't ask how he'd manage that without a car. She didn't care how he got there as long as she had someone to help her figure out what to do. A guy buying a coffee from a nearby kiosk gave her a wad of napkins and a sympathetic smile. She was too dazed by the situation to thank him. Not that napkins were much help, given the amount of vomit dripping down her front. Feeling queasy herself, she attempted to clean up the worst of it, then lifted Ellie again, who was crying pitifully.

"Trystan will be here soon," she told her, hoping desperately it was true.

Fifteen minutes later a black BMW pulled up at the taxi rank and switched its hazard lights on. When Trystan stepped out of the passenger seat, Beth had never felt such relief in her life.

"We're covered in sick," she warned him as he approached. "Ellie won't let me put her down and my arms are killing me."

Ignoring the state of them, he leaned around Ellie and kissed Beth's cheek. "We'll get you cleaned up and back to my place. Everything will be fine."

"I don't have any more clean clothes for either of us," Beth spluttered through tears. Blinking them away, she noticed the perfectly put together blonde-haired woman hovering in front of them.

"This is Jenny," Trystan said. "She's driving."

"Oh god, no," Beth said as Trystan took Ellie from her. "We can't get in your car like this. We're covered in vomit. Everything in the bag is drenched in sick too. We'd ruin your car."

"It's okay," Jenny said. "We brought towels and plastic bags. We'll figure it out."

Both women looked down at Trystan, who was talking softly to Ellie as he carefully stripped her to her underwear. He pulled his hoodie off and put it on her, managing to draw a smile from her as he joked about the size of it.

"I can't get in your car like this," Beth said, looking down at her top.

"Take it off," Jenny said. "You can have my cardi."

"I don't have anything on under it."

Jenny smiled lightly as she peeled her expensive-looking cardigan off. "Do it quick then."

While Beth changed in the middle of the busy pavement, Trystan loaded their bags and Ellie into the car. He covered her with a towel and gave her a bag in case she needed to throw up again.

"I'm so sorry," Beth said, holding Ellie's hand and registering the booster seat she was sitting on. "I wanted to surprise you but now it seems like the worst idea I've ever had."

Trystan twisted in the passenger seat and smiled at them both. "I don't think I've ever had such a smelly surprise." It got another smile from Ellie, whose face was ashen. "It's good to see you," he said to Beth, his tone serious.

"I should have called to check if it was okay for us to come. I'd planned to leave Ellie with Dee but then Ferne was ill... I should have known Ellie would come down with it too. I was grateful that she was so quiet on the train. It never even occurred to me it was because she wasn't feeling well."

"The poor little thing," Jenny said sympathetically as she manoeuvred through traffic.

"Do you have kids?" Beth asked.

"No." She glanced in the rear-view mirror, looking surprised that Beth didn't know that.

"The car seat ..." Beth said.

"Trystan borrowed it from a neighbour," she explained. "Do you mind if I put the windows down?"

"Please do. I feel terrible. Your car's probably going to stink for ages."

"Don't worry about it," Jenny said, seeming genuinely unconcerned.

Trystan reached his hand back and laid it on Ellie's knee while he asked how she was feeling. The smell of vomit made Beth feel nauseous for the entire drive. While she breathed slowly through her nose, she prayed that Ellie wouldn't throw up again. At least not until they were out of Jenny's car.

It seemed to take forever until they were outside Trystan's apartment building.

"I hope she feels better soon," Jenny said, handing Beth the car seat and towel while Trystan carried Ellie and the bags with ease.

"Thanks so much for driving us." After being worried about Trystan spending time with Jenny, Beth was now very grateful for her presence.

Jenny insisted it was no problem and told Trystan she'd talk to him soon before getting back into the car.

"This was the worst surprise ever," Beth remarked, following Trystan into the building and stepping into the lift behind him.

The doors closed when he pressed the button for the third floor. "I'm really glad you're here," he said.

"Are you?" Beth asked, looking sadly at Ellie, whose head was flopped onto Trystan's shoulder.

"Of course."

"You were in a weird mood all week. That's why I came … so we could speak in person." She breathed deeply as a wave of nausea swept over her. "I should just have called."

The lift doors pinged. "I really am happy you're here," Trystan said, leading the way to his door and handing over the bags so he could fish the key from his pocket. "I'm just sorry you had such a nightmare trip."

They switched to practicalities as Trystan led them into the bathroom to get cleaned up. He brought them towels and a couple of his T-shirts for them to wear, then left them and went to put their clothes in the wash.

Beth ushered a reluctant Ellie into the shower cubicle with her. After washing Ellie's hair, Beth put shampoo on her own but hadn't managed to rinse it out before Ellie started to cry. Opening the shower cubicle, she grabbed a towel to wrap around Ellie, telling her to sit on the floor while she finished in the shower.

"Do you need any help?" Trystan called before inching the door open.

"Maybe," Beth admitted.

He scooped Ellie up in her towel. "Let's dry your hair and get you tucked up in bed."

"Thank you," Beth said as he took her out of the bathroom.

Five minutes later, Beth wandered into Trystan's bedroom dressed in her underwear and one of his T-shirts. Ellie was similarly dressed on his bed with a bucket and a couple of towels beside her. Her eyes were drooping as Trystan gently stroked her hair. Once she'd nodded off, Trystan and Beth crept out and into the kitchen.

"I'm so sorry," Beth said, the noise of the washing machine churning behind her.

"It's fine." He wrapped his arms around her and she relaxed into his chest. "Are you okay? You're pale too."

"The sight and smell of all that vomit made me feel queasy," she said, her stomach rolling again at the thought of it. She inhaled steadily. "Jenny seems nice, by the way. I still have her cardigan."

"I'll get it back to her." He paused for a second, looking down at her. "I can post it."

Beth pulled back. "Do you think I'm a crazy jealous person … And I turned up here because I knew you were meeting up with your ex this weekend and I didn't like it?"

"No." His eyes were sympathetic as he gazed at her. "I didn't think that."

"I was very jealous," she admitted with a frown. "I didn't like the thought of you meeting up with her. But I mostly wanted to see you because Ellie told me that she'd asked you if you were her dad … and I think the question freaked you out."

"I was a bit freaked out," he said tentatively.

"You barely spoke to me all week."

"I know. I was just trying to get my thoughts in order." He tilted his head to one side. "Are you sure you feel okay?"

Taking a step back from him, she put a hand over her mouth as another wave of nausea swept up from her stomach. She dashed around Trystan and made it into the bathroom in time to lose the contents of her stomach.

CHAPTER THIRTY-FOUR

The afternoon and evening were an unmitigated disaster. When Ellie woke up and threw up all over Trystan's bed, Beth had little choice but to leave him to clean her up and change the bedding. Her stomach was agony and she didn't dare venture away from the toilet for the next couple of hours. At some point in the early evening she thought she was over the worst of it and crawled into bed beside Ellie, only to end up dashing back to the bathroom several more times.

Trystan kept checking on her and asking if she needed anything, but all she really needed was for him to stay out of the way so he didn't hear her puking her guts up. She supposed it would have been difficult to miss it given the size of his flat. Eventually he made himself a bed on the couch and told her to wake him if she needed anything or if Ellie woke up again.

In the early hours, Beth nodded off and slept fitfully until Ellie woke her up at first light.

"My tummy feels better," she declared, her chirpy tone only making Beth feel wearier.

"That's good," she managed to whisper without opening her eyes.

"Can we still go to the shop where Trystan got my nail stickers from?" Ellie asked eagerly.

"No. Mummy's not very well and you need to rest today." She blinked her eyes open to see Trystan creeping into the room.

"How are you feeling?" he asked.

"Pretty awful."

He set a glass of water on the bedside table, then lifted Ellie from the bed. "Let's leave Mummy in peace."

"Thanks," Beth murmured, then drifted straight back to sleep.

The next time she woke it was the middle of the afternoon and her phone was buzzing around the bedside table. Dee's voice was too loud in her ear when she answered.

"How did it go?" she asked in a rush. "I assume Trystan was happy to see you. Why haven't you replied to my messages?"

"I've been in bed," Beth mumbled.

There was a short pause. "You took Ellie with you, didn't you?"

"Yes." Beth managed a small smile. "I've been in bed because Ellie and I both came down with the vomiting bug."

"Oh, no. At Trystan's place?"

"Yep. Well, it started on the train." She explained everything, including Trystan and Jenny picking them up from the station and how sweet they'd both been about the whole thing.

"So, he was happy to see you?" Dee asked.

"Yes, I think so … he's been really lovely about the situation, but we haven't had a chance to talk." Her mind whirred to their brief conversation the previous evening. "He did say that he'd been freaked out by Ellie's questions last weekend, but he didn't seem bothered now. Although, it's Trystan – he'd be nice no matter what."

"At least you don't have to worry about his ex. If there was anything going on with them he'd never have brought her to pick you guys up."

"I suppose so. I can't think straight now. My head is pounding."

"I'll leave you to sleep. When are you coming home?"

Beth groaned as she realised it was Sunday and Ellie needed to be at school the next day. "I can't get the train back today. Ellie will have to miss school tomorrow."

"They'd probably advise you to keep her at home anyway. This virus is spreading like crazy."

"I need to sleep. I'll talk to you later."

She'd just set the phone aside when the door slowly opened.

"How are you feeling now?" Trystan asked.

"Terrible." She shuffled over when he sat beside her. "My stomach is cramping and my head is killing me."

"That's because you're dehydrated. Drink some water and you'll feel better."

"Every time I tried to drink I threw up again, so I gave up."

"You really need to drink."

"I know. I just don't want to puke again."

"You won't." He took her hand and pulled her to sit up, then handed her the water.

"Do you promise?"

He quirked an eyebrow, looking thoughtful for a moment. "Sure. Why not."

After a few tentative sips, thirst took over and she gulped a few more mouthfuls. "How's Ellie doing?"

"Way better than you. She ate some toast." He stroked the back of her hand as he smiled at her. "She was very annoyed that I wouldn't let her have jam on it. Then we did some colouring and played hide and seek. Oh, and she did my nails." He held up a hand to show off the pale pink polish.

"Cute," she said and lay back down.

"I think we're going to watch a film next. Do you want to join us?"

"I'll come in a minute."

"You don't need to. Go back to sleep if you want. I'll take care of Ellie."

"Thank you," she said, feeling utterly pathetic. "I can't face getting the train back today. Do you mind if we stay over again tonight?"

"I assumed you would. I can pick up my car tomorrow morning and drive you home."

"Really?" She relaxed further into the mattress at the thought of not having to get the train.

"Yes." He squeezed her hand. "Now rest. Give me a shout if you need anything."

As she watched him walk away, she was very glad they'd made the trip to London. As horrible as it had been to deal with Ellie getting sick on the train, she was very grateful that she wasn't at home alone and having to look after Ellie while she was ill too.

Trystan muted the TV when Ellie fell asleep halfway through the film. She was curled up under a blanket, her face the picture of serenity. His eyelids felt heavy too. He'd spent the previous night stirring at every sound in case Beth or Ellie needed him in the night. A nap would've been good, but his phone buzzed on the table just as he was nodding off and he snatched at it so it wouldn't wake Ellie.

"Hi." He spoke quietly into the phone, relaxing when Ellie showed no signs of waking.

"You've been ignoring messages," Kit said. "What happened with Jenny yesterday? Is she pregnant with your baby or what? The suspense is killing us."

Trystan squeezed his eyes shut, then gave a slow shake of his head. "No, she's not. Did you think she might be?"

"Noah and I were guessing why she wanted to talk to you."

"She's not pregnant," Trystan said, rolling his eyes and

sinking back into the couch cushions. "She's engaged to a guy who she works with."

"Wow. That was quick work."

"She seems happy. It was good to catch up with her."

"I'll message her later and congratulate her."

"Are you still in touch with her?" It wasn't much of a surprise. When he thought about it, it was obvious Kit would still be in touch with Jenny.

"It's hardly my fault you pick cool girlfriends. And you realise I was twelve when Jenny came on the scene. I'm closer to her than some of my brothers – I won't name names!"

"I don't have a problem with you keeping in touch with Jenny," Trystan told him lightly.

"Mum's still in touch with her too."

"I thought she probably was." He glanced over at Ellie's sleeping form. "Anyway, Beth and Ellie are here."

"At your place?"

"Yes. They came to surprise me yesterday but Ellie has a stomach bug and started vomiting on the train. Then Beth started with it shortly after they got here." He smiled as he thought back over the past twenty-four hours. "So they turned up covered in puke and I've spent the whole time cleaning and washing and looking after them …"

"You sound pretty cheerful about that."

"That's not all … This morning Ellie spilled coffee all over my work laptop." He'd decided not to mention that to Beth yet.

"You're still sounding very chilled about them puking all over your flat and destroying your stuff."

"I really like having them here … even though objectively it should have been a complete nightmare. It's been a strangely good weekend."

"So it's not just a holiday romance between you two?"

"I don't think so. You can probably stop sending me photos of St Mary's now."

"Because you're convinced about moving back? Should I start sending the photos to Beth instead?"

"No. Beth and Ellie are settled in Plymouth. There's no way they'd move, and I'd never ask them to."

"Don't tell me you're moving to Plymouth?" Kit groaned.

Trystan looked down at Ellie as she stretched her legs out in his direction. Gently, he curled his hand around her foot. "I'm definitely thinking about it."

CHAPTER THIRTY-FIVE

O n Monday morning Beth was roused by the sound of
music from the kitchen and wandered from the bedroom
to find Trystan and Ellie having a dance party. She hung back
and enjoyed a few minutes of watching without them noticing
her. Finally, she couldn't keep her laughter in any longer and
they both glanced up at her. She'd fully expected Trystan to be
mortified at being caught teaching Ellie dance moves, but he
only smiled coyly.

"You look better," he said while continuing to pop his shoulders to the beat.

"I feel it." She raised her eyebrows. "You're actually a very
good dancer."

He turned the volume down slightly. "When I was in
secondary school I went to hip hop classes twice a week after
school."

She grinned. "I bet all the teenage girls loved you."

"I was pretty popular in school," he replied, swinging his
hips in a way that drew attention to the perfect fit of his jeans.
"But not with any of the girls in dance class. They all hated me."

"I find that hard to believe."

"It's true. I got annoyed with them when they got the moves

wrong or if they were out of time. Apparently women don't like being told they're terrible dancers." He beamed as he twirled Ellie around. "The teacher was awesome though."

"Oh god. Did you have a thing with your dance teacher? I'm imagining a Dirty Dancing situation?"

"We're talking about me between the ages of twelve and fifteen. My sexual education didn't start until later than that." He grimaced as he glanced at Ellie, but she danced obliviously. "And my thing for forty-year-old women didn't start until *way* later." Grinning cheekily, he strutted over to Beth and held his hand out. "You up to dancing?"

"Not really." She slipped into his arms regardless, resting her head on his shoulder as they gently swayed together. "I cannot thank you enough for looking after us both."

"You're very welcome."

Ellie did a twirl on her tiptoes, then looked up at Beth. "I spilled coffee on Trystan's computer."

"Hey!" Trystan shot her a warning glance that was full of mirth. "I thought we agreed not to tell Mummy I let you drink coffee!"

"I didn't drink coffee," Ellie giggled. "It was Trystan's coffee."

Beth's eyes widened. "She spilled coffee on your laptop?"

"Yeah."

"Like a few drops or …"

"A whole cup. And I was tired so it was quite a big cup."

She dropped her head back to his shoulder. "I don't even have words."

"In that case, I'll go and get my car and I can take you two home before you wreck any more of my stuff." He poked his tongue out at Ellie as he walked across the kitchen. When Beth called out to him, he looked back and shook his head. "It was my work laptop, and I was probably due a new one anyway. Everything is stored on the cloud so there was no real harm done. Don't worry about it."

After the front door closed behind him, Beth glanced at the pile of their neatly folded clothes on the kitchen island, then down at Ellie. "What do you think? Is Trystan the loveliest man in the world or what?"

"I don't know, Mummy."

"Well I'm fairly sure he is," Beth told her confidently.

The journey back to Plymouth was relaxed and easy. They made a couple of long stops and it was dinner time when they arrived home. Eager to finally have a proper conversation with Trystan, Beth got Ellie ready for bed a little earlier than usual.

"Can Trystan read my bedtime story?" Ellie asked once she'd polished off a glass of milk in the kitchen.

"No," Beth said before he could get a word in. "Trystan's been driving all day. He needs to relax. I'm reading your story."

"Okay." Standing beside Trystan, Ellie raised her arms for him to lift her up then squeezed him tightly. "Can you bring me to school tomorrow?"

"I think so …" He looked to Beth for confirmation.

"We'll both take you," she said before switching the conversation to ask how long Trystan was staying.

"I'll need to head back tomorrow afternoon."

Ellie pulled on his chin to get him to look at her. "Can you do my hair in the morning?"

"Okay."

"Can you do a plait?"

"Um … sure." He gave her a kiss on the cheek, then wished her goodnight and set her down.

Beth pursed her lips. "Can you really plait hair?"

His eyes sparkled as he gave an ambiguous shrug.

Smiling to herself, Beth ushered Ellie upstairs and settled her down for the night. She walked back downstairs ten minutes later to find Trystan stretched out on the couch, his phone propped on his chest emitting a gentle murmur of a woman's voice from the video he was watching. He switched it off and sat up quickly when Beth cleared her throat.

She sat beside him. "Were you watching a tutorial on how to plait hair?"

"Nope." His smile lit up his face. "Definitely wasn't doing that."

"You're very sweet," she said, bumping her shoulder against his. "You're also very confusing. Last week I was convinced you were having second thoughts about being with me because of Ellie, but that really didn't seem to be the case this weekend."

He shifted to face her. "Last week I was freaking out because I thought I was completely out of my depth. You were right that spending time with Ellie on holiday was different to real life."

"And you thought you couldn't deal with it?" Beth asked, confused.

"I thought I was no good at it. When you were at work I felt as though I got everything wrong, but this weekend when Ellie was ill I looked after her fine."

"I'm not sure what you got wrong."

He sank back, running a hand down his face. "She asked me all these questions about her father, which I had no idea how to answer. I completely confused her."

"No, you didn't."

He huffed out a humourless laugh. "You wouldn't say that if you'd heard our conversation. Even *I* was confused."

"Ellie seemed pretty clear on everything when I spoke to her."

"But I didn't know how to answer her questions. And if I wasn't around, she probably wouldn't have been asking questions about her father, would she?"

"I was expecting she'd ask questions at some point."

"And you'd have known how to answer. I got completely flustered."

"I'm not sure what you think you said wrong, but what Ellie

understood was that families come in all shapes and sizes and not everyone has a dad … which is exactly what I'd have told her."

"But …" He tapped a finger against his front tooth. "There's a bit more to it than that."

"Yes, but she's five years old. That's all she needs to know for now."

"Okay. So I didn't completely mess up?"

"I'd argue you did, but only because you could have had this conversation with me earlier and saved me a week of worrying."

"You can't honestly have thought I had a problem with Ellie?"

"I didn't know what to think. You're so good with her, but you already told me you split up with Jenny because she wanted to get married and have kids and you didn't."

"It was never that I was against marriage and kids. I just didn't want that with Jenny."

"Really?"

"Yes. That became very clear to me pretty soon after I met you and Ellie."

Beth pushed her hair behind her ears. "Ellie's also been talking about wanting a brother and I wondered if that had put you in panic mode too."

"Not at all. Especially since she specifically wants Kit as her brother."

"What?" Beth asked, shaking her head.

He nodded. "She thinks he'd be a great brother. But she might also have got it in her head that he's her boyfriend, so you may want to have a chat with her about that."

Smiling widely, Beth reached for his hand. "So you really don't have any problem with the fact that I have a child?"

"No." He looked at her as though she was being completely ridiculous. "I love Ellie."

Beth stifled a laugh and schooled her features to a mock serious expression. "Really? You love *Ellie?*"

"And *you!*" He grinned, squeezing her hand as he sat up straighter. "I probably should have led with that. I love you."

Her heart felt as though it expanded to twice its size. "I love you too."

"Good." His lips brushed lightly against hers. "That's all that matters."

She wished it was as easy as that but couldn't put aside her niggling doubts. "I worry that one day all my baggage will be too much for you."

"I really don't see Ellie as baggage."

She shook her head. "There's also my dad."

"What about him?"

Beth breathed deeply. "This summer showed me that I could never leave him. I'd never get over the guilt. Which means that I can't leave Plymouth."

"I'd never ask you to."

"But that would mean that if things work out for us …"

"I'd move here," he jumped in. "I've already thought about it. Of course, we need to see how long-distance works out, but there isn't much keeping me in London any more. I could definitely see myself moving here."

"It seems unfair that you'd be the one to make all the sacrifices."

"Moving here to be with you would never be a sacrifice." He trailed his fingers over the back of her hand. "But we're jumping ahead. For now, let's see how long distance works out."

"Okay." She leaned to kiss him but pulled back at the last moment. "I really hate that you heard me throwing up."

"I didn't hear anything," he said, eyes bright with amusement.

"Liar!"

"At least we know this isn't just a holiday fling now." He raised a lone eyebrow. "Things felt pretty real this weekend."

"That's true. Nothing like a stomach bug to move a relationship out of the honeymoon phase."

"Just tell me it's not going to be like that every weekend?" he said, smiling lightly.

A laugh escaped her. "I seriously hope not."

He moved to kiss her, and her stomach filled with warmth at the thought of spending every weekend with him. Whatever was to come, she knew everything would be fine as long as they were together.

EPILOGUE

CHRISTMAS DAY

Multicoloured lights twinkled on the Christmas tree in the corner of Mirren's living room and the faint scent of pine needles hung in the air. A low hum of Christmas carols emanated from the sound system in the corner, while Noah and Ellie battled it out as the remaining two participants in a game of Junior Uno.

All eyes swept to Seren at the end of the couch as she let out a grunt of a snore. Kit rolled his eyes, looking down at her curled against his chest.

"This is the woman who claims not to snore," he said while Ellie giggled.

Seren blinked her eyes open. "What?" she muttered to Kit.

"Nothing," he replied, stroking her red hair as her eyes fluttered closed again.

"We should go back to the cottage soon," Beth said to Ellie. "It's way past your bedtime."

"I'm playing," she said with an impatient pout, which demonstrated just how tired she was.

"You can finish the game, then it's bedtime."

Ellie's eyes dropped to her cards, which were spread out on

the coffee table – she'd given up on trying to keep them fanned in her hand. "I can't go."

Noah shot Keira a look that sent her shuffling over to Ellie and tapping on one of her cards.

"Oh! I can go!" Ellie happily played the card.

Slouched on the couch with Trystan's arm around her, Beth felt the most relaxed she'd felt all day. Even so, she'd be glad when they were back in the cottage. Once Ellie was settled in bed she could give up with her fake smiles and false positivity.

Quietly, everyone looked on while Noah discreetly engineered the rest of the game so that it was over as quickly as possible – and with Ellie as the winner.

"That means it's time to go," Beth told her daughter, who beamed triumphantly.

"Not yet, Mummy. Trystan said we were going to dance after the game."

Beth smiled gently. "I think it's too late for a dance party."

"Don't listen to your mum," Trystan said, pulling his arm from behind Beth and giving her thigh a playful slap as he stood. "It's *never* too late for a dance party."

"She's been up since six," Mirren said, shifting in the armchair. "She must be ready to drop."

"One song?" Trystan said, looking pleadingly at Beth. He knew she could never say no when he looked at her like that.

When she relented, Ellie jumped up to high five Trystan.

"I'm not entirely sure how I feel about this," Kit said, then covered his mouth as he yawned.

"What?" his mum asked him.

He pursed his lips. "It's just been a while since anyone asked me to dance."

Turning in the doorway, Trystan barked out a laugh that made Seren jump awake. "After all the times you turned me down when I asked you to dance, I'd have thought you'd be relieved that I've finally found myself a willing dance partner."

"I know what he means," Noah said from his spot on the floor. "It always felt nice to be asked."

Trystan's eyes sparkled with amusement. "Would you like to dance, Kit?"

"No." The grin broke quickly on Kit's face. "Thanks for asking though."

"Noah?" Trystan said with a slight eye roll.

"No, thank you," he replied sweetly.

Trystan and Ellie took themselves off to the kitchen and a moment later, loud music blared, interrupted occasionally by Ellie's high-pitched laughter. Beth gave them five minutes, then coaxed them into leaving.

Ellie's eyelids were drooping as soon as she lay down in bed and Beth was surprised she managed to stay awake for the entirety of the bedtime story.

"When are we going home?" she asked as Beth set the book on the bedside table.

"In about a week."

"When can I play with Steph?" Ellie asked of the friend she'd made in the summer. They'd had a couple of playdates when they were over at half term as well.

"She's coming over to play with you the day after tomorrow."

"Good. I can show her my new toys."

"Did you have a nice Christmas?" Beth asked.

"It was the best Christmas ever."

Beth swallowed the lump in her throat, ignored the pain in her chest. "You were spoiled rotten." It wasn't only Mirren who'd showered Ellie with gifts, but the rest of the family too. Even Lowen had brought her a gift when he'd met up with them in the pub in the afternoon – a personalised bowl and plate to match the mug he'd made for her in the summer.

"Time to go to sleep," Beth said firmly as she clicked off the lamp. "Sleep tight."

"Mummy?" Ellie said. "I don't want to go home in a week."

"I know." It had been the same at half term – Ellie not wanting to go back to Plymouth. "We have to, though."

"Because of Grandad."

"Yes."

"Mummy?" Ellie said again, preventing Beth from leaving. "When we go home, will Trystan stay at our house all the time?"

"Yes." They'd explained about Trystan moving to Plymouth, but Ellie continually asked questions to confirm the situation.

"So he won't go back to London any more?"

"No. He's going to look for a new job in Plymouth."

"And he'll look after me when you go to work?"

"That's the plan, yes."

Trystan had been encouraging Beth to get back into wedding photography. While having the option felt great, she couldn't escape the niggling feeling that it wasn't the right path for her any more. In November she'd done some work for a local restaurant who were going through a re-brand. Taking photos of food for their website and social media had been a much more interesting project than she'd anticipated and had made her wonder what other areas of photography she might enjoy.

"Go to sleep now. Goodnight," Beth whispered and pulled the door behind her. She paused at the top of the stairs before venturing down to find Trystan leaning with his forearms on the kitchen counter.

"You look about as tired as Ellie is," Beth told him. He straightened up when she walked behind him and slipped her arms around his waist. Pressing her cheek against his back, she inhaled the scent of him and sighed loudly.

"Did you have a good day?" he asked.

"Yes."

"Really?"

She opened her mouth, but closed it again when she couldn't figure out how to respond. Apparently she might not have done such a good job of pretending to enjoy herself as she'd thought.

"I've been wondering about something," he said quietly.

"What?" she asked, feeling his shoulder blades rise as his muscles tensed beneath her cheek.

"Are you sure you want me to move in with you?"

Taking a step back, she pulled on his arm to turn him to face her. "Why would you even ask that?"

"Because I don't know if you're a hundred per cent sure. And if you have doubts, it would be better if you share them now."

She shook her head. "I don't have any doubts. I'm not sure why you'd think that."

"You've been in a strange mood for the last few weeks. Whenever I ask if you're okay, you say you're fine …"

"Because I *am* fine," she said in a rush, but the tears that filled her eyes told another story.

He tilted his head as he rubbed at her upper arms. "I don't know how to help you if you won't tell me what the problem is."

"It's nothing," she sniffed, stepping closer to him. "At least nothing to do with you."

"Tell me what's wrong. Please."

"I just …" She inhaled deeply as tears streamed down her cheeks. "It's the first Christmas in my life that I haven't spent with my mum." As a sob escaped her, Trystan folded his arms around her and she cried into his neck.

"I'm sorry," Trystan murmured after a few minutes. "I didn't think. I should have done."

"Mum always got so excited about Christmas. She loved everything about it. For the last few weeks your mum kept calling and telling us all her plans, and since we arrived she's been baking with Ellie and crafting, and she bought her all those presents. It was really nice of her but …" Beth paused for breath and pushed her fingers over her damp cheeks.

"It's all the things your mum would have done with her?" Trystan finished for her.

"Yes."

His eyebrows drew together. "You could have talked to me. I'd have told Mum to back off."

"I didn't want her to back off." Beth shook her head. "I love how she is with Ellie. I don't want her to stop. It's just hard for me sometimes."

"I'm really sorry. I knew there was something going on with you. I thought I'd done something wrong."

"No." Wrapping her arms around his waist she hugged him hard. "You make everything better. I don't know what I'd do without you."

He brushed her tears from her cheeks and dropped a kiss on her forehead. "Next time can you please talk to me instead of shutting me out?"

"I thought I was doing a good job of pretending to be fine. I didn't want to put a damper on Christmas when everyone else was so excited." The tears took some of her sadness away and she felt instantly calmer. "I can't believe you'd think I didn't want you to move in with us. The only doubt I have is whether you're really going to be happy living in Plymouth."

He shook his head. "How many times do I need to tell you that I don't care where we live as long as we're together?"

"I just think you'd rather live here."

"I'll be perfectly happy in Plymouth. I promise." He took her hand and led her into the living room, where they sank onto the couch.

"There's something else that worries me," she said, thinking she may as well get everything out in the open.

"Tell me," he prompted.

"Does the age difference between us bother you?" she asked, tentatively.

"No." He shifted to face her, propping his arm on the back of the couch. "Why? Am I too immature for you?"

"No." She gave his thigh a playful tap. "But I'm worried the age difference might become an issue in the future."

"Why would it?"

"Because when you talked about your ex wanting kids, you said you didn't want kids *yet*. What happens if you decide you want kids five years from now and I can't give you that?"

He looked thoughtful, which worried her. She'd fully expected him to wave away her concerns and say he was happy with her and Ellie and always would be.

"Do you ever think about having more kids?" he asked, his fingers grazing over the back of her neck. "Or did you always just want one?"

"I used to think I'd have more. When I had Ellie, I got more of the sperm stored in case I wanted to have another baby, so that they'd be full siblings. But it never felt like the right time to have another."

"But the sperm is still there, just in case?"

"Yes." She wasn't sure what his point was.

"So you didn't write the idea off completely?"

"No. I suppose I didn't."

He pressed his lips together, then twisted them to one side. "I'd like us to have a baby," he finally said, his blue eyes deadly serious.

Beth shook her head in sharp, jerky movements. "You ... what?"

"I already told you that when I was with Jenny, it was never really that I didn't want to get married and have kids – I just didn't want to do it with her. Everything feels different with you. I can absolutely imagine us getting married one day. And if you wanted to have another baby, we could. I mean, I'd like to."

For a moment, all she could do was stare at him. "You want us to have a baby?" she asked, slightly dumbstruck.

"Yes." He smiled uncertainly. "If you don't want to I'll also be very happy the way we are now. But if you were up for it, so am I."

"This isn't where I thought this conversation was going."

He took her hand, entwining their fingers. "What do you want?"

"I'm not sure. I didn't think a baby was on the cards for us." She bit her lip as emotions swelled in her chest. "But I'd love for us to have a baby ... I'd really love to."

"You don't need to decide right now," Trystan said. "You can think about it."

"You probably need time to think about it more too," she said, reining in her excitement. "We haven't even been together for six months. We definitely need to think about it more. Obviously ... It's not as though you were suggesting we have a baby immediately." Her mouth was spouting whatever sprang to mind and she couldn't seem to stop it. "Except we shouldn't wait too long because of my age. The longer we leave it the less chance there'll be." She paused to find him looking at her with eyes full of affection.

"I don't need to wait," he said calmly. "I know what I want and I have no hesitations. Unless you want to wait?"

"No." Her brain was struggling to keep up with the conversation, but her heart was way ahead. The thought of having a baby with Trystan filled her with joy. "I don't want to wait."

He smiled widely but his eyes flickered with uncertainty. "And you said you still have the sperm that you used for Ellie?"

The question threw her and she felt her brow crinkle. "Yes ... I mean I have access to it. Why?"

"I didn't know if you'd want to use that. So the baby would be Ellie's full sibling. I love Ellie and I'd love another baby, regardless of their DNA."

Beth slipped her hand around the back of Trystan's neck and twisted her fingers into his hair. "I love you so much. And I love that you'd be fine with that. But I'd rather use your sperm if that's okay?"

His eyes sparkled in delight. "I think I can probably get you access to some."

A laugh burst out of her and she leaned to kiss him.

"So we're really doing this?" he asked. "We're going to have a baby?"

"We'll try," she said, aware that they might be getting their hopes up for nothing. "It might not happen though ... we should keep that in mind ..."

"It's fine if it doesn't happen," he said, stroking her hair from her face. "I don't want it to be something we stress about. Let's try though. See what happens."

"Okay," she said, nodding her agreement, but knowing her hopes were already sky high and she'd be crushed if it didn't happen for them.

A delicious smile lifted his lips as he pulled her close. "Let's give it a go then," he murmured right before their lips met.

Beth pulled back abruptly. "Now?"

"Unless you've got something else in mind for the evening?"

Grinning widely, she leaned into him again. "I've got no plans."

BOXING DAY

The following morning, Beth was already awake when the door to the bedroom eased open. She managed to drag the bedding up over Trystan before Ellie got a full view of his naked backside.

"Morning," Beth whispered, pressing a finger to her lips before ushering Ellie out onto the landing. "Let's let Trystan sleep in today." She smiled to herself, thinking of their late-night activities, which would definitely have left him in need of a little extra sleep.

"I can't find my pony," Ellie said as they walked down the stairs. "The one that Keira and Noah gave me. Can I go to Mirren's house and see if it's there?"

"Not now. She'll still be asleep. We'll look for it later. Are you hungry?"

"Yes. But I want to find the pony. What if it's lost forever?"

"It won't be. We'll have some breakfast and then have a good look for it."

Ellie ate a bowl of cereal while continuing to complain about the lost toy. The two of them did a sweep of the cottage after they'd eaten but there was no sign of it.

"Can I wake Trystan up and ask him if he knows where it is?" Ellie asked impatiently.

"I'm sure it will be at Mirren's house." Beth checked the kitchen clock. It was still early, but she supposed Mirren wouldn't mind if she went in to look for the toy. The door was probably unlocked, and if not there was a spare key on Trystan's key ring. She plucked it from the counter.

"You stay here," she said to Ellie. "I'll go and look."

"It might be near the Christmas tree. Or in the kitchen."

Beth grabbed Trystan's hoodie from the back of the couch, pulling it on as she stuffed her bare feet into her trainers.

Outside, the air was crisp and everything was still except for the gentle swell of waves and the boats rocking on top of them out in the bay. Daylight seeped onto the horizon in a soft yellow glow and a gull shrieked on the beach as she stepped onto the lane. Pausing, she inhaled the silence and the sea breeze, smiling to herself as she wondered what the new year might have in store for her.

After inhaling her fill of salty air, she continued on her way. As she expected, the backdoor was unlocked at Mirren's place and she snuck quietly into the kitchen.

With no sign of the pony there, she moved to the living room. As soon as she switched the light on, she caught sight of the little horse sitting under the Christmas tree.

"There you are," she muttered as she strode over to it.

"What?" The croaky voice startled her so much that she walked into the coffee table, smacking her knee on the corner of it and cursing loudly.

"Sorry," she said, registering Kit lying on the couch with a blanket over him, his eyes squinting against the light. "Ellie left her pony here." With a watery smile, she bent to pick it up. "I thought I could sneak in and grab it without disturbing anyone."

"It's fine," he said through a yawn.

"I'll leave you to go back to sleep." Except when she reached the doorway he was sitting up, clearly not intending to resume sleeping. "Are you okay?" Beth asked on impulse.

"Yes."

She hovered by the door, feeling uneasy about finding him there. "Is everything okay with you and Seren?" It was none of her business, but she had a soft spot for Kit and hated to think he and Seren were having problems.

"Yeah." He blinked a few times. "Oh! You mean because I'm sleeping on my mum's couch? Everything's fine. We decided to stay here … partly because we couldn't be bothered to walk home and partly to avoid an argument about whose place we stay at." He rubbed his hands over his face, then glanced up at her. "We've been talking about moving in together, but she wants me to move into her place, which makes absolutely no sense since I own my place and she rents. But her place is bigger… it's kind of an ongoing discussion. But we're fine."

Beth hadn't been expecting so much information, and she was still slightly confused. "You're fine, but you're on the couch and Seren is …?"

"Oh!" Amusement flashed in his eyes. "She's upstairs, in the spare room. We both were, but she snores so I moved down here for some peace. Usually it's not so bad, but when she's had a few drinks it's not as cute any more. You did me a favour waking me up. Now I can slip back in to bed and she won't even notice I was gone." His smile was full of warmth. "She doesn't believe she snores. Or at least thinks I exaggerate about how loud it is. I've thought about recording her, but I'm fairly sure that wouldn't go down well."

"I can't imagine it would," Beth agreed. She was about to leave but dithered in the doorway. "Could I ask you a question?"

"Sure." He yawned. "Make it an easy one though. I'm not fully awake yet."

"Do you think Trystan's happy?"

Kit smiled. "That one's a bit *too* easy. He's definitely happy."

"Do you think he's happy about moving to Plymouth?"

"Yeah," he said, his tone even. "I think so."

Beth nodded slowly. "What does everyone else think about it?"

"How do you mean?"

She moved to sit on the couch when Kit shifted his legs out of the way. "I know he'd rather live here," she said, pursing her lips. Her conversation with Trystan the previous evening had made her think even more about how their future would look if moving close to his family was an option. "I keep feeling guilty that we have to stay in Plymouth because of my dad. Trystan insists he's fine with it and I guess I have to accept that since I don't think there's another option, but the more time I spend here, the more I realise it's not just him who it affects but his family too. Does everyone resent me for being the reason he doesn't live here?"

"No." Kit tilted his head. "It's not as though you took him away. It's been a long time since Trystan's lived here."

"I know but I get the impression you all expected him to move back someday."

"Maybe. But he's happy. And it's not as though you live that far away. I promise you, no one is upset with you about this."

"Not even your mum?"

"Mum's not upset about it. Although, that's probably because she thinks …" His eyes widened and he trailed off.

"She thinks what?" Beth asked.

"Nothing. Never mind. Ignore me."

"What were you going to say?"

"I'm not sure. My brain hasn't really woken up yet."

"Kit! Tell me what you were going to say."

He covered his face with his hands. "I don't want to. It'll cause drama and I'll be in trouble with everyone."

"Well, now I'm worried. Tell me what you were going to say."

"Fine." He dropped his chin to his chest. "Mum's got it into her head that you'll move here at some point. The three of you."

"Why does she think that?"

Kit shook his head. "I don't know."

"Okay." That didn't seem like such a huge confession. "Wait … you're not telling me everything, are you?"

He winced. "She hasn't taken any bookings for Peswera Cottage for this year in case you decide you want to move here."

"Are you serious?" Beth asked. "Trystan's completely chilled about job hunting because he'll have the rental income."

"The money isn't an issue. Mum can advertise the place at the last minute and still have it booked out for the entire tourist season. That's her plan. Trystan will be none the wiser. I should never have said anything."

"It's fine." Beth let out a breath. She should probably be annoyed with Mirren, but secretly she felt an odd sense of comfort that the cottage didn't have any bookings. "Mirren must be desperate for Trystan to move back here."

"She'd be over the moon if he moved back here. But it's also you and Ellie that she'd love to have around more. Especially Ellie. No offence."

"None taken."

"She loved having you here last summer." Kit sighed heavily. "I'll talk to her about the cottage though. Get her to start taking bookings for it."

Beth flashed him a grateful smile as she stood up, then stopped in her tracks halfway to the door. "Maybe you could wait a little while."

"How do you mean?"

Her thoughts were all over the place and she wasn't entirely sure what she meant. "Don't say anything to her yet … wait a few weeks so I have time to get everything straight in my head."

"I'm confused … are you thinking what I think you are?"

"I have no idea." She grimaced as she looked at him. "I can't leave my dad ... but I'm also really confused. Don't say anything to anyone, please. But don't encourage your mum to take bookings just yet."

NEW YEAR'S DAY

While the rest of the Treneary family had taken themselves off to the Mermaid Inn to see in the New Year, Trystan and Beth had opted for a quiet evening at Peswera Cottage. Once Ellie was settled in bed, they'd had an early night themselves, and Beth only briefly stirred when fireworks erupted at midnight.

When she woke again it was shortly before dawn. Lying in the dark, she reflected on the highs and lows of the previous year until the first hint of daylight crept around the curtains. Slipping out of bed, she pulled her thick knitted cardigan on over her pyjamas and drew the suitcase out from under the bed, feeling around inside until her hand landed on the only item in it.

Bringing her mum's ashes to St Marys had been a last-minute impulse, and up until then she hadn't even thought about scattering them. Now she felt a warm glow of hopefulness about the future and a compulsion to start the year looking forward instead of back.

As she stepped out of the cottage, dawn was arriving over Old Town Bay, and the clarity she felt in the gusty air was invigorating.

Walking to the end of the beach, she disturbed two sand-pipers who screeched in annoyance as they scuttled away along the water's edge. Beth clambered onto the rocks which marked the start of the jagged headland. High tide lapped at the seaweed-covered stones, and Beth matched her breathing to the gentle swell of the waves before unscrewing the lid of the urn.

She only hesitated for a moment before pouring out the ashes. Caught on a light breeze, they sparkled in the early rays of sunshine, then rested on the surface of the water for a moment before sinking below. Tears rolled down Beth's cheeks as she watched them disappear from sight.

Despite the rush of sadness, the stillness of her surroundings filled her with a sense of calm and she remained where she was, looking out at the warm hues of sunrise that seemed to change the colour of the sky and water from one moment to the next.

A sudden gust lifted her hair from her shoulders and drove a fine mist of sea spray into her face. She smiled to herself, imagining it was her mum, telling her not to stand around being maudlin.

Turning to move back to the beach, she caught sight of Trystan standing on the sand, his eyebrows knitted as he looked at her. Carefully, she picked her way back over the rocks, then took his hand to steady herself as she hopped back onto the sand.

"I did it." She set the urn down and draped her arms around his neck. "I scattered Mum's ashes."

"Are you okay?"

"Yes. It felt like the right time. And this was definitely the right place." A tumult of emotions whirred inside of her, but it was the feeling of hopefulness that she clung to. "Losing Mum was so incredibly hard, but I'm so grateful that she brought me here. To you."

He tightened his arms around her waist. "Me too."

"I think this is the right place for us too," Beth told him.

"How do you mean?"

Her gaze swept up to the cottage before landing back on him. "I think we should move here."

"What?"

"I think all three of us will be happier living here."

The skin around his eyes crinkled as his eyes narrowed. "What about your dad?"

"I'll go back and visit him regularly." Her shoulders rose and sank as she sighed. "I'm probably going to feel horribly guilty for leaving him, but if we stay in Plymouth, I'll feel guilty for putting him before us."

"You know I'd be perfectly happy to live in Plymouth. I don't want you to move here because you think it's what I want."

"I do think it's what you want." She smiled brightly. "But it's also what I want. And I know Ellie would love to live here."

"Have you really thought this through?"

"It's been on my mind since you first talked about moving to Plymouth. I never let myself think about it seriously because of Dad, but this week everything became really clear. This feels like home."

He quirked an eyebrow. "You should have told me you were thinking about it. We could have discussed it together."

"I needed it to be my decision."

"You know I'd never have encouraged you to leave your dad if you weren't comfortable with it. But as a relocation specialist I might have been able to offer different perspectives ..."

"Really?" She rolled her eyes. "Such as?"

A muscle twitched in his jaw and his eyes flashed with uncertainty. "There's a care home on St Mary's ... they take patients with Alzheimer's."

She shook her head while his words sunk in. "What?"

"If you were uncomfortable leaving your dad, you could look into moving him here. I don't know if it would work out or if it would be too unsettling for him to move, but it's a thought ..."

"Have you looked into it?"

"Only a quick internet search. I didn't want to mention it before because you seemed set on staying in Plymouth, and I didn't want you to think I wasn't okay with that."

"I don't know if he could move from his care home. I've never even considered it." She felt her brow furrow as she contemplated the idea. "It's definitely worth looking into." Whether or not it was a serious possibility, she was touched that he'd thought of it. With a hand on his cheek, she kissed him softly.

He broke into a wide smile when he pulled away. "Are we seriously moving here?"

"Yes!"

"When?"

"I don't know. You're the relocation specialist … how long will it take to organise?"

"Probably not very long."

"Do you really think you can find a job here?"

"Yes. I don't think that will be a problem."

"I'll need to figure out what I'll do for work," she mused. "But I'd be able to rent out the house in Plymouth, so that would be a bit of income."

Trystan nodded. "We might have to move in with Mum for a while. She'll already have taken bookings for the cottage."

Beth crinkled her nose. "I happen to know that she hasn't."

"What?"

"Kit accidentally let slip that your mum had kept the cottage free in case we decided to move here."

"Are you serious?"

"Yes." She laughed as he shook his head. "And I don't think we can really be annoyed with her about it."

"She's going to be so smug," he said, but his eyes twinkled with amusement. He hugged her so hard that he lifted her off the ground, making her laugh loudly. "Happy New Year, by the way."

"Happy New Year," she replied, rubbing her nose against his as he set her back down.

As they set off hand in hand up the beach, anticipation fizzed in her stomach at the thought of telling Ellie their plans.

The year had only just begun, but she had a feeling it was going to be a great one.

ALSO BY HANNAH ELLIS

Hannah has also written a series of children's books aimed at 5-9 year olds under the pen name, Hannah Sparks.

ABOUT THE AUTHOR

When she's not writing, Hannah enjoys spending time with her husband and kids. She loves to read and also enjoys yoga and jogging. And tea … she really loves a good cup of tea!

Hannah can be found online at the following places:

Facebook: @authorhannahellis

Instagram: @authorhannahellis

Twitter: @BooksEllis

Website: www.authorhannahellis.com

Feel free to contact Hannah at any of the above or email her at this address:

authorhannahellis@gmail.com

If you'd like to be kept up to date with news about Hannah's books you can sign up to her receive emails from her through her website:

www.authorhannahellis.com/newsletter

Printed in Great Britain
by Amazon

60747751R00180